SPIDER'S TRUTH

CHRISTA YELICH-KOTH

lovely to meet
you at the LC
Farmer's market!

CYEL-KR

(born in Milwaukee!)

COPYRIGHT

SPECIAL THANKS

Sandra Yelich: For your endless edits and continual help, this book is fantastic because of you

Claire Kirchhoff: For beta reading early on and giving me great feedback

Conrad Teves: For your amazing help with the cover art and feedback about the characters

Thomas Koth: For your thoughts and opinions in this strange world of kinda-sorta detective fiction?? Haha!

Kat Ross: For your help with the procedural process and for keeping me on track with the investigation

Stu Tighe: For letting me read to you in the car and giving great feedback about the characters.

Boston Police Department: For answering my questions to make sure I got things as accurate as possible.

1

February 29th
3 a.m.

Anya closed her eyes.

One. Two. Three.

She opened them. Her vision adjusted to the weapon's thermal scope. The colors flared against her retinas, reds and blues of hot and cold. The weight of the rifle sat comfortably against her shoulder, nestled as if it felt at home. Sawdust from the construction in the room tickled her nose, but she ignored the urge to scratch.

Adrenaline spiked through her when she spotted her target across the alleyway through the house window—plump, juicy.

Disgusting.

Anya clicked a special switch she'd designed for her gun and the scope slid over to night vision. Greenish glows burst against the black.

The target trudged through the rooms of the house, from the bedroom to the kitchen and then back again. A heavy-set woman in her late thirties, she had no husband, no children, no pets. Unless you counted the plethora of lace doilies which seemed to have bred along the counters, shelves, and tabletops inside her home.

Fat slob. What? Can't go to bed without stuffing your face first? Anya thought. Women like this shouldn't be allowed to exist. They were an offense against nature, against God. They took their life, their whole existence for granted, saturating it with grease, mold, and rot. The woman in her scope was tainted: a slovenly animal that deserved to be annihilated.

The ease of squeezing the trigger, feeling the recoil pop against her shoulder, and watching the bullet slice through the window and lodge into the woman's forehead tempted Anya. But that wasn't her job—at least, not tonight. Tonight she had bigger game.

This target would only be watched, to lead Anya to her true heart's delight: her real victim.

Anya smiled, showing her teeth. She was ready to hunt.

2

March 1ˢᵗ
3 a.m.

The moisture in Sean's mouth evaporated. Somehow he found himself standing in front of his 11th grade English class, getting ready to present his paper on *Romeo and Juliet*. Though completely prepared, when he looked down to read his report, blank pages greeted him. The snickers grew. Even the teacher giggled, wreathed in a ring of white lilies. Worst of all, Mara Swast, the most *gorgeous* creature ever to grace the halls of Martek High, was sitting in the lap of his arch nemesis, the captain of the swim team, Damien Andrews. She wore a white, beaded wedding gown and her sweet lips were locked against the jock's mouth, their tongues entwined, so wrapped up in each other they didn't even notice the whole class jeering at Sean's seeming stupidity.

The bell sounded in the background.

Sean awoke and sat straight up, his cheeks flushed from his nightmarish embarrassment. He reached over to the phone, whose early morning call pulled him from his adolescent nightmare, but the phone wasn't on the nightstand next to his bed.

No. That wasn't true. The phone was where it should be. *He* was out of place.

He wasn't in bed.

Sean rubbed his eyes and glanced at the clock on the nightstand. The bright red numbers came into focus and read 3:04 a.m. He'd slipped into unconsciousness on the couch after several drinks a mere two hours earlier. The television still flickered, though thankfully muted, as late-night television had transitioned into annoying infomercials.

Guided by the TV's light, Sean shuffled through his studio apartment. Though he'd moved in to one of the hundred or so apartments on Westland Avenue a year ago, the place still looked pretty bare. Not that there was much room for furniture or decorative items inside the 450 sq. foot apartment. Besides the bed, nightstand, couch, TV, and clock, the only other adornments to his sad little bachelor pad were a blow-up plastic Corona palm tree he'd won three years earlier in a drinking contest his friend entered him in, which he didn't remember playing, or winning for that matter, and a laundry basket overflowing with dirty clothes in the corner next to the bathroom.

Sean crossed the room and grabbed the phone. "Yeah?" he grumbled into the receiver, as the base of the phone tumbled off his tilted nightstand onto his floor, per usual. The uneven, cream carpeting caused the furniture to lean to one side. *And to think, I almost got an apartment with hard wood floors. As if my downstairs neighbors don't hate me enough.*

"Trann?" a deep voice asked through a haze of static from the other end of the line.

"You know it's me. It's *always* me," Sean said, putting the phone base back on the table.

"Never know when you might have. . .company."

Sean could almost *hear* the smirk on his sergeant's face. His superior knew Sean hadn't been in a relationship in over a year. In fact, he hadn't been *laid* in that long either. Sergeant Frank Millan took every moment possible to remind Sean of that fact.

"Ha, ha," Sean said sarcastically. "What do you want?"

"Same thing I always want in the middle of the night. I want to hear that pretty, sleepy voice of yours tell me how much you love me." Millan chuckled a gruff laugh.

"There aren't enough words." Sean stifled a yawn. He often wondered if other people would think it careless for him and his superior to joke when he knew the call meant the occurrence of a murder. When Sean had first become a homicide detective back in Philadelphia, the seemingly casual callous demeanor of some of the other detectives disturbed him. But after a while, he came to realize it kept them sane. Not that it ever hindered the process when dealing with a case, but they needed to keep things light as long as possible to prevent the horrors they dealt with from continually dampening their souls.

"What's the case?"

"Homicide," Millan replied.

"Details?" Sean asked.

"You need to come and see for yourself. It may be. . .I'm not sure."

Sean paused at Millan's words. Something about his tone caused a brief line of worry to wrinkle his forehead. "What's up, Sarge?"

"I'm hoping nothing. Now get your ass down here. We're at the Museum of Science."

"No pretty please?"

"With sugar."

"All right, I'm on my way. I'll be there in about. . .twenty minutes."

"There's even coffee."

"With sugar?"

Sean knew Millan had hung up because the static stopped. He smiled as he dropped the phone back onto its charger. He did have a cell phone, but his apartment building apparently had walls made of 20-foot thick cement. He got *less* than zero bars.

Sean rubbed his face and reached upwards, stretching his arms above him. His tight muscles pulled in protest, reminding him he should have stretched better after the Boston Police Department's basketball game yesterday against the Boston Fire Department—an ongoing friendly rivalry that took place once a year. It was usually one-sided—most of the cops who played embodied the stereotype of round bellies full of jelly doughnuts—but this year they had a secret weapon: Sean.

With his washboard abs, lean, well-muscled arms, and previous high school basketball experience, the entire police department decided Sean would win the annual basketball game for them. And they meant it. Sean must have scored nearly 80% of the points and blocked most of the other team's shots. Unfortunately, this also meant he had the most scrapes, cuts, and bruises from being pushed and tripped once the fire department realized Sean's abilities.

All in fun, though, of course.

Sean was new to the Boston P.D., having moved last year from Philadelphia. At twenty-eight years old, he wasn't by any means the youngest in the police department, but he was the youngest member of the homicide unit. He had a knack for solving cases that dead-ended, and he barely mentioned to his previous boss that he was *thinking* about sending out his résumé when he received six different job offers from all over the U.S., from Phoenix to Miami. But Boston had been the best deal: 14% pay raise, new division, and better hours.

At least, that's what the contract said.

Apparently the "better hours" clause only applied if you were *bad* at your job. Unfortunately, Sean was very, *very* good, which meant he got called for any and every case that seemed unsolvable, no matter where in the Boston area it took place and at what time a criminal felt like killing someone else.

Just one week I'd like to have someone not *die in the middle of the night. I mean, can't people pull triggers just as easily when the sun is out?*

Running his hands through his tousled, short, brown hair he walked across the small space, which made up both living room and bedroom, turned on the light in his tiny bathroom, and squinted as his eyes adjusted to the brightness. His normal reflection of a strong chin, sharp jaw, and smooth paled skin were marred by multiple lovely purple blotches of ruptured blood vessels from the game. He turned on the cold water, gathered some into his hands, and splashed it onto his face. Grabbing a small towel, he patted his face dry, and left the bathroom. As he crossed toward the closet, he stubbed his toe on the edge of his bed.

"Damnit!" he swore at the sharp pain.

And then the banging began.

"KEEP IT DOWN UP THERE! WE'RE TRYING TO SLEEP!" His elderly downstairs neighbor, Gerald, hollered through his ceiling as he repeatedly slammed something against it.

Maybe it's his wife's head.

"Gerald! Stop screaming! You'll wake everyone up!" his wife, Nell, yelled at him.

No such luck.

"HE'LL NEVER LEARN IF WE DON'T TELL HIM TO KEEP IT DOWN."

"Gerald! Shut the hell up! We're going to get evicted again!"

"THE DAY I GET EVICTED IS THE DAY MY GUN DON'T WORK ANYMORE! NO ONE IS GOING TO EVICT US, NELL. BUT THIS BOY UPSTAIRS..."

Sean grabbed a pair of jeans and pulled them on over his boxers as the couple below him kept fighting. He knew he hadn't woken Gerald up. In fact, Gerald often kept Sean awake. It seemed as though the 20-foot thick cement walls hadn't included the floors *between* the apartments, which were paper thin.

Gerald, an eighty-year-old, half-deaf, ex-American History professor, was awake every night until 5 a.m. The reason Sean knew this was because Gerald watched reruns all night and talked at the TV. At first, Sean had thought his downstairs neighbor was conversing with friends, until he heard him yelling at Charlie that angels don't really exist. Then that Hot Lips should really find some ice for her heat problem. And one late night that Darren should look behind him because Sam's witchy mother was right there, sitting on the fireplace's mantle, and couldn't he see her? She was right there! Why didn't he just look?

It had taken Sean a few months to get used to it, and when he was finally able to fall asleep through Gerald's mutterings, his own late-night phone calls began.

Strangely enough, the ringing phone didn't bother Gerald. Not a peep came from the couple below when Sean left his TV on all night. Only when he walked around in the early pre-dawn hours did the problems begin. Getting up to go to the bathroom in the middle of the night was a recipe for disaster. There would be Gerald, knocking something against his ceiling, yelling for quiet.

Everyone had spoken to the landlord about Gerald's incessant hollering. The landlord promptly replied he would take care of it, and then just as promptly did nothing.

How his wife, Nell, slept through it most nights, no one knew.

Sean's living situation wasn't ideal, but he didn't have the luxury of moving into a different building. His pay raise helped, but Boston was an expensive city, and he'd blown all his savings the year before on his "almost" wedding and now found himself back at square one.

Seriously, man, do not *start thinking about that.* But as he rubbed the feeling back into his toe, the thoughts came anyway—him standing at the end of a long aisle, sweat trickling down his neck into his rented tux as the seconds ticked away, until a figure came through the church doors. For a moment, his heart leapt, but then his stomach dropped when he realized instead of his bride-to-be, it was her mother.

Sean remembered the thick scent of lilies in the air—Angellica's favorite flower—as her mother scurried down the aisle to inform him about the change of plans.

Sean shook the memories as best he could from his head. That had happened a year ago. He was over it.

Then why haven't you had more than a couple lousy dates since you moved here?

Sean ignored his inner question as he searched through his closet. He grabbed a white T-shirt off the floor, gave it a quick smell to ensure its cleanliness, and slipped it over his head. The shirt stretched tightly over his well-muscled body—an attractive sight to most members of the opposite sex, and probably several of the same sex, too, but any kind of sex was the farthest thing from his mind. Not when he'd been called for a case.

Moving to the floor, Sean lifted up one of the blankets so he could see under the bed. He stretched his arm out underneath and grasped his sneakers, shoving his feet into them without bothering to lace them up. Crawling across the bed, he grabbed the keys on the table next to the phone. As he left his apartment, he hooked a finger around a pull-over jacket and tugged it over his head with one hand. On his way downstairs, he paused outside Gerald and Nell's—or Geriatric Hell as he'd come to think of them—and knocked on the door.

"I'm leaving. Stop yelling at your ceiling."

"You hear that you deaf bastard?" Nell hollered at her husband. "He's not even up there anymore."

"I CAN STILL HEAR HIM."

"You can't even hear. . ."

Sean had made it down the second flight of stairs as Nell's words trailed off. He pushed open the door and walked out into the cold, frosty air. His breath fogged while he made his way to his car, the air crisp as it entered his lungs. Though early springtime in Boston, without the sun, it felt colder than he expected, and he was glad for the jacket.

Sean approached his car. He pushed the key into the driver's side lock of his black Jaguar—a gift from the man who would have been his father-in-law. He popped the key into the ignition and started it up. The vehicle came to life with a growl that quieted to a purr. He hit the button for station 93.7 and started to back out of the parking lot as the music quietly pulsed from the speakers. Cracking his window to let some fresh air in, Sean pulled out onto the street, wondering once again what put that tone of worry in his Sergeant's words.

3

March 1st
3:30 a.m.

"You're late," Sergeant Millan said. Sean slammed his car door and trotted over.

"What are you talking about?"

"It's been twenty-three minutes." He handed him a steaming paper cup with a grin. Millan, a man in his late fifties, had deep brown skin, hard dark eyes, and a gristly white perpetual five o'clock shadow. His dark brown hair still remained thick, although it receded at the hairline, and white streaked his temples. Average height, average build, and a little soggy around the midsection. And though Catholic, when you asked him about it he would tell you "I love God, I love my family, and I help stop bad guys. Everything else is just lip service."

Sean took in a deep sniff of the hot coffee as the two of them walked toward the crime scene—a grassy area in front of the Museum of Science, a large brick building with white-trimmed windows.

"If I knew how much you missed me, I would've driven faster," Sean retorted.

Millan grunted a deep laugh. The laugh immediately turned into a cough.

"You want a smoke?" Sean asked.

"Only if your girlfriend gives it to me."

Sean smiled at the ongoing joke. A few months after Sean joined the Boston team, Millan had been x-rayed for a broken collarbone. The x-ray the doctor took revealed some shadowy portions he was concerned about. It had been a false alarm, but the day he left the hospital, Millan quit smoking. After 30 years, he just stopped.

Sean wouldn't have believed it were possible. He hadn't known what Millan looked like without a cigarette between his lips and smoke curling from his mouth. Other members of the team told Sean that Millan had scares like this before, but he never quit. Sean once asked the sergeant about it, but all he said was he'd made a promise to someone, and he meant to keep it.

Millan stopped coughing and raised an eyebrow. "Must have been some frat party."

Sean looked down. His University of Michigan jacket

appeared to be inside out, he wore two different colored socks, and he still hadn't tied his shoes.

"Well, you know me, always professional."

Millan grunted. "Luckily the woman you are about to meet won't care what you look like, seeing as how she's dead."

They approached the crime scene. Rolls of unwound yellow police tape hung around the perimeter, flood lights lit up the dark night, and flashbulbs flared from the forensics crew working the graveyard shift. Several different vehicles sat parked nearby, including three police cars, a fire truck, and the medical examiner's van. Frost had accumulated after the temperature dropped. The grass had gotten muddy from the score of people milling around. Sean reminded himself to watch his step.

"Why the fire truck?"

"First responder," Millan said. "They're packing up now."

Just as Sean glanced over at the uniformed men next to the huge, shiny red truck, a woman exited the medical examiner's van. Dr. Charlotte Salla.

"Why is *she* here?" Sean said out of the corner of his mouth to Millan. She was the chief medical examiner and normally wasn't called to come out to crime scenes.

"We need her. It's the first of the month, Trann."

Sean's body tensed up at those few little words. The medical examiner approached but Sean slid past her, lifting the edge of the tarp covering the body. There, a puncture wound at the base of the victim's neck, spread out across her left shoulder in spidery veins about an inch from the wound.

"Spider," he whispered. Before he could do anything else,

the medical examiner spoke up.

"Detectives?"

"You're just in time, Doc," Sean said to the coroner.

"Detective Trann, Sergeant Millan," she said, nodding in each of their directions. "You do realize," she continued, looking back at Sean, "that I am unable to remove the body from the crime scene before the forensics and detective teams have completed their work. Seeing as how the forensics team has just finished and you have just arrived, I appear to be early."

Her words grated on him and pulled him from his shock about the case. Sean resisted the urge to roll his eyes at the woman's condescending tone. *I swear to God, she is part Vulcan,* Sean thought. *Or a robot. She thinks she is so high and mighty compared to everyone else—like her opinion is the only one that matters. She doesn't even use contractions. Who doesn't use contractions?*

Millan leaned over to Sean as the medical examiner walked toward the victim's body. "Fifty bucks says *she* had company tonight and was. . .interrupted by this call."

Sean snorted a laugh, thankful for the break in tension. Except with dead people, he'd never seen the Ice Queen touch anyone. When he first met her a few months ago, Sean thought her quite stunning. No one really knew her ethnic background, but with her alluring eyes, high cheekbones, china doll mouth, and long dark hair, the latest polls were some kind of cross between Hawaiian, Native American, and Japanese. Not to mention her impressive credentials. Sean had looked forward to working with her, as the previous medical examiner may have been thorough, but seemed bored by his job.

But any interest in Dr. Salla as a colleague or otherwise melted away when she opened her mouth. She came off so *superior* to everyone else. He couldn't even be impressed by her knowledge or background because of how irritating it felt when she spoke to everyone like they were children.

Still, he sometimes found himself wondering just how cold her flawless skin really was. . .

The thought halted when he turned back to the scene.

"What have we got?" Sean asked with a nod to another detective, completely sobered. He chugged the rest of his coffee, already cooled in the brisk weather, and chucked the cup into a nearby waste receptacle. Sean already knew what Wilt would say—there is nothing.

"Young woman, mid-twenties, Caucasian," answered Detective Cam Wilt. He flicked his toothpick to the ground and licked his chapped lips. "She has no ID, no wallet, and no clothes."

Sean ignored the blatant littering, even if it was only a toothpick. Detective Wilt was definitely capable, but Sean was looking forward to the arrival of his new partner in a few weeks. His last partner, Detective Miah, left the week before to take a job overseas. Wilt's partner, Detective Juliette Tay, was on vacation back home to London. So Millan had paired Sean up with Wilt.

"Were any pieces of clothing found around her?" Millan asked.

Detective Wilt shook his head, his ear-length, oily, receding blonde hair flapping in the pre-dawn air. "Nope. We haven't found anything. And I mean *anything*. No footprints, no clothes, no drag marks, nothing. Forensics just finished taking what they need, but I don't know how much luck they'll have, either."

"It looks like she may have died from hypothermia," Millan said. "Her skin is waxy and her lips are blue."

"Think maybe she was doped up on something, stripped down for some action with a boyfriend, and got left?" Wilt asked.

"Don't you understand what this means, Wilt?" Sean asked. He couldn't keep the anger from his tone. If Spider were really back. . .

Dr. Salla raised an eyebrow, oblivious to the meaning of their conversation. "I assure you, I will come to a satisfactory conclusion. I have not done any tests. I cannot be sure she was under the influence of any mind-altering substances." She paused. "However, this situation may not have been chemically induced. Hypothermia victims often shed their clothing once they reach a state where confusion and disorientation set in. Once I perform an autopsy with a tox screen, I will give you my full report. If you are finished with the body, I would like to secure it." After Wilt nodded, Dr. Salla made a motion for her team to take the body to the van.

"Oh you'll find stuff on the tox screen," Sean said, slamming his fist into the palm of his other hand. "I can't believe it's Spider!"

Wilt's face paled. "Are you serious?"

Dr. Salla tilted her head. "This information seems important. May I inquire as to its significance regarding this victim?"

Sean's voice cut through the night air like a knife. "You'll find a specific toxin in her bloodstream. It is a type of paralytic agent. It simulates death, but the person can still see, hear, and feel. They just can't respond." He turned to look at the body. "This woman *did* die of hypothermia and she was aware of it the whole time. Unable to move. Unable to scream."

Dr. Salla turned back toward Millan. "The autopsy has not been performed. How can he know this?"

"I forgot," Millan answered. "You weren't working here when all this happened. The Boston P.D. dealt with a serial killer starting about a year and a half back. Six murders, each on the first of the month, from July through December. We were completely stumped. He'd send us notes with clues about what he was going to do and to whom. The notes were always delivered the day before he killed, but we never got to the victims in time.

"For six months," Millan continued, "Spider killed one victim on the first of every month. Like a rent payment. He would shoot them on the same spot on their neck, which would paralyze them. Then he'd dump their bodies somewhere and let them die in a different way while they were still aware of what was happening to them."

"Oh my. . ." Dr. Salla lowered her head for a moment in thought.

"We got a lucky break when Sean showed up."

Dr. Salla raised an eyebrow.

"The last of Spider's attacks happened about a week after Sean got here. He stayed up for twelve hours, poring over the case files, and then he figured out the clue."

"You located the last victim?" she asked.

Sean gritted his teeth. "Yes, but not soon enough. He died on the way to the hospital."

"And you believe this woman was murdered by the same man? This 'Spider' character?"

"The wound on the back of her neck matches his previous victims," Millan told her, pointing to the mark. "We can't be positive until the tox screen comes back, but this fits his M.O."

Dr. Salla rezipped the body bag. "I will inform you as soon as my examination is complete." She turned her deep brown eyes toward Sean. "I am very thorough, Detective Trann. Perhaps I will find something the previous medical examiner overlooked and we will prevent more deaths."

He flashed her a smile, though he felt confident she wouldn't find anything either. "Thanks, Doc."

She signaled to her team to close the back of the van. She and her group hopped in and took off down the street.

"I can't believe Spider might be back," Sean thought out loud as he watched the van disappear.

"We don't know for sure if it's him."

The two of them walked across the museum's courtyard to their cars.

"But you believe it *could* be him?"

"Well, the tell-tale veining on her neck makes me think it is." Millan reached habitually into his front shirt pocket. His fingers came up empty, no longer having a cigarette pack to grab onto. "But there's one difference."

"What's that?"

"You know how Spider always left a note? One with the clues about his murders?"

"Yeah?"

Millan cleared his throat. "This time there was no note."

4

March 1st
6 a.m.

Sean sat at his desk, sifting through case files. His facial features and body language may have appeared composed, calm, and collected, but inside he felt like a jumbled mess.

Could it really be Spider? The spidery-veined mark on the victim's neck did point toward that conclusion. Except there was no note—and Spider had always left a note. So maybe a copycat killer? But the details of Spider's M.O. were never released. A copycat killer wouldn't have known about the paralytic agent.

Maybe Spider wanted to throw the police off the scent by changing his pattern and no longer leaving notes? Or was it just some happy coincidence the body exhibited a web-like pattern on her neck in the same place as every other of Spider's victims?

Sean pulled off his jacket—he'd gone straight to work from the crime scene—and the sun rose slowly through the windows, heating up the building. His unlaced tennis shoes had left sloppy, muddy footprints from the front door to the evidence locker, where he pulled the case file on Spider, to his desk.

Sean rubbed his temples.

"Thought you could use this," a female voice said.

He looked up to see the receptionist, Mags, holding out a cup of coffee. She winked at him from behind her glasses.

"Is it. . .?" he asked about the coffee.

"It felt like one of those mornings."

Sean took the cup greedily, burning his tongue on the first hot mouthful, but he didn't care. The taste, dark roast with touches of hazelnut and something he could never put his finger on, relaxed him immediately. "You are a saint," he said as he blew on the contents of the mug.

"Don't tell anyone," she said.

"I never do." Sean watched her leave his office, her red maryjanes clicking on the tiled floor. She never dressed professionally, always in jeans and either a button-up blouse or patterned sweater, but the department didn't dare fire her. Mags was. . .unique. Rumor was she once had full scholarship offers to MIT, Stamford, and Cambridge universities in computer science. Another rumor said she'd graduated from all three. Although at 32 years old, the latter was hard to swallow, especially since those degrees would allow her to work anywhere from the Pentagon to NASA and she chose instead to work for the Boston P.D.

All Sean knew was she could get any information he wanted, always had a quick comeback, and carried her own supply of coffee, which she gave to Sean in dire situations.

Sean sipped on Mags' special blend as he reviewed the previous Spider cases.

Victim #1: Caucasian female, attended Boston University, and in a sorority. Good grades, devoted boyfriend, doting single father. She'd been found behind her sorority house inside a vacant garage. She'd been cooked alive, roasted over a slow-burning fire. The rest of her sorority house was away on their annual summer kayaking trip the last week of June. The victim had come down with a terrible summer flu and hadn't attended.

The note Spider left taped to the front door of District A1 the day before the discovered body had read "4 p.m. Don't you just *hate* getting the flu in the summer? It just seems so backwards, doesn't it?" The lines were followed by a set of latitude and longitude coordinates.

Millan, who had found the note originally, decided to follow up on it, even though it didn't seem to indicate any kind of foul play. He sent a squad car to check out the co-ordinates, which led to an abandoned warehouse with nothing inside. Millan dismissed it as a hoax—until the next day. One of the victim's sorority sisters pulled into the garage to park her car and found her friend's body. Millan realized that the coordinates in the note, if inverted, would have led straight toward the girl's body.

Needless to say when the second note arrived a month later on the 31st of July, Millan didn't take any chances. This note read "7 p.m. Can you imagine sinking when you aren't moving? How ironic after navigating the rivers so well." The sergeant began a search for any missing persons filed for that day and cross-checked the findings with boat owners or white-water rafters. He'd come up empty. The following day, the first of August, another member of the sorority house was found—the girl who'd found Victim #1. She'd been dog-sitting for her boyfriend and when he got back from his three-day trip, he found the bathroom door locked and the hall flooded. When he forced his way in, her found her dead in the tub. The tub had slowly filled with water until she drowned. Tox screen confirmed she'd been paralyzed, but aware, during the entire process. The medical examiner's report put time of death on the morning of the 1st, which meant she had still been alive when Millan received the note.

Millan then understood the note: the time gave 24 hours until the moment the victim died, the reference to the girl being a good river navigator was about the kayaking trip and "sinking without moving" denoted mode of death.

Millan thought they'd caught a break and found a pattern—some sort of relationship to the sorority. So when the third note arrived on the 31st of August, the police department thought they were prepared. The note read "9 p.m. All numbers all day will make him a dull boy. Can you count how many slices make the red river flow?"

Millan thought he had Spider beat. He focused on the

sorority as the connector; he monitored any male who had access to the group: two from the frat house opposite the sorority were attending the University on math scholarships and one of the girls had a fiancé studying to be an engineer. But when he checked them out, they were all fine. It wasn't until the next day, when someone found the body, that Millan realized his error about the sorority connection.

A 40-year-old Japanese accountant, Tam, was found dead in his apartment when his landlord, who had come up to collect the rent, found the apartment broken into. Tam had been attached to some sort of mechanical device which repeatedly sliced along his body, bleeding him slowly until he died.

Two more months followed, bringing two more notes, and two more deaths. The first was an elderly African-American man who'd been hung upside-down in an alley behind his restaurant until the blood clotted in his brain. The restaurant's chef found him the next afternoon when he took out the garbage at the beginning of his shift.

The last one was the worst: a twelve-year-old Caucasian girl whose head had been rigged in a vise that tightened continually until it crushed her skull. Her father found her the next morning when he went into the garage to get a tool. He thought his daughter was still asleep in bed.

Each death happened like clockwork: note on the last day of the month, frantic search that went nowhere, body found the next day.

The media had a field day with it, but without any major details, they spun their wheels. They hounded the police station at random intervals. They badgered the cops and their families about their ineptitude on the case. Calls flooded the precincts about fake notes, misleads, and mistaken sightings of the killer.

A few weeks before the sixth death, Sean joined the police department. He'd been brought up to speed on the serial killer's actions and jumped in on the search when the sixth note arrived on November 30th. It read: "7 a.m. Death is a terrible thing. Especially with uninvited picnic guests."

The group focused on parks because of the second part of the note. As Sean walked through a portion of wooded area, something occurred to him. He knew the note always came in two parts; one clue about something related to the victims themselves and the other about the manner of death. The police department assumed the "picnic guests" portion had been about the victim's location—but Spider never *gave* a location. Just something about the victim and something about the mode of death.

Sean sat on a bench to think. If the "picnic" reference dealt with the victim, then the first part "death is a terrible thing" should say something about the manner of death. But it didn't. It just said it was terrible.

What if we switched them around? he thought. *What if the second part had to do with the manner of death and the first part deals with the victim? Then the "death" reference deals with the victim directly.*

Sean called Millan and told him his theory. Willing to try anything, Millan met up with Sean and they went over other options.

"'Death is a terrible thing'," Millan had repeated. "Maybe this victim is a mortician? Or works for a funeral home?"

"But for those people, death is just a job. When is death terrible?"

"When it's unexpected or happens to someone you love."

"So not funeral homes, just *funerals*." Sean paged through the newspaper to the obits section to see if any funerals were held that day. It was a Tuesday, so they only found two: a very elderly man who'd died peacefully in his sleep after several months battling terminal cancer and a young 15-year-old Puerto Rican girl who'd been hit by a car and killed unexpectedly.

"Must be someone in the girl's family," Millan said, already making a call for a police car to head over to her house. Sean and Millan drove over themselves to find the whole family asleep and very much alive. The family of the cancer patient was checked as well, just in case, and they were all fine, too.

"We missed something. What did we miss?" Sean paced. "I know it's this girl's family. But we missed. . ." Sean leaned closer to the picture from the paper of the girl—it had been cropped, but he could still see part of a hand of someone who'd draped his arm around her.

"There's a boyfriend," Sean said. "She had a boyfriend!" Sean sped to the girl's family's house at 6 a.m.—one hour until the 24-hour limit expired—and pounded on the door until someone answered. He quickly explained the situation and got the boyfriend's address. He raced over there, calling for an ambulance and backup to meet him. He drove straight across the lawn, jumped out of his Jag, bounded toward the front steps, and smashed through the door.

The woman inside, sipping coffee, screamed at the abrupt entrance, spilling her hot drink all over her lap.

"I'm with the Boston P.D.," he said, showing his badge. "Your son, Jesse, may be in danger. Do you know where he is?"

The woman kept screaming and started babbling in Spanish.

"Alto!" Sean pulled at his couple of years of high school Spanish and told the woman to stop. "Estoy con la policía. Where is. . .uh. . .I mean, donde está Jesse? Es posible que algo malo pasó. ¿Entiendes? Something bad. Algo malo."

The woman stifled her screams and pointed up the stairs. Sean sprinted up the staircase as he heard the ambulance arrive outside.

The boy's room appeared empty.

"Damnit!!" he yelled, kicking the chest at the bottom of the boy's bed. The chest moved about a foot to the right and as it did, a massive number of ants scattered from a hole in its side.

Fire ants.

Sean blinked once. "*Uninvited picnic guests. . .*"

"Oh, God. . ." Sean broke the latch on the chest and yanked the top open. The boy lay huddled inside, covered in a mass of tiny moving dark spots.

Sean pulled the boy out of the chest, brushing away as many ants as he could, ignoring as they changed their palettes to his own flesh. A sick scent of honey and barbecue sauce filled the air—the mixture had been poured over the boy.

Sean heard steps on the stairs. He looked up and saw the ambulance crew enter the room.

"Fire ants," he told them. "He was locked in with them."

"We'll take it from here," an EMT said, pushing Sean aside. As they put the boy on the stretcher, Sean saw his chest move spasmodically. The boy was still alive!

He sat for a moment at the end of the boy's bed, stunned. Slowly he came around and called Millan to tell him the good news.

"I'll meet you at the hospital," Millan told him. "With any luck, this teenager saw Spider. Good job, kid. Good job."

Sean closed the file on Jesse with a sigh and stretched back in his chair. Whether the boy had seen Spider or not remained a mystery. The injuries he sustained were too massive. He died in the ambulance on the way to the hospital.

Sean had received a commendation from the city and the media did a whole story on him. He went along with it because the precinct needed the positive PR. Luckily, when nobody appeared the following month or the month after, the media frenzy died down.

Sean jumped as Millan rapped on his door.

"Go home, kid. You look like hell. There's nothing we can do right now."

Sean rubbed his face with his fingertips. "Is it really him? Is he back?"

"Truth be told, I almost hope it is. You figured him out

once and it kept him away for a year. We can figure it out again."

"And if it's a copycat?"

Millan spread his meaty hands on Sean's desktop. "Then he'll screw up somewhere and we'll nail his ass, too. But for now, go home and get some sleep."

Sean gulped down the last of his coffee, which was cold. He hadn't realized he'd been perusing through files for over six hours. "You'll let me know if something else comes up?"

"Of course. Until we have anything confirmed, I'm on media duty. We are going to try and keep this as quiet as possible, so don't talk to anyone about it. But if it is Spider, everyone is going to be in on it, possibly even the feds."

Sean nodded. "I'll be back in later then."

"You'll be back in tomorrow," Millan insisted. "It's still technically your day off and I am going to need you at full speed."

"All right, tomorrow. You'll call me, though, if—"

"I will," Millan interrupted. "I promise."

5

March 1st
2 p.m.

When Sean woke several unrestful hours later from a dream about Sergeant Millan as a giant spider-man planting lilies around the latest victim, he found he'd somehow managed to shove both pillows off his bed in different directions and get completely tangled up inside his sheet, to the point where he literally had to untie a knot that worked its way around his ankles.

Once free, he staggered into his bathroom and turned on the shower as hot as the temperature gauge would go, which landed somewhere around lukewarm. When Sean once complained about the lack of hot water, his landlord told him that if it wasn't cold, it must be hot.

Still fully dressed, Sean stripped out of his clothing and sighed at his dried muddy shoes. Without a second thought he tossed them into the shower. He wasn't about to pay $2.00 to wash them in his apartment building's coin laundry machines. On that note, he threw his mud-spattered jeans in there, too.

Kicking the clothes to the side of the stall, Sean let the water rush over his head, face, and skin. His mind swirled with thoughts about the case, but images of his dream kept intermingling with the facts, and he realized he'd been standing for several minutes without accomplishing anything.

Sean soaped up, scrubbed his shoes and jeans the best he could, and hopped out of the shower, wrapping a towel around his waist. After placing the shoes in the sink and draping his jeans over the shower door to dry, Sean headed back into his living space and went straight for the couch to watch some bad TV—anything to keep his thoughts at bay for a bit.

He found it hard to focus at the moment on the case when elements of his dream made his stomach feel queasy. Why did there have to be lilies in his dream again? He couldn't wait until he didn't care about his ex-fiancé anymore. Television often quieted his mind until he could refocus.

On the way to the couch, he smashed his foot into the edge of his bed.

"God damn son of a bitch!" he yelled, spinning around and shaking his foot. "I swear to GOD if I kick you one more time I am retiring you to the curb and sleeping on the couch for the rest of my—" In the middle of his rant, Sean noticed an envelope on his floor that lay halfway under his thrown pillow. He bent to pick it up, then froze.

On the front, in evenly spaced typed letters, read the words "SEAN TRANN." Every instinct in his body went into high alert. He immediately ran to the window to see if he could make out anyone suspicious running away, but the street appeared empty. He climbed over his bed, losing his towel in the process, and checked the door, which was locked. He unbolted it before peering down his hall. Nothing.

With quick steps he hustled back to his phone and dialed Millan, all the while staring at the letter on the floor.

"Come on. Come on!" he said to the rings on the other end.

Finally Millan answered. "I told you I'd call you if—"

"I'm pretty sure Spider left the note in my apartment," Sean said, cutting Millan off. "I'm staring at it right now. I think it was under my pillow. I didn't get it yesterday because I fell asleep on the couch. Bastard was *in* my apartment before I got home!"

A moment of silence. Then Millan spoke quickly, his words coming fast. "All right, don't touch anything. I'm sending a squad down there. Did you hear or see anyone last night?"

"No one."

"Hang tight. I'm on my way, too."

Sean dressed quickly and paced next to the letter, thinking about all the places he'd touched in his apartment, contaminating the crime scene. About twenty minutes later, his intercom buzzed.

Sean pressed the button.

"It's me, Mil—" it hissed, cutting off Millan.

Sean hit the key to allow entrance to the outer door and unlocked his own, cracking it a bit.

Millan entered first, followed by a uniformed officer and two individuals from forensics, one toting a camera.

"You all right?" Millan asked.

Sean snorted. "I'm pissed."

"You'll need to give your full statement down at the station. I'll stay here and make sure everything gets locked up. The place will be a mess though when you get home." He nodded to the forensics team, already pulling out their dusting kit.

Sean grudgingly accepted leaving his apartment and drove to the precinct. Once there, he went through the logistics and waited for Millan in his office. Detective Wilt arrived and awkwardly patted Sean on the shoulder.

"I heard what happened. Creepy."

"Thanks," Sean said. The idea that Spider had been in his apartment suddenly hit him. The hairs on his arms raised.

Millan came in shortly after and took a seat behind his desk. Sean shrugged off his unease and focused on his boss, whose dark face looked pinched and long.

"Buckle up, boys," Millan said. "This is now top priority. As far as we can tell, the note is from Spider."

6

March 1st
8 p.m.

Sean felt like an idiot. If he'd just slept in his bed instead of crashing on the couch, he would have found the note sooner. Maybe they would have had enough time to find the woman before she died. "This is all my fault—"

"Knock it off, right now," Millan interrupted. "There is no way you could've known this was going to happen. Spider always sent the letters to the police station. It is *not* your fault."

Sean stood with his hands in his pockets as Millan read the copy of the note. "'Three a.m. Unusual cold snap we're having. Good thing she's used to it.'"

Millan handed the printed copy to Sean. "We've got an ID on the victim; she's from Alaska. She just moved here a month ago. Lilia Jonah. Twenty-three. And the cold snap must refer to her death by hypothermia."

"Well, it fits with his previous letters," he said, handing it over to Detective Wilt. "Two sentences, one about the victim's identification, one about the victim's death. Unless someone shows us evidence to the contrary, I think we should assume we are dealing with Spider again—or at least someone who knows him intimately."

"I agree," answered Wilt, spitting his toothpick toward the trash. Luckily, he made it. He scratched his forehead at the receding hairline before tucking his oily blond hair behind his ears. "I'll let Detective Tay know as well. She was involved when this mess first started. She'll want to know what's going on."

"She's still on vacation in London for the next week," Millan put in. "Don't bother her with it until she gets back. We already found the victim associated with this note and Spider won't bother us for another month."

"Gotcha." Wilt turned toward Sean. "We'll keep a squad car outside your building to keep an eye out for Spider."

Sean wondered about that. Squad cars helped to show a presence, but that may not be the best route to take. "Before we do that, do they know how he got into my apartment? The doors and window were locked."

Millan shook his head. "We're still looking into it. The locks don't look like they'd been picked. Do you know anyone who has a spare key?"

"No. . .wait, yes, I mean, the landlord does."

"Yeah, I got people tracking him down. Apparently he's out of town, so he's got an alibi if nothing else. He's supposed to be back in the morning. First thing for sure, we are changing those locks tonight. Don't give the key to the landlord until we've checked him out and find out what happened."

Sean thought for a moment. "That sounds good. As for a squad car. . .I don't know. If Spider wants to send the notes to me directly, then a car might scare him off. I'd rather just set up a camera inside my apartment. Be more discreet."

Millan nodded. "That sounds like a good plan. Try and get that installed when you can. We can help you with that through the department, but it'll most likely take a week or two."

"That sounds fine to me. I don't really feel like trying to install it anyway. I think if Spider could get into my apartment, he could have killed me at any time. I think he's just trying to rattle me. I'd rather catch him in the act."

Wilt scratched the back of his head. "Then I'll call forensics and have them look over the note—see if they can get any prints off it."

"It's in the works," Millan replied. "If it is Spider again the evidence will be the same: an Office Depot number ten envelope, a standard piece of white stock printer paper, and the words typed on an electric typewriter."

"Okay. . .then I'll let the local FBI agency know so we can access them again if we need help."

"Already done," Millan said. "The previous Behavioral

Science Unit agent we worked with has been sent everything up-to-date. Hopefully he can glean something new from this recent killing and give us a better idea of what type of killer we're up against, but honestly, I feel like the FBI is grasping at as many straws as us."

Wilt threw up his hands in mock frustration. "Fine! Is there anything I *can* do right now?"

"You can get us some coffee."

Wilt blinked at the Sergeant.

"Extra sugar in mine," Sean said with a grin, jumping in on the joke.

"You guys are assholes, you know that?" Wilt began to leave the room.

Millan grunted a laugh that turned into a cough.

"And get the Sergeant some smokes while you're out!" Sean called out.

"And get Trann some action!" Millan hollered in response.

"If I get a woman and a pack of smokes, you think I'm coming back here?" Wilt joked back as he walked out of the office.

The two detectives laughed, breaking the tension. Sean could feel the tightness in his shoulders dissipate a little.

Millan's grin faded. "I'm not happy with the fact we're right. All we can do right now is our jobs, but I'm worried it won't be enough, considering our past failure." He threw the note on his desk. "Fucker isn't going to be back for a month and then we have twenty-four hours to find his next hostage."

"Well, we'll start at the beginning. Check the autopsy

again. Interview the family. Dig apart this victim's life. We'll find a connection."

"We don't even know if there *is* a connection. This guy could just be picking them at random again." The frustration in Millan's voice made his words sound guttural.

Sean tapped at the note on the desk. "There is something to this. I mean, if this guy weren't getting something out of all this, he wouldn't go through the trouble of thinking up elaborate ways to kill his victims. I mean, why not just set a bomb on a timer? Why the notes?"

"Maybe he's playing with us? Using us like lab rats to see if we can figure things out?"

"Maybe. I don't know. And that's the problem." Sean sighed. "Why did he disappear for a year? Because I found that sixteen-year-old while he was still alive? The kid died. We didn't win." He thought for a moment. "Spider went into hiding for months because he was so pissed about it. You know how I know that? 'Cause he sent that note *to my place*. It became personal for him."

"Which means you have a target on your back. If *anything* out of the ordinary happens, you let me know. I mean it. This guy knows where you live and he's a cold-blooded killer."

"Trust me, I'll let you know." Sean stood, the chair scraping against the floor.

"So where are you going to start?"

"I'm going to see a medical examiner about a dead body."

7

March 1st
8:30 p.m.

Dr. Charlotte Salla pulled the sheet up over the body in front of her and removed her bloodstained gloves. She tilted her neck from one side to the next, trying to remove the annoying kink that had embedded itself in her stiff muscles. She'd been poring over the body of Lilia Jonah for the past several hours, ever since she called Sergeant Millan and told him the victim's tox screen showed traces of succinylcholine, the neuromuscular blocking agent Detective Trann had described. There was some sort of time-release of pseudo-cholinesterase mixed in to keep the succinylcholine active, since normally the effects of the paralytic only lasted between ten and forty minutes.

Whatever the killer's identity, he or she was very adept in science. Charlotte had never seen this type of drug interaction before.

She felt excited to be involved in a possible serial killer case. It would be her first. Being new to the Office of the Chief Medical Examiner, she was anxious to prove her abilities to her colleagues and the police department. Except this serial killer's choice of targets perplexed her. So far no one had found a pattern. Charlotte, however, swelled with determination to discover one.

The answer must be somewhere on the body. The answer was *always* on the body. She simply needed to find it. Some clue. Some angle the previous examiner missed.

Not that he'd been unqualified, having been the Chief Medical Examiner at the Suffolk County ME's Office for over two decades. But Charlotte's eyes were fresh. And very, *very* sharp. Within the first month of her transfer from Honolulu to Boston, she spotted two flaws in Dr. Walsaw's previous findings—including one that freed an innocent man from prison for a crime he hadn't committed. When Dr. Walsaw retired, Charlotte was offered his position, which she accepted immediately.

Still, part of her wondered if she'd been here during the initial Spider murders, maybe she would have found something Walsaw missed.

Charlotte put her hands on the table and bent forward to stretch her back. At twenty-six, she became the youngest doctor ever to be chief medical examiner in Suffolk County.

She'd excelled in college, completing it two years early, and now after med school, found herself in a prestigious line of work.

She let out a sigh, closed her eyes, and gave herself a moment to regroup. She should grab a few hours of sleep, but felt so close to figuring out—

Her eyelids snapped open at the knock on the door. She looked over and saw Detective Trann waving at her through the lab's glass door. She walked over and let him in, as he didn't have a key card to enter this area of the morgue.

"Detective Trann? I am surprised by your visit. I assure you I will deliver my full report when it is complete."

Sean entered the room, his gaze flickering briefly onto the cadaver, and grabbed a pair of purple nitrile gloves. Charlotte noticed he'd showered at some point since viewing the crime scene—probably slept as well—and she wondered for a moment about her own personal hygiene. She hadn't left the lab since she and her team recovered the body from the scene of the crime in the pre-dawn hours.

Since she didn't like feeling less prepared or less put-together, she switched her rationale. Her lack of time spent showering and sleeping simply meant she was more dedicated to her job.

"Only wondering what you have so far." Sean leaned back against the wall of coolers, drumming his gloved fingers on the metallic doors.

"I have given my up-to-date findings to your Sergeant every two hours."

"I know. But sometimes I like to hear things in person.

Do you mind giving me a recap?"

She pursed her lips for a moment. "Very well. The victim was injected with the same paralytic agent as found in the previous Spider victims. The drug kept her alive but unresponsive to stimuli. When the body became exposed to the elements, she eventually died of hypothermia."

Sean stilled his hands. "That's it?"

Charlotte sighed. "I am afraid so. I can find nothing unusual about the puncture wound or the means in which she died. There is nothing distinctive about this body compared to all the others. In fact, there is no common thread between any of them and I have been very thorough." She gestured toward the body. "For example, there are different genders, different races, and different ages. Some are above average height, some below. Some have high BMI's, some low. I compared many different regions of the body, but there is no common factor. Some had tonsils, some did not, some have appendices, the rest had been removed. Dental history is diverse, from braces to dentures. Different joint problems, healed broken bones—some have never been to a hospital at all. Some dye their hair, some are natural. Some have fake fingernails, some are painted, the rest plain. Two are virgins, the rest were sexually active. One woman even has six toes. There is nothing that connects these victims. The only thing I know for sure is that lying on this slab in front of us is an attractive twenty-three-year old woman who died a fruitless death in a horrible manner." The words came out with an edge to them.

Sean cleared his throat. "Well, I'm sure you're doing your

best."

Charlotte took a deep breath and composed herself. "I apologize for the outburst."

Sean snorted a laugh.

Charlotte looked at him sharply.

"I'm sorry," he said, holding up his hands in a defensive manner. "It's just. . .you call that an outburst?"

Charlotte felt the touch of a smile reach her lips.

"To be honest," he continued, "it's refreshing. No offense, but you kind of come off as. . ." he trailed off.

"As an Ice Queen?" Charlotte finished, an eyebrow raised.

Sean flinched. "I was going to say unsympathetic."

"Of course." Charlotte knew it was a lie. She'd heard the term "Ice Queen" whispered under coworkers' breaths. She knew she came off as cold and calculating. This wasn't the first department to name her in such a fashion.

But she somehow found it endearing he pretended otherwise.

"The drugs injected into the victims are not easy to attain," she said. "They cannot simply be purchased at a local pharmacy."

"Yeah, we know. That's what the last M.E. said as well. We looked into it, but no one could find where it's coming from. No hospital or lab has reported anything missing or any lost shipments during that time frame. We think maybe Spider stored it early on or ordered it from out of the state, maybe even out of the country. Could have even had it purchased through someone else. Just another dead end so far, but we are still looking into it."

He gave a half-hearted smile as he peeled off his gloves. "Thanks anyway for your time. I'll be in touch." Sean began to walk away.

"Detective?"

"Yeah?" he asked, turning around.

"I will determine the connection between these victims. I promise."

He stared at her for a moment, studying her. "You know what? I believe you." He then glanced at her quickly from head to toe. "But don't forget you have a month to figure it out. You don't have to skip meals and showers during that time." He tossed the gloves in the trashcan next to the door on his way out.

"Noted," she replied, trying to stay professional, but feeling self-conscious by the fact that she felt so disheveled.

Especially when he looked so good.

8

March 7th
7 p.m.

Anya followed the man through her weapon's sight. Twilight twinkled in the background. This area of park remained empty save for one jogger. She waited until he moved past the trees, which blocked her view. As soon as her shot was clear, she fired.

The dart made a *whizz* sound as it flew through the air. It hit the target dead on—back left of his neck. The man collapsed.

"Hit," Anya said to herself. She dismantled her rifle and loaded it into a padded black case. She walked down two flights of rickety, rusty fire escape stairs as a gray van pulled up next to the body. In a swift motion, Anya grabbed under the unconscious man's armpits and dragged him up the ramp that extended from the side of the van. She flipped him over onto a thin mattress rigged with straps. Closing the door behind her, she strapped the man down, securing him as the van pulled away from the parking area.

"Make sure you turn his head to the side so he can breathe," the driver of the van called out. "You always forget that!"

"I remembered, Violet," she yelled back as she quickly turned the man's head. "I'm not stupid." Anya re-pinned a few wisps of her blonde curly hair back into her barrette.

Once the man was secured, Anya made her way into the front seat of the vehicle. She buckled herself in and turned toward Violet, a woman in her forties with short, wavy black hair and soft brown eyes. Her cinnamon-colored skin stood out against her white teeth as she smacked her gum.

"Piece of cake," Anya said, putting her feet up on the dashboard.

"Uhn. . .don't talk about cake. You know I'm on a diet."

Anya assessed the driver's physique—the skin underneath her chin hung slightly loose, her arms a touch less toned than normal.

"How could you let yourself go like that?" Anya asked.

Violet looked over at Anya's 5'7", 120 pound perfectly toned body. "When you get older, you'll understand. Besides, you know how it is when you get in that groggy state. And we were in it for so long this time." With easy turns, the van steered through the streets, the remnants of the sunset tipping the horizon in pinks and reds.

Anya nodded and sat back in her seat. She *hated* being in her groggy state. It always felt like some strange dream, going through the motions of someone else's life. The first time she'd come back from that state she found she'd gone tanning. *Tanning!* She couldn't believe she'd done that to her own body. UV damage was completely unacceptable. She cried for days, scrubbing her skin to remove layer upon layer of skin cells, trying to rid herself of the imperfection, which did nothing but leave her pink and sore.

Truth had helped her. Truth made her see it hadn't really been her, not when in the groggy state.

"Well at least it's over. And now we are back doing what needs to be done." Anya looked in the back of the van at the unconscious man. "This one will be fun."

9

March 8th
Midnight

Sean walked into his apartment, yawning. A week had already come and gone and they'd made no more progress on Spider. They finally figured out how someone gained access to his apartment, though the lead dead-ended. The spare keys to Sean's apartment were missing from the landlord's giant key ring.

When questioned about anyone who had access to his place, the landlord remembered he'd hired a dog walker the previous month when he went on vacation for a weekend. The service was all through his smartphone—he had an app where the dog walker selected him and a lockbox with the key to his apartment was left for the walker. No physical transaction took place between the landlord and the walker. When they tracked down said employee, it was revealed that the employee in question had used a stolen driver's license and only went on the one walk for the landlord's dog.

The police department urged the landlord to change the outer locks, which, after much complaining, agreed he would. Sean received his new keys for the outside of the building a few days later and now had them and his shiny new apartment lock keys hanging next to his door.

The police department continued by asking the landlord to send out a memo of concern to the residents about suspicious behavior or persons to be reported. The landlord flat out refused, saying he didn't want to cause a panic and receive a hundred phone calls a day about everyone's neighbors.

Sean shifted his thoughts back to the case, though his tired mind didn't much want to comply. Dr. Salla's full report came back almost verbatim to her original diagnosis. There simply wasn't anything on the body. She'd appeared disillusioned when she turned in her report.

Sean found it unsettled him to see her that way. She was usually so calm and collected. And she seemed more than distraught, as if defeated. With most coworkers, Sean would have asked her to grab a bite or get a coffee and talk about it, but with Dr. Salla? He had no idea how to approach her.

But right now, it didn't matter. Sleep beckoned him. Even though nothing new had risen about the case, he felt exhausted. It was as though everything from when he'd first moved to Boston came flooding back, simply because Spider returned. All his pain from the almost-wedding that ended so abruptly. His urgent need to get out of Philly and move somewhere else, *anywhere* else, as fast as he could. His guilt at finding Spider's last victim not quite soon enough. Soon enough to stop the killer, yes, but not to save the boy.

And since they hadn't *caught* the killer, he was back.

Sean couldn't think about it anymore. He slid into his bed, fully clothed, and wrapped his arms around his pillow.

A full night's sleep and a day in front of the couch since I have off tomorrow. . .

BUZZ!

He blinked repeatedly. *What? Who?*

The intercom buzzed again—a shorter burst, as if hesitant.

Sean got up, rubbing his scruffy face, and pressed the intercom talk button.

"Yeah?" he asked, looking over at the clock. It read 2:16 a.m. He must have fallen asleep.

A staticky voice answered. "De—ctive –ann?"

"Yeah?"

There was a pause on the other line.

"Who is this?" he asked as his sleepiness began to bleed away.

"It's Doc— Salla."

"Doctor Salla?" Sean paused, stunned. Why was the medical examiner outside his apartment? "What are you doing here? It's two in the morning."

"I realize it is la—, and I apolo— for a— in—veni—"

"Look, my intercom is shot. I can't understand you."

A pause. "May I c— up?"

"Uh. Sure?" *What the hell is she doing here?* He buzzed downstairs to let her in and stuck his head out of his door. The elevator in his building had been broken since he moved in—thankfully he only lived on the third floor—so he watched the end of the hall until she emerged from the stairs.

"Here," he said, motioning her over.

She crossed in front of him through the threshold and he closed the door.

"Uh. . ." he began. He watched as she surveyed his tiny living space, her almond-shaped eyes curious. He cursed himself for the overflowing piles of dirty clothes that seeped from his closet, covered the end of his bed, and slopped their way onto his couch. "Do you. . .do you want to sit down?"

"Thank you." She made her way over to the couch and gingerly sat on its edge. She tucked loose ends of hair, which had fallen from her long, dark braid, behind her ears. Her hands lay folded on her lap and her feet rose up on tiptoe. She wasn't wearing her tell-tale white doctor's jacket, but her clothing still remained reserved, as if she'd come straight from the lab and merely taken off her coat before she got here.

Sean nonchalantly shoved the dirty laundry from the back and arm of the couch and sat next to her. "So. . .uh. . . what can I do for you?"

"I would like to consume an alcoholic beverage. Do you have any beer?"

Sean blinked in surprise at the unexpected question. "You drink beer?"

She arched an eyebrow. "Yes."

"Sorry, I just. . .never mind. I'll get you one." Sean was glad he turned away from her because his face felt hot. *Get a hold of yourself! Why are you so nervous?* He grabbed two Rowhouse Reds—Philly beers—popped their tops, and handed one to Dr. Salla. He sat down slowly, about to ask if she wanted a glass, but instead watched as she drank down half the bottle in seconds.

"Are you alright?" he asked.

"No, Detective Trann, I am not. Not in the least." She took another swig from the bottle. "I cannot determine what I am missing. I do not understand it. It has been a week and I have gleaned no new information from this body or the previous victims. I know the connections are right in front of me, but I cannot see them."

Sean took a swig. "I hate to burst your bubble, but there might not be a connection. And even if there is, maybe you just can't see it?"

She shook her head slowly, her eyes staring forward at the blank television. "But you would be wrong, Detective. The link is there. And I have already seen it. I am simply unaware of what it is."

"There's no way you can know that."

She turned to look at him. "This killer, this Spider, works in patterns. The notes are all set: two sentences, two clues, two meanings. The days they are sent are always the same. Everything is methodical. Everything follows a blueprint. Which means there is a pattern with the bodies as well." She downed another portion of her beer.

"That makes sense, but it's still an assumption. Maybe

everything follows a method, but the bodies are random."

"There is a method to every madness, Detective."

Sean searched his brain for the reference. "That's. . . Shakespeare, right? Hamlet?"

Dr. Salla nodded. "Most experiences we define as insanity seem perfectly sane to those experiencing the sensation. Therefore, unless their actions are controlled by someone else, they *believe* what they are doing makes sense."

"But what if we can't figure out their 'sense?'"

"Is that not the job of the detective?"

Sean coughed on his swallow of beer. He couldn't tell—her face was blank—but he thought maybe she'd just told a joke.

It couldn't have been. She must have been insinuating I should have figured this out already, too.

Still, that would be an insult. She liked to state facts—even if they were void of tact—but she didn't seem spiteful.

Sean changed the subject. "So then. . .why are you here? I mean, not that the visit isn't nice, I guess, but. . .my place?"

She looked down at the nearly empty bottle as she rolled it between her two hands. A strand of hair fell loose from her braid and framed her face. Sean had never seen her look so—vulnerable. He felt something inside him stir at the thought she was actually a human being. And in this state, when her guard was down, it made her more beautiful than usual.

Sean shifted on the couch, embarrassed with his body's physical reaction. He would not be the guy to take advantage of someone in this situation.

"I am not sure why I came here," Dr. Salla continued. She

looked up at him. "Please understand, Detective, this is very unusual for me. I do not fail. Ever. I never have. And so I find myself desiring company that can. . .that will. . ."

"Someone who might understand?" Sean's ego hummed at the thought that she'd picked him over anyone else to confide.

Dr. Salla nodded. "I have never felt desire for this type of companionship before." She smiled and her next words knocked Sean's ego down a few pegs. "Do not misunderstand. I am not speaking of a romantic entanglement. I simply need to. . ." she paused.

Sean understood. "You need to vent."

She thought over the word. "Yes. To vent."

It may not be a "romantic entanglement" as she put it, but something had changed between the two of them.

Sean smiled and clinked his bottle against hers. "Then vent."

10

March 8th
7 a.m.

"Detective Trann. You need to wake up."

Using every ounce of will power he could muster, Sean forced his eyes to open. He was lying on his stomach on the couch and currently staring at Dr. Salla's bare feet on the carpet.

He wanted to ask when she'd taken off her shoes. Instead, he said, "Uhhh..."

The Chief Medical Examiner stooped down and turned her head so he could see her face. Her braid hung to one side—all the strands perfectly in place.

There's something not right about that. How can she look so pretty when I feel like such crap?

"I found a note," she said.

Sean was still analyzing her degree of attractiveness and didn't realize at first what her statement meant. Suddenly the words made sense.

Sean sat up with a start.

"Jesus!" he said, clutching his swimming head. He waited for a few moments until the world balanced. "Okay," he said, massaging his temples. "Did you just say you found a note?"

She nodded and sat next to him. "Yes. It seems as though someone slipped it under your door. I discovered it when I awoke." She pointed to the floor. A white envelope with SEAN TRANN lay there.

Sean glanced at it, the words blurring slightly. "What time is it?" he asked as he rubbed his eyes. *And how much did we drink?*

"It is seven in the morning."

"Seven." he repeated. "Seven? We fell asleep like an hour ago." His vision cleared and he took in all of Dr. Salla's appearance—she looked perfect. No dark circles. No wrinkled clothing. No messy hair. "How can you look so good?"

"The note," Dr. Salla said, gesturing to it. "We can discuss my appearance another time. Please focus. The clock is ticking."

Sean shook his head to sober up. He didn't feel drunk, just really groggy. "Okay, let's get this started. I'll get ready while you give Millan a call, but you'll have to use my land line. Then we can head over to the station."

"May I accompany you? I did not drive my vehicle here last night."

"You didn't?" he asked, surprised. "Why not?"

"I was unsure if you would have alcohol and on the chance you would, I did not want to drive under the influence. I took a taxi."

"You really do plan for everything, don't you?"

"I did not plan on receiving this note."

"Yeah. Good point. Okay, I'll wait until you're done with the phone call and we'll take my car. Except. . .can you drive?" He looked at her through bleary eyes.

"I am not impaired."

"Are you sure? You didn't get any more sleep than I did."

A twitch of a smile touched her lips. "I am not impaired," she repeated.

Sean shook his head, which made the room sway. "I'll take your word for it. But. . .it's a stick."

"I am capable." She looked him up and down—he stood in his boxers, blinking repeatedly.

Sean quickly grabbed his pants as Dr. Salla began the call to Millan. He tried to think as he buttoned them. He didn't even remember taking them off. And he didn't even feel self-conscious that he'd been standing in his underwear.

He looked down at the floor next to the couch. Several empty beer bottles lay there with a bottle of vodka, about three-quarters empty, next to them. He was by no means a light-weight and could handle a few drinks, but though some of the memories came flooding back—he was pretty sure he was the only one who drank the vodka—they seemed blurrier than his vision. *Oh, God, I hope I didn't make an ass of myself. I remember her talking about the case, going over different aspects of the bodies, and then somehow I switched to the vodka and. . .*

Had anything happened between the two of them? Please *don't tell me I made a move on her. But maybe she responded?* Everything still felt so hazy, just flashes of color, that Sean couldn't be sure. And how could he ask without insulting the good doctor either way?

Sean could hear Dr. Salla's side of the conversation as he finished dressing.

"Sergeant Millan? This is Doctor Salla, Chief Medical Examiner at the Suffolk County. . .yes, this is Detective Trann's home phone line. . .no, I did not show up this morning. . .hold on. . ." she turned toward Sean. "He has asked me to tell you to pick him up a pack of smokes."

Oh, God! Sean left his shoe untied and grabbed the phone. "No time, Millan," he said over the Sergeant's laughter. "We found a note."

The laughter died. "What? It's only been a week!"

"I know. But it's here."

"Damn! We just got approval to install the security camera in your place for today." Millan sounded garbled for a few moments, as if yelling to someone while covering the phone. His voice came back clear. "We don't have time to wait for forensics for the note. They will meet you here and get your keys to check your place, though I doubt they'll find anything. Wrap up the note and bring it. I'm already getting the word out. See you soon."

After Sean hung up, he finished dressing while Dr. Salla slid the envelope into a plastic sandwich bag from his kitchen.

The two of them left the apartment quickly.

Sean threw Dr. Salla his car keys and hopped into his Jaguar. As they began to move, he couldn't help his gaze—it kept flickering back to her. There was the chance something had happened between them. Except he woke up on the couch. But did that mean she'd slept in the bed? Or at all? How could he find out?

"Um. . .Doctor Salla?"

"Yes, Detective?"

"Last night is. . .sort of. . .a blur. . ."

"You removed your clothing to show me different areas where you'd been assaulted during your life, to prove to me you've made mistakes as well. You fell into unconsciousness on the couch. I slept for an hour in your bed." She turned her head away from the road for a moment and looked into his eyes. "Thank you."

Sean was glad she'd turned her view back toward the windshield. She'd somehow managed to know exactly what he was thinking and how to respond so he didn't feel like an idiot.

Even with his buzzing head, Sean came to a realization. Dr. Salla was kind of amazing.

"Where is the best place to stop?" she asked, bringing him out of his thoughts.

"Stop for what?"

"Cigarettes for the Sergeant."

Sean groaned. "Just—just drive."

11

March 8th
7:45 a.m.

"Okay people, I want to hear those wheels turning," Millan called out in a gruff voice. "We have less than twelve hours to find this victim before he's dead. Think! What does this clue mean? I want every possibility on the table now, no matter how strange or farfetched. Wilt, take notes." Millan passed around cups of coffee as he, Sean, Dr. Salla, Detective Wilt, and three other cops who were on duty that morning surrounded the Sergeant's desk. The space was small and cramped, but Millan had cracked a window and the outside air, though cold, felt refreshing.

Forensics left a few moments earlier with the original

document for analysis after making a copy. They said they'd let Millan know if they found anything. Dr. Salla offered to stay and assist, even though she had the day off, because she didn't want another body heading her way if at all possible.

"All right," Sean said, holding the printout. "I'll read the clue again. 'Does anybody have any quarters? This man made his living that way.' Remember, one clue has to do with the victim's identity and the other with the way he is going to die."

"The second half seems self-explanatory," Millan told them. "The man makes his living somehow related to quarters—money, or change specifically. So let's think of some occupations that could fit this statement."

"Homeless man," Sean said immediately. "Someone who asks for change."

"Bank teller," Dr. Salla added. "Someone who deals with giving change."

"Casino worker," one of the cops said.

"Restaurant worker."

"Change machine operator."

"Someone who asks questions."

Everyone turned and stared at Wilt.

"What?" he asked. "The first sentence is a question so maybe it's a guy who asks questions all day."

Silence.

"Uh," one of the officers chimed in, his Boston accent heavy, "what job is a guy who asks questions all day?"

"I don't know," Wilt answered, chewing on a toothpick. "A question-asking guy?"

Millan closed his eyes momentarily. "Just write," he told Wilt. "Okay, so we have some possibilities. Anything else?"

More silence.

Sean thought for a few moments. He watched specks of dust float through the bands of sunlight that streamed through the Sergeant's blinds. His head pulsed as his brain worked, but he ignored the pain. Something felt wrong about the group's answers. He felt they were taking the clues too literally. Spider always liked to twist things so they looked one way, but really meant something else.

"What if Spider's playing with the words?" Sean offered up. "Quarters are change, but what if he doesn't mean money."

"What do you mean?" Dr. Salla asked. She'd managed to seat herself in the chair across from Millan—a plethora of male coworkers stood in a semi-circle behind her.

"Well, maybe it means 'making something different' kind of change. What's a job that changes things?"

"Like an interior decorator?" one of the cops suggested.

"Exactly! Or like an architect."

"Except they build things, they do not necessarily change them," the medical examiner cut in. She leaned forward in the chair, elbows on her knees. Several rays of light streaked across her face, highlighting her eyes and lips. "How about people that change *people*, not just material objects? For example: a therapist."

"They do change people emotionally." Sean's thoughts drifted. He took in Dr. Salla's porcelain skin, her high cheekbones, her arched eyebrows. Her facial features were quite flawless. People would pay for her facial shape. "But what about a physical change? Like a plastic surgeon?" Sean added.

Wilt was going to suggest something when Millan waved to interrupt him. "We have plenty to start with right now." He slapped a meaty hand on the blonde detective's arm to show it wasn't personal he'd cut off his answer. "Remember, we have less than twelve hours to sort through this, come up with ideas, and follow through with them. If we have time, we'll add more later." Millan looked at Wilt. "What do we have so far?"

Wilt removed his toothpick and tucked it behind his ear as he read off his notes. "Homeless man, bank teller, casino worker, restaurant worker, change machine operator, interior decorator, architect. . .oops, that got cut, therapist and plastic surgeon."

One of the cops gave off a low whistle. "That's still a long list. There's no way we can find everyone in Boston who does all those jobs."

"Is there a way we can narrow the list down?" Dr. Salla asked. Sean didn't fail to notice how several of the guys standing behind her dropped their gaze as she took off her sweater and sat back in the chair—her v-neck blouse was cut modestly in the front, but it didn't matter if you stood directly behind her.

The idea bothered him. Yeah, he joked with Millan about how long it had been since he'd been physical with a woman, but he always tried to keep his attraction to others on his own time, not while at work. Plus he didn't like the idea of ogling co-workers and he *really* didn't like them all looking at Dr. Salla that way.

"Let's see if we can narrow the list down," Sean cut in, waiting until each cop's eyes were back on him. He ticked off each type of person on a finger. "Homeless: they definitely ask for money for a living, but there's no way we can check them all. Bank teller: they just exchange money, they don't really give change. Casino worker, same thing, although there aren't really any big casinos here, so it wouldn't be too hard to check out. Restaurant worker—we may have to leave that in there, which could cause a lot of problems because of the volume of servers out there. Although it seems like Spider's past clues have been very specific—not too many options—if we just find the right one.

"Change machine operator," he continued, "works on machines that give change, but doesn't give change to people directly. But it is pretty specific. Might be worth looking into. Interior decorator, definitely changes things. We should look into that. Therapist? Them, too. And plastic surgeon— changes things in a pretty drastic way. Keep."

"So we've narrowed it down to the local casinos, interior decorators, therapists, and plastic surgeons for sure, then change machine operator and restaurant workers for as long as there is time." Millan looked around the group. "Does that sound okay to everyone?"

Everyone nodded.

"All right. Ramsey," he said, talking to one of the cops, "get your whole team in here. I want everyone on this. Now!"

Ramsey ran off to start making phone calls.

"Wilt, I want you to call Detective Tay. I know she just got back from her vacation today, but she can take time to settle in after this is over."

"On it." Wilt left the office to call his partner.

The Sergeant turned toward Dr. Salla. "Doc, you don't have to stay if you don't want to, but any extra set of eyes and ears we have on this will help. Plus, you're already familiar with the case."

"It is not a problem, Sergeant. I would prefer not to work tomorrow. The only way to do that is to prevent another victim from dying."

"Good to have you on board. Since Detective Wilt will be pairing back up with Detective Tay and Sean's new partner isn't scheduled to arrive for another few weeks or so, maybe you could ride with him?"

Dr. Salla stood and tied her sweater around her shoulders. "That would be acceptable."

"Great." Millan leaned over toward Sean. "What's your pick, kid?"

Sean swirled the leftover coffee dregs in the bottom of his paper cup and thought for a moment. "I don't know. We haven't come up with the way the victim may die, so even if we find the right guy, we have no idea where he could be."

"Except most of the victims were found near their places of residence or work," Dr. Salla reminded them.

"That's true." Sean blinked his bleary eyes. "Which leaves restaurant people in hundreds of restaurants, every worker at the casinos, all the interior decorators and any places they've ever worked on, and all plastic surgeons and their places of business." He let out a huge sigh and rubbed his forehead. "I'll take whatever needs the least amount of man power. That is if the good doctor here would be so kind to help me by continuing to be my chauffeur."

"I thought you smelled like you crawled out of a bottle," Millan interjected.

"I might be still in it."

Millan eyed him. "Do you need to go home? I won't have you mucking up this case or getting it dismissed because you're still drunk."

Sean straightened up a bit. "I'm sorry, Sarge. My head hurts a bit, but I'm not still drunk. It's mostly lack of sleep. I promise. You know I wouldn't do anything to screw up this case."

"I will help," the medical examiner told Millan. "I do not mind driving Detective Trann until his headache dissolves." She looked at the list. "We will pursue. . .plastic surgeons. The number of clinics in the area is small. The list of doctors will most likely be short."

"All right," Millan agreed with a nod to Sean. "Call me if you need anything."

"Just a couple of aspirin and a shot of espresso and I'll be peachy-keen."

12

March 8th
8:30 a.m.

"If you need to vomit, please let me know and I will stop the vehicle." Dr. Salla clicked on the Jaguar's turn signal as she took a left. They were headed toward their first plastic surgery clinic. Since the clinics would not give out personal information over the phone, Sean and Dr. Salla decided to drive to each place individually, show ID, and ask for information on any surgeons who were absent that day. If anyone wasn't present, the two of them would do a thorough sweep of the area, while back at the office Mags would look up the individual's home address and message it to them. Probably not the most efficient plan, but without any idea of the method of death, they didn't have much of an alternative.

"I'm fine," Sean said through gritted teeth. He willed himself not to think of the remnants of bad coffee churning in his stomach. "We are all fine here."

Dr. Salla looked at him with an eyebrow raised. "It is just that you have turned a very unique shade of green." She shifted seamlessly as she drove Sean's Jaguar around the curve.

"You've just never seen me out in natural light. My green-skinned alien undertones shine through when exposed to the sun," he joked. He looked over at her. "Is that. . .is that a smile?"

The medical examiner's smile lingered for a moment as her eyes danced toward him. "Contrary to popular belief, I *am* human, Detective Trann."

"Please, just call me Sean. You've earned it. You've slept at my house, you're driving my car, and you've seen me both drunk and hungover. I think that qualifies you to use my first name."

"Very well, Sean."

A few moments of silence passed.

"Well?" he asked.

"Well what?"

"Aren't you going to tell me your first name?"

She looked over at him, briefly. "Why?"

"Well, it's usually polite when one person offers theirs for the other person to do the same."

"You qualified your reason for telling me your first name because I slept at your house, drove your vehicle, and have seen you in several stages of inebriation. You have not done those same things for me, so why should I tell you my first name? If you only offered your first name to be polite, then the reasons you gave are meaningless. And if that is the case, why say them at all?"

Sean squeezed his head in frustration. "I *swear* you are part Vulcan," he muttered under his breath.

"Did you say something?"

"Not that I wanted you to hear." He let out a deep exhale. "Look, those reasons were a *shared* experience. Just because I didn't sleep at your house or drive your car doesn't mean. . .you know what? Forget it. You are absolutely right. I didn't do any of those things so. . .just call me Detective Trann again." He crossed his arms and stared out the window. Sidewalks, freshly wet from the night's frost, sped by. *Why on Earth did I think I should bring her along on this case? I tried to show an inkling of humanity to this woman and she reverts right back to her robotic tendencies. Maybe last night was a fluke. Maybe I read too much into it. Maybe—*

"Charlotte."

Sean turned his head toward the driver. "Excuse me?"

"I understand your explanation about a shared experience. I believe it is valid. My first name is Charlotte. Although I would prefer you address me as Doctor Salla when we are at work."

"Of course." Sean turned his head away. For some reason, knowing her first name made her an actual person. More specifically a woman. An exceedingly attractive woman who might not be as ice cold as he'd always thought—

Knock it off! You are trying to stop a killer and save

someone. This is not the time to be thinking about this crap! Sean's focus shifted back to the case. "First clinic," he said as they pulled into the building's parking lot. "Let's hope we get lucky."

13

March 8th
5:15 p.m.

"Guess number six wasn't lucky, either."

"Six clinics in almost nine hours," Charlotte said, ignoring Sean's comment. He'd made the same remark at each clinic when they didn't find the victim. She never believed in luck. She trusted in hard work. But if she *did* believe in luck, it would be nice to have some right now. "Between getting permission to search through all the doctors' names, attaining the phone numbers of those who were absent from work today, then traveling to the houses of those who did not answer to ensure they are all alive and accounted for. . ." She shook her head. "We have less than two hours and with the heavier late-day traffic, we will not complete our list in time."

"Sergeant Millan is in the same boat." Sean slammed his hand against the steering wheel. He'd been sober for quite some time—massive quantities of coffee and two burgers from a drive-through helped—and told Charlotte he felt better driving, giving him some semblance of control in the situation. "I wish we could've further narrowed down the list somehow. Like there's something we missed."

"There most likely is," Charlotte said quietly.

"Don't start," he warned her. "This is not your fault. You told me yourself you scoured those bodies and there is no common thread. Spider is picking these people at random. Even forensics can't find anything on this guy."

"There *must* be something," she countered. Charlotte looked through the windshield and pointed up ahead. "My office is only a block away. I am of no use to you anymore. You are no longer inebriated. I would like to examine the reports again. Maybe I will find something in the next couple of hours."

"Don't torture yourself."

She glared at him. "You understand the probability of you and your team finding this victim in time are statistically insignificant, correct? And yet you continue, just in case. Can you blame me for wanting to do the same, only in my field of expertise?"

He opened his mouth, but paused before saying, "You're right. If the situation were reversed, I would not want to be cooped up in a morgue when I could be out looking for the killer."

With a swerve, Sean drove down the street and pulled over. "Call me if you find anything."

Charlotte opened the door with a nod. "You will be first on my list."

14

March 8th
6:30 p.m.

Head. Arms. Torso. Legs. Check.
Hands. Feet. Faces. Check.
Organs. Tissue. Muscle. Check.

Charlotte sighed for about the fortieth time in an hour. She had gone through her notes and all the previous reports on Spider's victims and still hadn't found a connection. She even reviewed the most recent victim's body again.

But she couldn't find anything. She asked the chief lab technician, Dr. Len Knottes, to look over the logs with her as well, but he came away just as stumped. He'd left her alone to grab them some food, but Charlotte barely registered his absence.

There is no connection between any of these victims. She hissed out another sigh. Number forty-one. But this sounded angrier. Only a half hour remained before the next victim would die. And then there would be another body for her to log. She had everything she needed to determine why Spider chose his victims, yet she couldn't see it. Even though the chance these killings were random could be a possibility, Charlotte knew based on her psychological and medical background that the specificity of leaving notes, having a timetable, and the personal focus on Sean meant in all likelihood the victims were specific as well.

"What are you missing?" she asked herself. "It must be right in front of you. What is it?" Charlotte leaned her hand against the table. Her blood-slicked glove slid clean off the edge and her face banged onto the metallic surface.

She pulled off her gloves and gingerly patted her nose as tears sprung into her eyes. "Wonderful," she muttered. "Simply wonderful." The pain was surprisingly minimal, considering the loud noise the impact made, but her nose definitely felt tender to the touch. Pushing off the stool, Charlotte made her way toward the women's restroom. She examined her nose under the harsh fluorescent lights, and relief washed over her to see no visible damage. Splashing cold water on her face, she checked the mirror one more time. She really didn't want a swollen nose because she'd be seeing the whole police department soon when they called about the next victim.

Not that a swollen nose would be so terrible. She could

have a huge lump. Or bruising. Broken blood vessels which would make her face red and blotchy. Patchy. Imperfect.

Although it took a lot of time and effort, Charlotte felt very concerned about looking perfect as often as possible. She had been born with irregularly shaped, strawberry-colored birthmarks covering her arms and legs. They faded over the years and by age seven were completely gone, but the extensive teasing she endured, even after they'd gone away, had sent her home in tears almost every day from school. The children would associate her discoloration with her intelligence level, calling her names like Disease-freak, Patchy-retard, and Strawberry No-brains.

Though simply immature names which held no logical merit, to an elementary school child, they were devastating. She'd been so happy when her family moved from Seattle to Portland in the fourth grade. No one at her new school knew about her previous condition. She still garnered a reputation and was treated coldly by fellow classmates, mostly female, but for different reasons. Now they envied her for her beauty, resented her for her intelligence. These dissociations she could handle, even cultivate. She kept herself aloof on purpose, putting her studies and eventually her career before friendship.

Not that she hadn't ever had friends, but they seemed to be circumstantial—the teenage girl she studied with during high school for exams, the study group she met with weekly in college to review essays, the other individuals in her residency program at Johns Hopkins. But once she completed each of those steps toward her career, those people in her life faded out as she moved on.

Still, she always feared someone, somehow would find out the truth. That her compliments weren't deserved. And that someone would point her out in the middle of a moment of triumph and pronounce her a phony and her birthmarks would return full-fold, darker and more hideous than ever.

Charlotte knew the impossibility of spontaneous reemergence of her birthmarks, but no matter how far along she'd come, she always wanted to obtain perfection, even if only on the surface.

On the other hand, she knew it wasn't healthy to fixate on such an unobtainable goal. She supposed that was one reason she went to Detective. . .to *Sean's* house the night before. She wanted to—how had he termed it?—vent. To have someone listen to her problems and know she *had* problems.

It might have been the reason why most of her relationships ended up so short-lived, both platonic and romantic. She consistently went out of her way to be perfect, and couldn't tolerate imperfection of any kind in others, which included normal life problems in her partners.

And yet the last ten hours, most of which was spent in the small space of a car with Sean, hadn't been as awful as she thought they would be. She'd been, to be honest, relaxed.

"Look at it this way," she said to her reflection, "at least you are not saddled with an extra toe like the fourth victim. Although I suppose you could always wear closed-toed shoes." She snorted a laugh. And then she became very still.

At first she felt ashamed for cracking a joke about a

victim, though she wondered if Sean would have laughed, but then another thought struck her, hard.

"I do not believe it. . ." Charlotte bolted from the restroom back into the lab. She frantically flipped through all the notes, opening the pages to specific points, and laying them out side by side.

"The things they have in common are things that are *un*common."

She looked at the clock on the wall, its face the representation of her enemy: time. But it read 6:40 p.m. Not too late. Only 20 minutes left of the twenty-four hours, but if she could get a hold of Sean quickly enough. . .

15

March 8th
6:40 p.m.

"I'm looking for *what?*" Sean asked as he slammed on his brakes. The bus in front of him had stopped abruptly as a passenger raced to catch it. Sean craned his neck, the phone slipping in his hand as he looked to see if he could pass the bus. The last clinic hadn't panned out. He could still make it to one more and check on any absent persons in the last 20 minutes.

"I can barely hear you," he continued into the phone, jerking the wheel to the left. He raced around the bus, making an illegal right turn in front of it. He ignored the bus's horn. "You're breaking up." He shook his head at her garbled response. "Get some place with better reception and call me back."

Sean drove in silence for a few minutes, weaving in and out of traffic, before his phone rang again.

"Detective Trann," he answered.

"Is this better?"

"Yeah, much," he answered Charlotte. "What's going on?"

"I found the connection," she said, panting.

"Are you okay?"

"Yes. I ascended three flights of stairs at a rapid pace to call you back. Our elevators are out of service."

"So you think you found a connection?"

"Not *think*, Detective. Know."

"What have you got?"

There was a pause as she gulped in a breath. "The connections between the victims are idiosyncrasies in or on their bodies. Each victim had something about him or her that is or was abnormal. I did not realize this pattern because two of the victims' abnormalities could not be determined from an autopsy analysis. The problems, however, would have been noticeable while he or she was alive."

"What do you mean?" Sean asked.

"I will explain later. Call the department. Have them search through the medical records for our last group of plastic surgeons. Tell them to look for anything medically unusual about them. They are who we need to focus on."

"Medically unusual?"

"Yes. Anything, such as extra digits, glandular problems, a non-functioning gall bladder, anything out of the ordinary.

The more unusual, the better. If anyone on the list has a unique medical condition, go to that building first."

"I'm already almost at the next building."

"But if I am right, you will know for sure. Please, Detective. . .Sean. Trust me. And hurry."

Sean looked down at his phone, now quiet since Charlotte had hung up. He pulled into the clinic's parking lot. He called Mags at the police station and took a few moments to explain.

"You want me to search through people's medical records? That's not legal," Mags told him. "Those records are confidential."

"Mags," Sean said, "don't give me that crap. I know you can hack your way into any system you want. Why do you think I haven't fired you even though you *suck* as a secretary?"

"The coffee?"

"Please Mags. We are almost out of time." Sean's stomach clenched.

A couple moments of silence passed. "Give me a few minutes."

Sean let out his held breath and waited on hold, drumming his fingers on the steering wheel. He stared at the clinic, feeling like he should be in there asking questions. He could at least *start* to check out the place. If Mags couldn't come up with anything, then at least he'd continued with his search.

Sean turned off the car and opened his door.

"Detective?" Mags asked.

Sean paused, halfway out of his car. "Go ahead."

"Doctor Fred Folger was born with his heart on the outside of his chest. Doctor Sly Hops was born deaf. Those are the only two that popped up with anomalies remaining on your list."

"Either of those sound more abnormal to you?"

"Heart on the outside? Pretty freaky."

Sean nodded in agreement, even though Mags couldn't see him. "Call his clinic, see if he's there. It'll save me the time. In the meantime, give me his home address and I'll make my way over."

"On it."

Sean disconnected the line as Dr. Folger's address came in through his computer system.

"Fuck!" he cursed. "It's on the other side of the city." He radioed the squad car closest to the house. Millan answered.

"I have a hunch," Sean said. "I'm sending you an address. Do me a favor and—hold on, I'm getting a call." Sean picked up his cell phone. "Detective Trann. Yeah, Mags. He wasn't at work today? Got it. I'm sending Millan to the address. Check out the other doctor, just in case." Sean switched his line back to the Sergeant. "Millan? Send whoever is closest to this address. I'm about twenty minutes away with traffic and we only have about ten minutes left."

"Why this place?"

"No time. Just trust me."

"You've got it, kid."

Sean hung up as the phone rang again. "Trann. . .yeah, Mags. The deaf doctor was at work? Then it must be the outside-heart guy. I'm on my way to Doctor Folger's."

The twenty-minute drive was the longest of Sean's life.

16

March 8th
7:15 p.m.

Sean pulled up to a split-level red house on Harvard and Glenway behind several other police vehicles and one ambulance. He'd received the call a few minutes earlier that he'd been right: the victim lived here. But the fact that the ambulance still sat in the driveway boded ill.

Oh, no, Sean thought. *It's like that kid Jesse all over again. They got to him, but we were still too late.*

Sean hopped the chain link fence surrounding the place, raced up the short set of stairs past an EMT, and tried to go through the open door.

"Hold it. You need booties," said a forensics agent. Sean

quickly protected his shoes with the plasticky-cloth coverings and entered.

The scene was a mess.

Blood splatters covered the cream, carpeted floor of the living room. Chunks of flesh littered the leather furniture and sleek, black appliances. The salty, metallic smell of blood filled his nostrils

Pieces of body hung from ropes tied to metal clasps in the ceiling. A strange metallic box with a gear sat attached to the center of the ceiling next to the overhead light. A thick line of wire led from the contraption to each of the four cornered metal clasps and one line hung loosely toward the front door.

Sean closed his eyes and looked away. When he opened them, he spotted Millan sitting in the kitchen, the EMTs giving him oxygen. His normally dark skin was a ghastly shade of pale, yellowish-brown. Splotches of blood and possibly flesh speckled the front of his shirt.

"Millan!" Sean cried out, rushing over. "God! Are you all right?"

Millan pushed away the oxygen mask. "It's my fault, kid. It's all my fault. I couldn't. . .the paralytic must have worn off. I couldn't tell what he was saying before. . .and we just went in so fast and—" Millan threw up. He wiped his mouth with a towel provided for him, his hand shaky. The EMT told Millan to put the oxygen mask back on his face.

"I'm sorry, Detective," the medical technician told Sean, "he's in shock. We need to take him to the hospital."

"I understand," he replied. He gave Millan's shoulder a squeeze and then found Detective Wilt. His partner,

Detective Juliette Tay, stood next to him. She was an exceptional detective and Sean had even asked to be partnered with her, but Millan said Wilt would be a better fit. Her freckled cheeks had flushed red, as if she'd been running, but Sean wondered if she simply didn't want to vomit. He didn't envy her coming home from her week-long vacation to this. Not to mention the jet lag—she'd been back to visit her mother in London.

"Wilt, man, what happened?"

Wilt rubbed the palm of his hand across his lips, his normally smooth demeanor lost. "I got here just minutes after the Sergeant did, so this," he said, gesturing to the mess in the room, "had already happened."

"Which was what, exactly?"

Wilt pointed at the ceiling and spread his fingers outwards. "The man was quartered—as in pulled into four pieces. His arms and legs had been cut almost clean through, while a cauterizing mechanism followed along, to ensure he wouldn't bleed out first. Then, when the contraption completed, it would jerk him apart."

Sean's stomach tightened. "Oh my God. That's what the clue meant when it referenced 'quarters.' Fucking sick bastard."

Wilt nodded. He swallowed hard and turned his head, unable to continue.

Detective Tay continued for her partner, her British tones clipped and crisp. "Apparently, he was tied to the four clasps. When Sergeant Millan arrived and broke down the door, it triggered that," she said, pointing to a metallic geared box on the ceiling, "which caused the ropes to pull apart rapidly and. . ."

Wilt made a ripping noise.

"So that's why Millan thinks it's his fault." Sean let out a sigh. "But the guy would have died at seven o'clock anyway."

"That's the stickler. The Sergeant and his team arrived with four minutes to spare. If they'd have gone in slowly. . ." Wilt shrugged.

Realization hit Sean. "The man tried to tell them not to come in. Millan said the man was yelling, but he figured he wanted help, and they were in such a hurry. . ."

"Exactly." Wilt looked at the four body parts hanging from each corner of the room. "The man would have most likely lost both arms and legs, but without the blood loss from the final rip, he may have lived. But after all of this, I don't know if he would have wanted to." He shivered. "At least maybe he could have given us an I.D. on Spider."

"Did you determine his defect?" a female voice asked from behind them, startling the trio.

Sean whirled around. "Hey, Doc. You remember Detectives Wilt and Tay."

Charlotte nodded at each detective in turn. "Welcome back, Detective," she said to Tay. "I was told you were on vacation. England?"

"That's right," Tay answered. "Went to visit my mum. Did *not* expect this as a homecoming."

"Understandable."

Sean indicated Charlotte with his thumb. "Doctor Salla is the reason we are here at all. She found a connection between the victims. Abnormalities on their bodies. This guy was born with his heart on the outside of his chest," he said, answering the medical examiner's previous question.

Charlotte nodded, surveying the room. "The body will be difficult to examine, but nevertheless, there may always be a chance the murderer left something else behind."

At that moment a member of the forensics team came over. "Sorry everyone, but you need to clear out. We've got our work cut out for us. I'll send you the photos of everything and notify you when we finish."

"Okay," Wilt replied. He looked a little overwhelmed. Tay patted him on the shoulder.

"Then I will speak with Sergeant Millan about arranging transport of the body," Charlotte said.

"Millan went to the hospital." Sean took a few moments to explain what happened.

Charlotte's brow furrowed. "With four minutes to spare, a hurried entry seems the most logical choice. The Sergeant chose the most direct and timely course of action. He could not have known what would happen. His logic at the time does not appear flawed."

"Logic may be nice for math problems, but it serves as poor reassurance when there's a dead person involved," Sean said.

Charlotte looked puzzled, as though she couldn't understand why logic would not solve everything. "Well then, Detective Wilt, since you are the senior officer, I would like you to let me know when I can remove the remains."

Wilt looked surprised. "Sure."

The four of them made their way out of the living room, giving the scene a wide berth. They could see a small crowd of people gathering outside while some officers set up police tape to keep them at bay.

"We're not going to be able to keep this one out of the press." Wilt let out a low whistle as a piece of the victim's arm fell from its harness. "Sometimes I hate my job."

Tay sighed. "I need a bloody vacation."

17

March 9th
12:30 a.m.

Sean had never been happier to see his crappy apartment. After almost five hours of typing up the report, questioning neighbors of the victim, medical examiner findings, typing more on the report, speaking with the Chief of Police—who suggested creating a task force with Sean in the lead— rereading old files, dealing with the press who'd not only heard about the previous day's murder, but also the week's before and planned to run the story on the late evening news, checking in on Millan, and typing the conclusion of the report, Sean had finally been able to go home. His head pounded, his fingers felt cramped from writing and typing, and after getting through the entire day on one hour of drunken slumber, he felt ready to sleep for a week. Since he only had the next day off, a week couldn't happen, but knowing he didn't have to go into work tomorrow seemed good enough for the moment.

Although sleeping for a whole week may give me just enough time before Spider's next attack. But who knows now that he's changed his pattern? There could be another note in two months. Or two days. He looked up at the wireless security camera above his door and felt better knowing that it, and the one in the hall that could see the outside of his door, might help catch Spider next time around. The landlord hadn't been completely pleased, but when Sean assured him only the outside of his door would be seen, and that it would be set up through his own internet and wouldn't cost the building anything, he allowed the small camera in the hall to be installed.

A squad car now sat parked outside of Sean's apartment—more of a show for the press that something was being done than a hope of catching someone breaking into his unit. Mostly the officers ended up shooing away reporters who would dig through the garbage or harass people going in and out of the building.

Sean didn't care at the moment as long as it didn't happen tonight as all he wanted was some quality time with his pillow.

Peeling off his shirt and sliding out of his jeans, Sean laid down on the bed, face-up. He stared at the switched-off ceiling light and let the day's events flow out of him. He envisioned himself like a giant colander with pinpoint holes where his stress drained out of him. Every time a thought came in, whether an image of the crime scene, a picture of Millan in shock, or the repetitious questions he had to type up for his report, he sent them draining through the sieve. His breathing became rhythmic. His muscles unwound. He closed his eyes and felt himself submerge into the dark abyss of unconsciousness.

BZZZZZ!

"For fuck's sake!" he yelled. He stomped out of bed to the door.

Bang! Bang! Bang! "Keep it down up there!"

"Shut UP, Gerald!" Sean yelled at his floor.

BZZZZZZZZZZZZ!

Sean slammed his fist on the intercom. "Who the *fuck* is it?"

"Sorry to bo—you, Detec—Trann," one of the officers from the patrol car said. "There is a young wo—down here who—knows you. Her na—is Angellica."

All the blood ran from Sean's face. The intercom swam before him, a vivid swirl of tan and gray.

"I know you're up there!" Gerald hollered from below. *"People are trying to sleep!"*

Sean didn't hear it. *Angellica?* he thought.

"Sir? Sh—we let her up?"

"Quiet, Gerald! He's got the cops outside."

"Good! I can tell them what a loud punk this kid is!"

"Sir?" the intercom crackled.

"Uh. . ." A thin layer of sweat sprouted across his forehead, which apparently transferred from the moisture that normally would be in his mouth. Sean's tongue felt like dry sandpaper. He couldn't make any words come out. Instead he hit the button to allow her to come in.

"Ohmygodohmygodohmygod. . ." She was here. She was coming up to his door and he couldn't seem to form words or thoughts.

Get a hold of yourself! Using the doorknob, Sean steadied his wobbling knees. He jumped at the timid knock.

He didn't remember opening the door. It was just open, and she stood there, looking as much of an angel as he remembered.

"Hey, Sean," Angellica said, a tentative smile on her face. "I—uh, I'm sure I'm the last person you ever expected to see. . . ever *wanted* to see, maybe."

Sean said nothing. He did nothing except stare at her blue eyes, her curvy lips, her smooth skin. Her hair fell longer, past her shoulders, and it curled up at the ends into tiny blonde waves. She looked tired, but still beautiful.

"What do you want?" The words came out forced and guttural. He'd really wanted to say he didn't care what she wanted, he just wanted her to stay forever, to not say anything. To just come in, close the door behind her, and forget everything that happened. Start over. Together.

But the crushing pain in his heart prevented these thoughts from becoming words. It warned him that although she appeared an angel on the outside and once told him to have faith in their love, that it would lead them through forever, no matter the obstacles, it was all a pack of lies.

A look of pain flared briefly in her eyes at the tone of his voice.

Part of him wanted to apologize.

Part of him enjoyed it.

"Do you. . .do you mind if I come in?" She eyed him in his boxers and glanced into his apartment. "I mean, if you're. . . if you're not busy?"

Sean grabbed the shirt and pants he'd removed when he arrived home and tugged them on. He hoped she didn't see his hands shaking. How he wished Charlotte was here right now. Or *any* girl for that matter.

"Yeah. Sure. Why not." The words were clipped, monotone.

Angellica walked into the room and her eyes flitted over his place. "Cozy."

"What do you want?" he repeated. A thousand thoughts raced through his mind. Had she come back for forgiveness? Did she regret what had happened between them? Was she sorry for how things had ended? For leaving him at the altar? For cutting off all communication with him?

Did he even want to hear her apologize?

Would he want her back if she did?

Angellica took a seat on the couch. "No small talk, huh?"

When she walked past him a scent floated through the air—lilies. Her perfume. It triggered a thousand memories: lying on a blanket on the hood of his car staring at the stars, holding her close during their wedding dance lessons. He remembered smiles, kisses, the feel of her head pressed against his shoulder when he'd wake. Her fiending for coffee in the morning. Her nervous habit of chewing on the side of her thumb.

But those were memories. Part of the past.

Except she was here now, in the present. So close. Real. Tangible.

He stood, arms crossed, just staring at her.

"Right, no small talk." She clucked her tongue against her mouth. Her next words came quickly. "So here's the thing. I got this letter in the mail, about two weeks ago. There were two pages. The first page said I was to bring the second page to you, in person, before the first of the month, or there would be consequences." She shuffled through her purse, looking for the letter. "I blew it off—I mean, I'm sorry, but I thought maybe it was some lame attempt from you to contact me. . ." she trailed off and handed him the letter. "Here's the second page. The first page seemed like nonsense. I turned it over to the Philly P.D. anyway and they filed it and said not to worry about it unless another letter came, and another one never did."

Sean opened the page. He read it and his eyes widened.

It was a note from Spider. *Sean— You stole twelve. Every week until the quota is met.*

"Did you have the police department run it for prints or DNA testing or anything?"

She shook her head. "I didn't know it was important. Not until I saw on the news tonight about the murders. They said the page was too contaminated, but would send it along to the police here. I saw on TV you were one of the lead detectives on the case."

"Why didn't you call me and tell me right away?" he snapped at her.

"It—the letter says I was supposed to give you this in person. I-I didn't know. I thought it was a prank!" Angellica chewed on her thumbnail.

"That'll be really reassuring to the victim's family."

Her eyes grew large with horror. "God! Sean, I'm so sorry! It was the soonest I could get here! I've been having a hard time at home, not really feeling the best, and then I couldn't get off work until—"

"Please," he said, turning his head and closing his eyes for a moment, trying not to think about maybe some boyfriend bringing her soup while she lay sick in bed. "I don't care about your personal life. Not anymore." The sting of the comment hung in the air for several moments.

Sean let out a deep breath. As much as he wanted to hurt her for what she'd done to him, he couldn't let her think she'd gotten someone killed. "It's not your fault." He turned toward her—saw the tears dance in her eyes. "Really," he reassured, sitting next to her on the couch. "There's no way you could have known what would happen. You tried to get here in time. This death is *not* your fault."

She pressed her lips together, as if afraid to speak.

He wanted to reach out, to comfort her, but the fear clenching his stomach held him back. He didn't want to care about her again. He couldn't.

Could he?

"Listen," he began, wondering if he would regret what he was about to stay. "It's late. And you are obviously. . .not in the best state of mind. You should just stay here, get some sleep, and then you can drive back to Philly in the morning."

Angellica went back to chewing on her thumbnail. "I don't know, Sean. I mean, you have police outside and things seem crazy right now—"

"I don't know how good I feel knowing this monster sent a letter to your house. To be honest, I'd rather you were here, where I can keep an eye on you."

She dropped her hand. "You sure?"

He laughed. "Not really. But I think so."

The beginnings of a smile touched the corner of her mouth. "Okay. I guess I could stay here. On the couch is fine."

Now it was Sean's turn to feel horrified. "Oh, God, no. I mean, I meant stay here, in Boston. Like a hotel. I didn't mean—"

She flushed. Full-on reddened face. "I'm sorry. I thought you meant—'cause you said—I'm such an idiot!"

"No, no, it's okay. Really. And actually, maybe you should stay here. I mean, I already have the cops stationed outside. I can let them know and I'd be here and you're already here and it's late—"

She stood as if to leave. "No. I couldn't. I'm too embarrassed now."

"It's really okay. Really."

She paused, her face returning to its normal pale color. "Are you sure. I mean, *really* sure?"

No.

"Yes."

"Okay. Then I'll stay." She looked around his place. "I am

really sorry I wasn't here sooner."

"It's okay. How could you know what this meant?"

She hesitated and sat back down, her small frame hardly denting the couch cushion. "What *does* it mean?"

Sean reread the letter out loud. "'You stole twelve. Every week until the quota is met.' It means he blames me for losing twelve victims over the twelve months he didn't kill anyone and to make up for it, he is going to kill one person every week until he catches back up."

"You mean if I would have come here before the first of the month I might have given you enough warning to prevent *two* deaths?"

"We don't know *what* would have happened if you would have come earlier. Maybe he was planning a trap or wanted to use you against me. I don't know. All I do know is now we are aware the victims will come every week so we'll be better prepared."

Angellica's face hardened. "I want to stay and help."

Sean hesitated before speaking. "It's not that I wouldn't appreciate it—"

"This isn't for you," she said, her tone determined. "This is for me. You expect me to just mosey back home while this guy is killing other people, especially since I didn't take him seriously to begin with? Screw that! He brought me into this mess and now I want to be a part of taking him down."

Sean treaded lightly with his words, not wanting to insult her. "I don't know how much help you could be. I mean I don't know what you could do. You're not exactly authorized for anything."

"It doesn't matter. I'll do something. Whatever you all need. Coffee runs, getting copies, whatever I can do." She paused, abruptly. "I mean. . .well, as long as you're okay with it." She rubbed her fingertips across her forehead. "God. Listen to me! Here I am going on about what I want and just barging into your life after. . ." she swallowed. "After what happened between us."

Sean started to say something, but she stood again, cutting him off. "Look, just. . .never mind. This is—I'm sorry. . .I just. What was I *thinking*? I'm just going to go to a hotel and leave in the morning and. . .I'm sorry. Ugh! I'm such a bitch!"

"You're right," he told her. "You are a bitch."

Angellica's jaw dropped.

"You royally fucked me over," Sean continued. The words spilled from his mouth, out of his control. Words he'd had pent up inside him for months. Things he never got to say because she'd refused to see him. "You left me at the altar on our wedding day. You ran off without a word and left me, alone, without any way to talk to you about it. You are a gigantic mega-bitch. And I don't know what that means for your karma."

He held up his hand to stop her from speaking. "But you *don't* deserve some psychopathic asshole making you feel like it's your fault someone died when *he's* the killer. Or putting you in an awkward situation so that you can't help. This shit is on him, Angel, not you."

Angellica sat back down, stunned. Gradually, a soft smile spread through her lips. "You're the only one I ever let call me that, you know?"

Sean hadn't even realized he'd called her Angel. "Yeah, well. . .old habits and all that."

Slowly, Angellica leaned forward. She kissed him gently on the lips.

"I'm sorry," she whispered, tears in her eyes. "I'm so sorry. For everything."

Oh, God. She just kissed me. She's so beautiful. I want her so much.

He could feel his body responding to the several months of no physical contact. His skin tightened, his fingers spasmed, his body quivered.

She was saying something. He didn't know what. His brain had shut down. A different part of his body was now directing him.

"Shut up," he told her. "I don't want to hear it. Any of it." He grabbed her by the shoulders and kissed her, hard. She resisted for less than a moment before wrapping her hands around his lean shoulders. In one swift motion, he picked her up off the couch, her legs straddling his midsection, and made his way toward the bed. She'd already pulled off her shirt, her black bra heaving as her breath quickened.

Sean threw her down and slid her toward the wall. He crawled on top, fighting hard to never let his lips part from her body for more than a second. Her skin was already slick with sweat and his hands slid against her thighs as he pushed her skirt up to her waist.

Her hands moved as if possessed, running across his back, through his hair, the back of his head and neck.

He kissed her skin, nibbled her earlobe, chewed on her

shoulder. Her skin tasted salty and sweet. The smell of her perfume intensified when mixed with her sweat and it overwhelmed his senses.

With one hand he slid underneath the bra's silky fabric and was lost on soft skin—with the other, he rummaged inside his nightstand, praying, *praying* for. . .

Oh, thank GOD! he thought as his fingers wrapped around a plastic package.

Her eyes were hungry as she tore it open and assisted in applying the contents. As soon as she was done and safety had been established, Sean thrust inside of her.

"Oh, Sean!" she cried out, her eyes rolling back into her head in pleasure.

He bit his lip. The immediate and intense stimulation was almost unbearable. He breathed out slowly, willing himself to hang on to the feeling, which intensified every time she moved her hips.

Her fingernails bit into his back as she encouraged his motions. When this wasn't enough, she slammed her hands against the headboard, pushing against his rhythm to intensify the thrust.

"I'm there!" she cried out. She squeezed her legs together around him, her head arched back.

The whole bed rocked off the floor.

Sean reached a point of pleasure so intense it felt like pain. Eyes closed, his leg muscles cramped tight, but he couldn't feel it. He was immersed in the moment—a surge spread throughout his entire body and then it rushed into one spot—the pinpoint of his explosive release.

Only one other thing penetrated that moment—Angellica's high-pitched squeal of ecstasy, which came at the same time.

18

March 9th
Noon

Sean opened his eyes slowly. The sun shone through his slanted blinds, casting layers of light through the small room.

He looked beside him and saw Angellica nestled into his arm, the wisps of hair around her face curling from the humidity of her sweat. The bedsheet was wrapped loosely around her lower half, her bare shoulders and back exposed to the bands of sunshine.

He smiled.

And then felt sick to his stomach.

Oh man. What did we do? This is not how things were supposed to go. Did this even mean anything to her? Is she still going to stick around? Do I want her to? What do I say? What do I do?

Angellica stirred and opened her eyes. She smiled.

"Good morning."

"Afternoon, actually," he told her, nodding at the clock.

"Good afternoon then." She reached above her and stretched, her slim arms leaning against the headboard.

"So," she said.

"So."

"Want to talk about what happened?"

"I think we both know what happened," he replied.

"You know what I mean."

"I do."

"We don't have to talk about it."

Sean sighed. "We probably should."

"Yeah." She paused. "I'd kill for a coffee."

He glanced at his kitchen. "I don't know if I have any."

She shrugged. "It's okay. I'll pick one up later."

Silence.

"So. . ." Sean began again.

This time Angellica sighed. "I don't know why it happened. It was amazing. It was wonderful. It was the best sex I've had in a very long time."

"No need to stroke my ego."

She shook her head and rolled over onto her side, facing him. "I'm not. It's the truth. We never had problems in this department."

"I didn't know we had problems in *any* department."

She tucked a piece of hair behind her ear. "I know. And I

don't think now's the time to discuss that."

"You mean it takes longer than a year for it to be the right time for you to tell me why you stood me up at the altar?"

Angellica exhaled forcibly and stood, pulling the sheet around the rest of her body. "That's not what I meant."

"Well what exactly do you mean, Angellica?" His frustration leaked into his tone of voice. "I mean, seriously, what am I supposed to do with this?" He sat up in bed as she got dressed. "You show up here after a year and a half with a letter from a killer that has been tormenting me and we have a night of mind-blowing sex and I'm supposed to be okay that you don't think it's the time to talk about what happened?"

"God," she said, as she slipped her shirt over her head. "This was a huge mistake. I don't even know what I was thinking last night. I should have just given you the letter and walked out."

He stood up from the bed and roughly pulled on his jeans. "So why didn't you?" he snapped. "Why did you stay? You didn't have to. No one made you. No one made you kiss me. No one made you leave these scratch marks on my back."

She whirled around and glared at him. "Sean. . .!" she started. Then her breath ran out of her. "I can't—I can't explain what happened last year. I know that's not what you want to hear, but it's the truth. I just—I just couldn't marry you. I had a massive panic attack the day of our wedding—blacked out and everything. It wasn't just about marrying you—it was that I'd be married to your job, too. The violence, the late nights, the worrying about if you'd be alive every day.

And raising a family in that? I just couldn't."

"And you couldn't tell me that at any point before the wedding day?"

She shook her head and sat back down on the bed. "Yes, no, I don't know." She barked a sharp laugh. "This is why I avoided you. I didn't know how to tell you. You are your job. I was scared you'd also leave it for me and resent me for it. I thought this was better."

"And last night?"

"Last night?" She paused. "Last night was. . .I don't know the answer to that, either. All I know is that I knew I would feel good with you and that's all I wanted. It's selfish, but it's the truth."

"Well at least you told me the truth about something," he shot at her.

"Yeah. I deserve that."

Sean scratched his head. "Do you. . .do you regret last night?"

Angellica looked up at him. "No. I don't think I do. I don't know if what happened last night means anything, but I don't regret it. Being with you is always wonderful."

"I don't regret it either. But I don't think it should happen again. There are too many. . .complicated emotions about you, and what we did won't help keep them straight in my head."

She nodded in agreement. "I'm sorry. For all of this."

"I know. I also know you didn't plan it."

There was a moment of silence. He hated her for being here, for reviving all these emotions, but the thought of her walking away again burned in his chest.

"So are you still thinking about sticking around?" he asked.

"Is that okay?"

"I know how hard it would be for me to walk away if I were in your shoes."

Angellica chewed on her thumbnail. "I don't want to cause any more problems."

"I don't know how you could *possibly* cause more problems than what you've already done."

"Having crazy sex with you couldn't have helped." She slid the edge of her thumb over her bottom lip.

Sean felt his body stir as he thought about it. "Probably not. But we decided we weren't going to do that again."

"Yeah," she purred, spreading her hands across the sheet. "We did decide that, didn't we?"

19

March 9th
4 p.m.

Three hours later, after a second round of "we're not going to do that again," Sean drove to the police department with the letter. He told Angellica to stay at his apartment, explaining about the wireless cameras on his door and in the hall to reassure her of her safety, and letting the patrol car outside know about her. He told her someone would want to question her about receiving the note, but figured she could use some sleep first, and to come down to the station later. He gave her his keys to lock up when she left, saying he'd get them back when they met up.

Sean hadn't thought Millan would be at work,

considering what he'd been through the day before, but apparently he didn't want the time off. Sean didn't push the subject as he updated his boss on the situation.

"Angellica is here?" Millan asked.

"Yeah."

"Staying at your place?"

"Yeah."

"And Spider sent her this letter to give to you?"

"That's right."

Millan looked over the note. "He's really pissed off at you. I mean, sending your ex who stood you up at the altar to bring you the news that he's going to kill every week instead of every month?" He shook his head. "That's fucked up."

"You're telling me?" Sean replied. "I'm the one with the woman in my apartment." He leaned back in the chair across from the Sergeant's desk and drummed his fingers on the arm. "What the hell am I going to do?"

Millan rubbed his chin, his fingers scraping over his stubble. "I don't know, kid. All I do know is don't sleep with her. It'll screw up everything even more."

Silence.

"You didn't."

Sean gave a weak smile.

Millan rubbed his fingertips against his eyelids. "Rookie mistake, kid. You just opened up a huge can of pain."

"She and I talked about it. It's—"

"Fine," Millan cut in. "Oh yeah, like no one's ever claimed that before. You've probably even said it'll never happen again, right?"

Silence.

"And it did already, didn't it?"

"Well. . ."

Millan laced his fleshy hands behind his head and chuckled. "Unfortunately, I've been there, so I can't preach. I just don't envy you the aftermath."

Sean shook his head. "Really, it's—"

"Fine. Yeah, whatever you say, kid."

Sean felt anger rise up. "You seemed all gung-ho about it a couple of days ago when you thought I'd slept with Doctor Salla."

"Having sex with a hot, super-smart medical examiner is much different than rekindling the flame with an ex who ditched you on your wedding day. You know this. Don't get defensive about it."

Sean bit back a retort. He knew the Sergeant was right. He wouldn't be arguing if he'd thought sleeping with Angellica was a good idea.

"I'm an idiot, aren't I?"

Millan laughed his harsh laugh. "More like human." He paused. "Which is pretty much the same thing when sex is involved."

"Too true." Sean resumed drumming his fingers on the arms of the chair. "Well at least we know for sure that Spider will strike again in six days."

"Unfortunately, we can't do much until then."

"What about Doctor Salla's corpse connection? I mean it must help somehow to know that each of the victims has some sort of medical unusualbility about them."

"Unusualbility?" Millan asked, his eyebrow raised at the made-up word.

"You know what I mean."

"We're looking into it," Millan replied, tossing a file across the desk for Sean to look at. "It's helpful, but getting permission to look through the entire Boston population's medical records for abnormalities is impossible. And even if we could, do you know how many people have something about them that isn't 'normal?' We can't really narrow anything down until we learn about the next victim."

"So until we get another clue."

"Pretty much."

Sean cracked his knuckles. "This guy really set this up well. Even though we discovered the connection between the victims, we are still at his mercy, because we can't do anything about it until we have the next set of clues."

Millan took a slug of coffee. "And since he's anticipating how we operate, we're going to start second-guessing ourselves every time we approach a possible victim's location. I mean, Spider knew we'd go in fast and hard at that last place. He had it rigged that way."

Sean didn't envy Millan's experience. Millan had been a cop for over 30 years—he'd probably seen his fair share of gruesome scenes—but to be responsible for having a guy get ripped apart. . .

"Listen," Millan continued, taking the file back from Sean, "go home. There's nothing more you can do today. And sleep in tomorrow—I don't want to see you until eleven in the morning, you hear me?"

"Like I can feel relaxed with Angellica around."

"Send her to a hotel. You know we can put guys on her to keep watch. She's not your responsibility anymore."

"I know, it's just. . ."

"It's just she was your girl."

Sean nodded. "Stupid, huh?"

"Of course it's stupid," Millan said, automatically reaching into his empty shirt pocket. "I told you—I've been there."

20

March 9th
6 p.m.

Sean walked into his apartment, a ball of nerves. He knew Millan's idea of sending Angellica to a hotel was smart, but he found it very hard to *want* to send her away.

It's better this way though. You and she aren't going to get back together, so you should just separate yourself from her as much as possible.

And then he saw her.

It wasn't as if she was standing in her underwear or holding a big gun or dressed like a school girl or any other cliché male fantasy, she was just sitting cross-legged on the couch, her hair tucked behind her ears, sun shining on her face, eating a sandwich, watching TV.

She looked beautiful.

"Hey," she called out, turning her attention away from the television. "In the mood for some really awful evening TV? You missed the soaps, but I'm sure there will be some bad sitcoms coming on soon." She smiled.

Sean's heart felt like it was going to expand out of his chest.

"Sounds like a blast," he said, his voice catching in his throat. "How did it go at the precinct?"

"Fine. I just gave them a statement, but since I didn't have anything except when I received the note and coming here, they finished with me pretty quick."

Sean wanted nothing more than to climb onto the couch and wrap his arms around her. Instead he said, "We need to talk."

She put her sandwich down. "Is everything all right? Did anything new happen with the case?"

"Yeah, no—it's fine," he told her, shrugging out of his jacket. "Millan said there's not much we can do 'til the end of the week. It's about you staying here."

She let out a sigh. "It's not going to work, is it?"

"Not for lack of wanting on my part. But it's probably not a good idea."

"So what do you think?"

He took a seat next to her. "Millan said we can set you up in a hotel and put an unmarked car outside to keep an eye on the place."

Angellica chewed on her thumbnail. "Do you think I'll

be safe?"

"Yeah. You'll be fine."

"Sean. . ."

"You will," he reassured her.

"But you don't like it."

He leaned back against the arm of the couch and turned to face her. "I don't like you being out of my sight, but if you refuse to go back home, then it's the best we can do."

She smiled. "You always were protective of me."

"You always meant a lot to me."

There was a pause.

"If you really think I'll be safe, I'll go."

"I think you'll be safe."

"Then I'll go."

Sean hesitated. "Right now?"

"Is there a reason I should stay?" she said, a smirk tugging at the corner of her mouth.

21

March 10th
9 a.m.

Sean woke up and stretched—and hit Angellica in the face. "Ow!" she cried out.

"Sorry," he said sheepishly, kissing her nose. "Better?"

"I may need some more kisses later, just to make sure," she said with a smile. She reached over and grabbed her bra. "And some clean clothes!" She shrugged. "Well, it'll give me an excuse to do some shopping while I'm here."

He climbed out from underneath the sheets, away from the warmth of her naked body, and went into the bathroom. "Do you want to grab breakfast before I drive you to your hotel?" He splashed his face with cold water and squeezed a glob of toothpaste onto his toothbrush.

"Don't you have to go into work?" she called back.

"Noh till evelven."

Angellica stuck her face into the bathroom. "What?"

He spit. "Not till eleven."

"You detectives sure are slackers," she joked.

He scrambled out of the bathroom and grabbed her around the waist, throwing her to the bed. "We just like to take our time," he said in a low voice.

She giggled and squirmed out of his grip. "That I know," she teased. She was already in a bra and underwear and proceeded to slip a shirt over her head. "I just didn't know that applied to *all* areas of your life."

"Guess I've changed."

She paused while buttoning her jeans. "You have changed, Sean," she said, her tone serious. "You're not the same man you were a year ago."

"Heartbreak will do that to you," he mumbled. He knew she'd heard him, but she didn't respond. The topic of what had happened and what was going on between them now hung in the air like a dark cloud, but Sean didn't really care if they didn't talk about it. Things felt so good with her he didn't want to spoil anything.

"So, breakfast?" he said more loudly, turning the conversation back to a lighter tone.

Angellica pulled her hair into a loose ponytail. "Sounds delish. And definitely a coffee."

"You and your coffee."

She grinned. "Some things *don't* change."

22

March 10th
2 p.m.

"You appear to be in a pleasant mood."

Sean looked up at the speaker. "I guess I am." He gestured across his desk. "Have a seat, Doc."

Charlotte sat down, crossed her legs, and tossed her braid over her shoulder. She eyed the overflowing piles of papers and multiple coffee cup rings that surrounded the computer on his desk.

"What brings you to my humble, and exceedingly messy office?" he asked.

"I wondered how the search has been going for upcoming possible victims, after the medical abnormality link was established."

Sean nodded his head in the direction of several boxes packed full of medical reports. "It's kind of come to a standstill. We just don't have the bodies to sort through all the information. Mags and several others have been doing computer searches and she's been printing out whatever she can find for others to sort through, but it's still not a narrow enough search margin. And even if we do find leads. . ." he shook his head.

"Mags. . . she is your receptionist, correct?"

"Yeah, but way more than that. She's a genius when it comes to computer systems—could probably hack the pentagon if she wanted to." He took a slug of coffee. "Not that it matters. There are just too many people who have things wrong with them. And there seems to be no other defining pattern on the victims, except that they had something *abnormal* about them."

Charlotte tapped her fingers against her thigh. "I was concerned it would still be an issue. If there is some deeper pattern at work as to why these victims were chosen, I cannot see it."

"You've already seen more than most. Than *anyone*, actually." Sean couldn't help but be impressed by the medical examiner's skills. She'd managed to find a pattern out of a *non*-pattern. It kind of reminded him of himself and how he found things in cases that others missed. It was probably why he was such a sought-after commodity—he wasn't a hard-ass, shoot-first-ask-questions-later type of detective, more the kind who solved cases that couldn't be solved. And Charlotte seemed similar to that.

Not like Angellica. She can't even figure out how Sudoku works.

Sean dismissed the thought. He didn't care about that fact with Angellica. She was amazing, even if they didn't have puzzle-solving in common. And just because he and Charlotte did, didn't mean anything.

It doesn't matter. Nothing ever happened with Charlotte and Angellica is back so who cares who I have more in common with? Even if I can't be in the same room as Angellica and not have things be awkward unless we are having sex or talking about getting coffee or something else as trivial.

Sean dismissed the spiteful thought. He was just still mad at Angellica. That was all.

He brought his attention back to Charlotte as she responded to his comment.

"Yet finding that connection is still not enough." Charlotte looked around the area, taking in the hustle and bustle of the other officers, the tapping on keyboards, the laughing at bad jokes. "Do not misunderstand," she continued, watching as one detective who was imitating a botched robbery proceeded to bash his head into the office's sole hanging plant, which sadly looked as if it had been neglected for weeks. "I am not pitying myself. I am merely stating a fact."

"So no late-night beer fest tonight?" he said with a smirk. He said it as a joke, but part of him didn't think the idea would be so bad. Then he mentally kicked himself. *Idiot!*

Angellica is in town! You can't have Charlotte over.

And yet why not? He and the doctor weren't involved. There was nothing going on between the two of them. So Charlotte *could* technically come over and it would be fine. Just a friend hanging out...

"I would not want to intrude on your limited reunion time with Angellica," Charlotte replied.

Sean's mouth fell open in shock. Did she just read his mind? "How the hell do you know about that?" he stammered.

Charlotte shrugged. "Most people like to gossip. And the—what is the term—ah yes, *juicier* the news, the more people want to talk about it." She tilted her head, as if pondering. "I suppose that this information about you would qualify as exceedingly juicy, seeing as how I had three people tell me on separate occasions."

"Three...who?!" He looked around the office floor as if everyone he worked with was a traitor.

Charlotte shrugged, non-committal. "Co-workers of yours, I assume. I have not worked with any of them directly."

Sean fumed. Who the hell was talking? How did anyone even know? The only person he'd told was Millan. Well, and the guards posted outside his apartment building knew about Angellica. And the guards that took over after the first night she'd spent there. And Wilt who'd read the note this morning and wondered how Sean found it. And Tay because she'd been telling Sean about her trip to London and he'd somehow told her about Angellica. And the mail guy who Sean had spilled his guts to because he was bursting with happiness this morning and wanted to tell someone all about it. And. . .

"I'm such an idiot," he mumbled.

"That also seems to be the general consensus," Charlotte added.

"Nice. Rub it in."

There were several moments of silence.

"Well, thank you for your time, Detective," Charlotte said, standing. "If anything else opens up in the case, please let me know."

"I didn't mean for you to leave."

She paused, her hand on the back of the chair. "I know. But from what I have heard, you have been thrown into several chaotic situations at once. I understand your inability to keep up a conversation with me."

"Great," he muttered. "Something else I'm unable to do right now."

She hesitated before speaking. "I have found, however, that when one's head is in disarray, a radical technique called 'venting' seems to work wonders." She nodded. "Good day, Detective."

Sean smiled as Charlotte walked away. But then he wondered about her statement. If he *did* find himself wanting to vent, who would it be with? Angellica or Charlotte?

23

March 12th
10 p.m.

Anya was supposed to do something. And whatever it was, she was late for it. But the pounding in her head made her not able to think straight. Something about a hotel. Was she supposed to go to the hotel? Was she supposed to target someone in a hotel? And was she supposed to travel? No, not exactly.

It was starting to come back to her.

No one would be angry at her. It would be okay. She was still within the time frame.

Although this was one assignment she was *not* looking forward to. In her opinion it was a waste of time.

But no one ever asks the executioner what *they* think.

24

March 13th
11 a.m.

"This is Detective Trann," Sean said, answering the phone at his desk with a smile. He had a feeling Angellica's voice would be on the other line. The past few days they had been nearly inseparable, physically mostly, and it felt incredible. Even better than things before. Though their discussions still weren't about anything substantial, Sean didn't care. He craved this high he hadn't experienced in a year—and he wanted it to continue.

Sean *had* managed to finally let Angellica sleep in a hotel. He really didn't want her to go since things had been going so well between them, but he knew it was starting to affect his professional life and he couldn't afford that right now. He'd been late to work every day this week because of his lack of desire to leave her side. And the week's countdown to Spider approached soon.

To make sure she felt safe, they decided she would report to the unmarked patrol car each time she left from or returned to the hotel. Also at the beginning of each shift, the new officer on duty would check in on her room. And just in case she wanted to, Sean made her a set of spare keys, so she could go to his apartment if she felt scared at the hotel.

But they still spent most of their time together and it didn't mean they couldn't have lunch, which was what Sean assumed the phone call was about.

He felt surprised when a male voice spoke back.

"Hello, Detective Trann. This is Officer Alonzo. I was assigned as one of the patrol members to cover your guest, Angellica, while she stayed in the hotel."

Sean vaguely placed the name to a heavy-set, caramel-skinned man about Sean's age. "Right, Officer. What can I do for you?"

"Sir, I don't want to alarm you, but she wasn't in her room when I checked to start my shift. We wondered if she was with you."

Sean's heart jumped into his throat. "What?"

"We wondered if she was with you," he repeated. "The officer I replaced said she didn't check in with him when she left, but maybe she forgot?"

The phone shook in his hands. "There's a serial killer who contacted her directly. I doubt she *forgot* to tell you. I'm pretty sure you lost her!" He nearly screeched it into the phone. Several cops around him turned to stare.

"Uh, Detective, I'm sure—" the officer stammered.

"If something happened to her. . . I'll. . ." His fists tightened. "Don't move. I'll be right there." Sean threw the phone on the desk, not even bothering to hang it up. He flew from the precinct, nearly knocking over three officers on his way out as he struggled to call Angellica at the same time. They grumbled obscenities at him, which he ignored, as her phone went straight to voicemail.

Sean sped through the streets, ignoring traffic signals, cutting across lines of cars. Horns blared at him, but he couldn't care less. Angellica was staying in the Midtown Hotel, just a couple of blocks from his apartment, but the 10-minute drive from the precinct seemed longer. When he reached the hotel, the car squealed to a stop and he parked right in front of the entrance, blocking a fire hydrant. Hopping out of his car, he followed the officer inside to Angellica's room. After a lack of response from banging on the door, Sean used the spare key card left with the patrol officer to enter.

"Angellica?" he cried out, bursting inside. Everything seemed in order, but the room appeared vacant. "When's the last time anyone saw her?" he demanded.

"Last night, when you dropped her off," Officer Alonzo said.

"Maybe she's still in the hotel then," Sean rationalized. "Call for backup. Block all the exits. We'll scour each room, each bathroom, each *mouse hole* until we find her."

Officer Alonzo didn't bother to argue.

The next hour was a nightmare for the hotel staff and patrons. Sean and multiple officers entered into every nook and cranny the building had, from its roof to its kitchen pantry. They knocked on each door and, although they weren't allowed to enter unless given permission, they lucked out as everyone allowed them access.

"Ohmygodohmygodohmygod. . ." This was the mantra spilling from his lips when Millan arrived on the scene.

"Sean!" the sergeant called out. "What the hell is going on?"

Sean was sitting on the edge of a hideously patterned chair in the hotel's lobby. He ran his fingers through his hair as his eyes remained wide open, staring into the ground.

"Sean!" Millan repeated, grabbing him by the wrist.

Sean looked up. "Oh god. He took her. The sonofabitch took her!"

Millan's chocolate-colored eyes looked confused. "Who took her? What are you talking about?"

"Spider!" Sean's voice rose. "Who the hell do you think? He took Angellica!"

"*What?* Are you telling me you got a note? It's a day early, though. . ." Millan trailed off when he saw Sean shaking his head.

"There's no note," he answered.

"Then how do you know he took her?"

Sean glared at Millan so fiercely the older detective took a half-step back.

"Who else would take her?" Sean growled.

Millan sat on the arm of the chair next to Sean. "Why do you think she's been taken?"

"She's missing!" Sean said, as if that meant it was obvious she'd been kidnapped.

"Sean. . ."

"Don't," Sean responded, turning his anger on Millan. "Don't tell me it's in my head. You know Spider is out to get me. You *know* it's personal. Who better to target than my. . . than Angellica?"

"But why a day early?"

"Why the hell not? Maybe he's tired of following a pattern. Maybe he just wants to fuck me over. How the hell should I know why he's doing any of this?" Sean couldn't think straight. If that psycho took Angellica. . .if he'd allowed her to remain in Boston and she got hurt because of it. . .if he never saw her again. . .

Millan patted Sean's shoulder, his gesture one of comfort. "Listen, take some deep breaths. We'll go over everything again, step by step. We'll find her."

Sean ran a shaky hand through his hair. "Yeah," he said, "but in time?"

25

March 13th

Angellica opened her eyes. Her head felt stuffy, as if full of cotton. The smell of sewer water reached her nose. She looked around and wondered where she was. She was *definitely* not in her hotel room. The plain beige walls and scarlet bedding had been exchanged for gray cinder block and a steel bed with a thin, soiled mattress.

She stood up from the bed quickly as one of her hands pressed onto a wet spot.

Oh God, I hope that wasn't from me. But her pants felt dry. She groped around, looking for her purse which carried her phone, but couldn't find it.

She surveyed the rest of the room in search of a door.

She couldn't find one.

Angellica's hands began to sweat. She wasn't the biggest fan of enclosed spaces. Most of the time she took stairs instead of elevators if she could. She'd even traded her underground parking spot for one outside so she wouldn't have to drive down the ramp, deeper and deeper underneath her condo back in Philly.

Don't panic. There has to be a way out. Otherwise how did you get here?

How *did* she get in here?

Oh my God. Someone must have drugged me. The killer? Spider?

Angellica's heart raced. Her breath quickened. She was stuck somewhere and the killer had brought her here and she was going to die.

I've got to get out!

Angellica frantically searched around. The concrete walls gave no indication they were anything but solid. No windows. No doors. No anything.

She glanced up. There was a rectangular chunk of ceiling that looked like it had been removed, but it was lined with bars. Thin streams of light shone through around the edges.

I must be in a basement. Or a cellar. Or a vault. Oh God. Don't think that he buried you alive and you get to slowly suffocate for the next 24 hours.

"Hello?" she called out, tentatively at first.

"Hello!" Her louder yell gave no response either. She lifted the end of the bed and banged its metal legs repeatedly on the floor as she screamed for help.

Nothing.

"Fuck." Angellica wasn't much for swearing, but the word seemed appropriate. And it wasn't like there was anyone around who could hear her.

She walked around the small room, feeling the walls, finding them tight. No cracks, no breaks. There *had* to be another way out.

"Fuck," she repeated. Maybe she could tilt the bed on its edge and climb it to reach the bars in the ceiling and somehow pry them open? It wasn't the best plan, but at least it was something to do.

"*Don't be alarmed.*"

Angellica whipped around at the disembodied voice, letting go of her grip on the bed's frame.

"What? Who—"?

"*You're safe,*" the voice continued. It was low and sharp. And definitely female.

Female? Does that mean it's not Spider? Or is Spider a woman? "Safe my ass!" she said out loud. Her restraint for foul language disappeared. "Where the hell am I? And who are you? Why did you bring me here? Forget that. Just let me out!"

"*It is necessary for you to be here at this time. I apologize for the inconvenience.*"

"Oh. Wow. Thanks for the apology. I feel much better now." Sarcasm dripped off each word. Her anxiety came back full fold, knowing she wouldn't be able to leave. Her throat tightened, her breath wheezed, her stomach balled into a knot.

"Would you like something to eat?"

Food was the *last* thing on her mind. But the question intrigued her. The voice had said she was safe, and if it wanted her dead, it probably would have killed her by now. *Unless it's just toying with me.* On the other hand, she didn't know how long she'd be kept here and she didn't know if the voice would offer food again.

Her stomach unclenched slightly. It still wasn't ready for food, but Angellica didn't want to take the chance this was the only time food would be offered. "Yes," she replied.

There was a grinding and the light widened, pouring through the grate in the ceiling. A packet fell through the bars and dropped onto the floor. Angellica picked it up as the window closed. She tried to see her kidnapper, but the light came behind and all she could make out was a silhouette.

The packet felt warm. Angellica opened it to find a bowl-sized portion of noodles in a red sauce with vegetables. A plastic spoon was included in the packet.

"There is a canteen full of water in the corner. There is a light above it for you to use."

Angellica made her way over to the corner and found the light. She turned it on, her eyes narrowing at the sudden brightness. The toilet was clean at least, and the canteen sat on top of its tank.

"I take it I'm going to be here awhile?" Her anxiety spiked, sending shots of adrenaline through her like jolts of electricity.

"You will be here until it is necessary for you not to be here. Once again, I apologize for the inconvenience."

Silence.

"That's it?"

Nothing.

"Hello?"

More silence.

"Great," Angellica said to herself, her breathing ragged as she chewed on her thumbnail. "Just great."

26

March 13th
11 p.m.

Sean felt terrified. It had been twelve hours since he'd received the call from Officer Alonzo that Angellica disappeared from the hotel. There was no trace of her. No note showed up from Spider. Nothing.

He sat on his sofa in his apartment—it still carried the faint smell of lilies from Angellica's perfume—and a million thoughts raced through his mind. What if she was hurt? Or dead? What if Spider was hurting her? Doing things to her... sexual things...

"What am I going to do?" Sean asked Millan, who sat next to him on his sofa. "The only thing I'm doing is sitting on my ass running through every horrible scenario she may be experiencing."

"You can't think like that," the older man said, running his hand across his stubble. "You don't have any idea what happened to her. And to be honest, if it is Spider, I feel like we would've gotten a note. The bastard would've been *way* too eager to gloat about something like this." Millan paused, hesitating about what to say next. "Did you call her family back in Philadelphia?"

Sean snorted and rolled his eyes in exasperation. "What the hell would I say to them? 'Hey, ex-almost-in-laws, your daughter, who left me at the altar without a word, has been with me the past several days, back to our old tricks as a matter of fact, until she was kidnapped last night by a diabolical killer who has a personal vendetta against me.' Yeah. That would go over *real* well."

"No," Millan said slowly, dragging out the word. "I meant have you called them to see if she went home?"

The words hung in the air.

"What are you saying?" Sean's chest tightened.

"I just. . ." Millan paused. "I just mean this wouldn't be the first time she left you without saying goodbye."

The room felt thick with silence. Sean's hands were balled into tight fists, his knuckles white from the pressure.

"No," he whispered, shaking his head. "She wouldn't have. . ." But he couldn't finish the sentence, even to convince himself. She *would* do it. She had before. He wanted to say it was different this time, that the two of them together were different, but were they really? She'd been here for, what, five days? Maybe she had freaked out, especially knowing another murder would happen soon, and left. Maybe she had a husband back home who had called her and she'd gone back to him...and a kid...and...

Sean stood abruptly from the couch. He walked straight to the fridge, grabbed a beer, and drank the whole thing down without taking a breath. It didn't help. He couldn't get the images out of his head—Angellica having a laugh with her husband as they sat on their porch in matching rocking chairs, looking out over their immaculate green lawn, waving at their neighbors over a white picket fence. Sean could picture her telling a lie about staying with a girlfriend who was having guy troubles and how she would never leave again because her friend was pathetic and whiny and—

Sean threw the bottle against the wall, spraying shards, embedding slivers into the carpet.

Millan stood, tense.

Get a grip. You don't know anything. You don't know where she is or what she's doing and until you do, you aren't helping the situation. Sean took in and let out several deep breaths. It helped, but his anger was still strong. "This is such bullshit. I can't believe the options for the woman I love is she has either been kidnapped by a psychopath or ran off and left me—again. I just can't deal with this. I can't..." He turned away from his superior, pissed at himself for losing it.

Millan said nothing. He simply walked over and opened the cabinet above Sean's fridge. He pulled out the mostly empty bottle of vodka.

"Here," he told Sean after opening the bottle. "Try and

get some sleep. I'm here all night, in case Spider makes a move. But you need to rest. That's an order."

Sean took the bottle and drank several gulps. He grimaced at the raw taste of the warm liquor sliding down his throat and then crawled onto his bed. He felt like a kid being told what to do by his father, but to be honest, it felt good not to make any decisions. He'd been barking orders all day and it had gotten him nowhere. He even made officers fingerprint the hotel, but besides in her room, no sign of Angellica existed.

Sean heard Millan turn on the television, turn off the overhead lights, and resume his position on the couch. He was watching some rebroadcast of an old baseball game. The Red Socks against the Robins maybe? The sound rumbled too quietly and Sean couldn't make out what the commentators said.

Sean pulled another swig from the bottle. He'd never been very involved in watching sports. He played a bit in high school, soccer mostly, but his school's football team had sucked so there wasn't much prestige in being a football player.

*Swimmers though. . .*he thought, floating on the edge of sleep. *They were the hotshots. . .*

27

March 14th
4 a.m.

"Are you hungry?" Violet asked. She wrung her fingers nervously. This wasn't usually her job. Although she was responsible for choosing the method of elimination, she wasn't used to carrying out the punishment. The Third usually did that, but circumstances being as they were. . .

"Please let me out of here!"

She repeated her question. "Are you hungry?"

The woman kept in the cell below her paused. *"Yes. But please, tell me where I am."*

Violet opened the gate and dropped the packet of food. Her heart raced. She felt exhilarated. Was this what it was like for the Third every time she killed? Was this how good it felt to deliver justice instead of just determining how it would happen?

There was the tearing of tin foil followed by the sound of someone eating.

"You have been judged," she told her captive, reading from a piece of paper, "and have been found unworthy." She listened as the woman below gagged on her food.

"You will suffer for the way the world has suffered with you in it. The poison is slow and will turn your organs into liquid, your blood into paste, your skin into sand. And balance shall be restored."

There was the sound of attempted retching.

Oh crap, she thought. *I should have shot her with the paralytic first, then put the poison through an IV. Ah well. Once she falls over I'll go in and inject her anyway. Guess this is why I don't usually do this.*

The woman below coughed, her voice sounding weaker. "*Please! No! I haven't done anything wrong.*"

"*You* are wrong."

The gate shut with a slam.

Violet secretly smiled. She could get used to being the executioner.

She could get used to being the Third.

28

March 14th
6 a.m.

Damien Andrews, captain of the swim team, was walking through the hallway of Sean's high school, handing out lilies to everyone who walked past. He came closer to Sean, a twisted evil grin on his face, a spiderweb mark on the side of his neck. . .

"Sean! Wake up!"

Sean bolted awake. "Wha. . .what is it?" The smell of vodka issued from his mouth.

"We got a note."

Shaking away the remnants of his nightmare, Sean's eyes

adjusted to the brightly lit room and he watched Millan sit next to him on the bed.

"Where did you find it?" he asked. He looked at the envelope through the plastic bag.

"Taped to your showerhead."

"My—how the hell did someone get it here?" He climbed out of bed and walked into the bathroom. Sean stared at the showerhead, willing it to tell him who the killer was, but it merely dripped in reply.

"I don't know," said Millan from behind him, frustrated. "The note says four a.m. NO ONE has been here since we got here at eleven last night. There is no way anyone could have gotten in two hours ago and planted this."

"It must have been put in before. . ." Sean said softly.

Millan spun around. "What?"

"I haven't taken a shower since yesterday morning. I haven't looked at the showerhead since then. Someone must have gotten in and taped the note up before you and I got here."

"But doesn't Spider always leave the note after he kidnaps the victim? Wouldn't he have left it here at four in the morning?"

Sean shook his head and cleared away the rest of his tiredness. "He's been changing the rules left and right. Maybe he's been watching my building. Maybe he planned the time, but he knew he couldn't get in here once I came home. I don't know. All I know is that if this note didn't get planted while we were here, it must have beforehand. But that doesn't change how much time we have left to find Angellica."

"There's more. I went to check your security footage—no go."

"What do you mean?"

"I mean there hasn't been anything recorded for a couple days. It showed an error message saying it wasn't connected to any network."

Sean glanced over at his modem—the lights were all off. His stomach dropped as he made his way over to the device. He checked the back and sure enough, the plug hung on the edge of the socket, not quite inserted into the outlet enough to draw power.

He straightened up, dumbfounded. "I didn't think about it. I've been running around for the past two days and everything going on with Angellica—I haven't exactly cared about doing something like checking my email from home." Sean punched into the wall, denting it slightly, and pulled his pained hand away. "Fuck!"

Millan handed Sean a different bag with the letter inside. "It's fine, don't worry about it. Focus on this. I had gloves and I didn't want to wait for forensics. We needed to know what this note says." He got up to open the door. "While you read it, I'm going to ask what they saw." The two officers assigned to the patrol car entered a few minutes later.

Sean blinked his eyes a few times, not understanding why Millan wasn't upset due to lack of video. "What who saw?" But Millan waved him off. Sean read the note out loud to himself as Millan demanded to know what the inside of the officers' asses looked like, since their heads were so far up them.

"Four a.m.," Sean mumbled. "Nice world, huh? How can we tell if it's good anymore when everything around us is toxic?"

Sean tried to think about what the note meant, but he was distracted by the conversation next to him.

"What do you mean, no one's been here?" Millan hollered. "Obviously *someone* has been here. There's a note!"

"But it's the truth," the younger officer put in. His face was as rosy as his curly red hair. "Nobody has come through this hall except you and Detective Trann last night."

"Then how the hell did this note get here?"

The young officer stepped forward; though fear appeared in his eyes, his face remained determined. "I'm telling you, sir, I have been stationed here since ten last night. No one else has been through here."

"You were here all night?" Sean asked, indicating the other officer as well. "Wait, I thought you were parked outside in the car?"

The older officer stepped up, his steely gray eyes wide with nervousness. "Millan ordered someone to remain in your hall, sir, after the missing person's report."

"It might have happened earlier yesterday," Millan said. "Who did you relieve?"

The older man stammered a reply. "Uh. . .I'm not sure. I'm. . .uh—I'm new here. In Boston, I mean. And to the force. Just passed the exam three weeks ago. They, uh, gave me this duty—said it'd be a piece of case. . .I mean cake—for training purposes—"

The younger officer furrowed his eyebrows and cut in. "I

think it was Holden? Or Hoffen? Something like that. Older guy. Like fifty. Real thin, brown hair."

"And glasses," the other officer chimed in.

"Doesn't anyone know each other?" Sean grumbled.

"We've been mixing with other districts, sir, to pick up the slack."

"I bet it was Holden from A-seven," Millan said. "I'll check in with him and ask him if anything happened on his shift." He pointed at the note. "And we gotta get that to the station and figure it out." He pointed at Sean's bedside table.

"Clock's ticking."

29

March 14th
7:30 a.m.

Everyone was assembled around Sean's desk. They'd each heard the note and already compiled a list of possible victims. Millan issued orders, sending out pairs of officers to look through the likeliest possibilities.

Sean sat in his chair, frustrated, confused, and sulking. The clue didn't seem to have anything to do with Angellica. They'd come up with potential victims from environmentalists to toxic waste dumpers to anyone who taught global studies. But Angellica didn't fit any of those descriptions.

Could what Millan said before be true? Could she have

left again without saying goodbye?

Though he knew the possibility existed, he couldn't make himself contact her family to find out. And since *technically* a person wasn't missing for at least 48 hours. . .

Sean felt sick at the thought. Here he was, using a dumb excuse not to find out if she merely skipped out again. Especially since everything pointed to the fact that Spider's new victim was *not* Angellica.

He felt a pressure on his shoulder and looked up to see Millan standing next to him. "We need you out there," he told Sean.

"I know." Sean was angry at the way his voice trembled. He balled his hands into fists and forced himself to focus. He needed to be out there helping them find whoever Spider did have. And if Angellica still didn't show up by the next day, he would accept the idea that she'd simply left and then make sure someone contacted her family to double-check.

A voice called out from the doorway. "Could I be of any use?"

Sean looked over at the voice and saw Dr. Salla leaning against the doorjamb. Her eyes rested for a moment on Sean, a look of concern within them. She looked so simple in black dress pants and a button-down cream shirt. Sean felt an instant relief at seeing her there.

"I did not receive a call," she continued, "but calculated that if a note had been delivered, you would all be assembled here this morning to discuss its contents." She looked around at the scrambling officers. "I see my assessment was accurate."

Millan motioned for her to come in. "Right on target.

We did receive a note—taped in Sean's shower this time." He handed her a copy of the clue. "But there has been an additional variable this time around," he said, motioning to Sean.

All of his relief at seeing Charlotte trickled away at his embarrassment. He steeled himself to speak and stood. "Angellica's gone," he said, "and we thought Spider kidnapped her but it looks like she just took off. Variable done. Let's get this asshole." He stormed out of the office, brushing past the medical examiner, but he didn't care. He was ashamed his failure with Angellica had to be publicly told to his coworkers, not to mention Charlotte. His head pounded, his eyes felt tired, and on top of it all, someone was probably going to die.

* * *

Charlotte watched with concern as Sean pushed his way through the heavy front doors of the station. She didn't need her keen powers of observation to notice the difference between now and the previous times she'd seen him. Even when upset about the case, his demeanor had been one of anger, not one of despair.

"He is not all right," she noticed out loud.

"No," Millan said, shaking his head. "But somehow he has to be. We need him."

30

March 15th
Midnight

They'd had no luck. They eliminated everyone on their lists and had not found a single person missing or dying or dead. The entire Boston Police Department, minus a few routine patrol officers, were once again aggregating around Millan's desk, poring over the words in the note, trying to find any other meaning they may have missed since only four hours remained until their victim died. Officers packed Millan's office, sending waves of body odor into the main area every time the door opened and closed.

After the fifth cop had spoken to Sean about another option that led nowhere, his coffee-scented breath adding to the other aromas of the room, Sean told Millan he needed some fresh air.

But as he sat in his Jaguar outside the precinct, staring into the blackness of the night, he felt more frustrated. There'd been a brief heat wave the day before and the weather compensated by adding a new type of humidity. Low-lying fog covered the streets and although it was spring, it looked like Halloween. Street lamps shone into the mist and the light collected into pools of bright vapor that swirled around the nighttime bar-hoppers.

Sean didn't even notice. He looked outside, but saw nothing.

He started at a tap on his window.

He lowered the pane.

"Did Millan send you?" he asked. One of the street lamps shone behind the figure so he couldn't see any facial features, but he recognized the medical examiner's voice.

"No. I decided to come see if your trek outside the building has helped."

"It hasn't." He paused. "Anything new up there?" he asked. He'd been outside for about 20 minutes.

"No," Charlotte answered, leaning her hands against the window frame. "Nothing new."

Sean felt too resigned to care. He *wanted* to care. He mentally yelled at himself to snap out of it, do his job, suck it up. Anything to motivate him. Somewhere inside he hated himself for giving up while there was still time. But it seemed hopeless. They'd looked through all the options. Everyone was doing what they could.

He hadn't even noticed Charlotte left his side of the car until the passenger door opened and she sat next to him.

She gave a long sigh, staring out the windshield.

"We are in need of your capabilities," she said softly.

He wanted to tell her to get the fuck out of his car.

He said nothing.

"This individual," she continued, "this *Spider,* writes his notes in a way that no one but you seems to understand. We need you to turn off your thoughts and your emotions and focus on the words. Do not think. Do not feel. Just react." She paused, pulling out a slip of paper, and began to read. "'Nice world, huh? How can we tell if it's good anymore when everything around us is toxic?'"

The words flittered around inside Sean's head, a messy goo-ish twisted set of letters that meant nothing to him. Pressure built in his head, an ache forming just behind his eyes. He closed them, wanting to shy away from the world.

"Sean. Tell me a profession and a method of dying."

In the darkness, the words tightened into a pattern. He focused on her voice. Specific words jumped out at him: *world, toxic.*

"Job," he said, the word coming out clipped. "Something in which we view the world. Not a job involving the world, but a job in which we see it." He paused. "A company with a logo that has a picture of the globe."

"Death," he continued. "A way for something to become toxic." He looked out at the swirling low-lying clouds, reminding him of puffs of poisonous gas. "Poison," he told her.

He quickly turned toward her and his mind came back to

the present. And then he thought of what he'd just said.

"Oh my God!" he exclaimed, panic rising in his throat. "When we first met, Angellica worked for a travel company that had a globe as their logo: TravelAmerica."

Charlotte's face paled. "It seems Angellica may be involved after all. I promise, we will find her. We will search any TravelAmerica buildings here in Boston. Spider has always kept his victims either close to their homes or businesses, and her home is in Philadelphia, which is too far away, so it must be related to the business." Charlotte put a hand on his arm, a gleam in her eye. "Poisons have antidotes. We still have over three hours to find her. And we will."

31

March 15th
2 a.m.

Sean had been wrong. He would have given his life ten times over to have Angellica safe and sound in her own home snuggled with some other guy and him with his heart broken rather than riding behind the ambulance that raced her to Massachusetts General Hospital. He didn't even watch traffic—all he saw were the flashing lights on top of the white wagon, his ears full of the sound of a siren.

They found her a half hour ago. She'd been locked in the cellar of one of Boston's TravelAmerica headquarters. It was scheduled for demolition the following week because they were opening a new office across town.

The only odd thing revolved around Angellica's state of being.

She told them she'd been fed, given a change of clothes, slept semi-comfortably once her mattress had dried out, and, as far as she knew, was completely void of poison. She hadn't suffered any torture at all.

Still, no one wanted to take any chances, so they rushed her to the emergency room to get checked out.

Terror consumed Sean at the thought that somehow the poison wouldn't take effect until 4 a.m. and he'd have to watch her die. He knew it was improbable, since Spider usually tortured his victims for the entire 24 hours, but anxiety never listened to logic. Plus Spider seemed to be changing his rules so who knew what might happen.

The doctors cleared her, saying there were no known toxins in her system with two hours to spare, but Sean couldn't believe it. They insisted she was fine, that Sean could take her home whenever he wanted, and that there was no kind of poison known that would lie dormant and then suddenly erupt inside her body.

Millan had also tried to be reassuring, reminding Sean that Spider had lost this time.

But Sean wouldn't be appeased until the clock read one minute after 4 a.m.

He and Angellica stayed in the waiting room after she had been checked out, since a bed couldn't be used up for a person who wasn't ill, no matter what police officer wanted her there.

3:57 a.m.

No change. Angellica still looked fine. Tired, but fine.

Sean shifted uncomfortably in his chair. *Why do they keep this place so warm?*

3:58 a.m.

Angellica's eyebrows began to furrow. She looked concerned, worried. Was something wrong? Was it starting to happen?

"Sean?" she asked.

Oh, God! It's started! He looked up at the clock. It read 3:59 a.m.

"Sean? Are you okay?"

"Am I. . .?" His voice cracked. He realized he was breathing heavily. Sweat dripped off his forehead and into his eyes.

4:00 a.m.

Her face blurred. Could poison do that? And why were the lights dimming?

"Sean!"

Her voice came from far away, down a tunnel of blackness.

32

March 15th
4:30 a.m.

There is a saying that when a person is more embarrassed than they've ever felt before, they wish the Earth would open up and swallow them.

This was how Sean felt about a minute after opening his eyes.

A horde of nurses hovered over him, as well as Angellica and Millan. Their bodies were silhouetted by the harsh, florescent, white lights of the hospital's lobby ceiling.

"He's coming 'round," one of the nurses exclaimed, her thick glasses magnifying her eyes to a bug-like extreme. Her breath was warm on his face and smelled of cheese.

"Oh, Sean!" Angellica exclaimed, awkwardly trying to give him a hug.

"What happened?" he said, inhaling a lock of her hair.

"You fainted."

Dead silence.

"I-I *what?*"

"Passed out, pro'bly from panic," the nurse told him, pushing her glasses up the bridge of her long, straight nose. She spoke in a thick, southern drawl as she helped him to his feet. "Happens son-tines when a young buck like you gets too excited-like. Betchoo were really worked up about the little missus here."

Sean felt Angellica grab his hand.

"I passed out," he said.

He looked up at Millan, whose dark face was almost purple from holding in his laughter.

Oh, man. I'm never going to hear the end of this at work.

Sean ran his fingers through his hair. He then had a moment of panic wash over him and turned toward Angellica.

"How do you feel? What time is it?"

"I feel fine," she said, squeezing his hand. "And it's almost four fifteen. I think we're in the clear."

He held her gently by the shoulders, kissed her, and stared into her eyes.

"You should go back to Philly" he told her. He hadn't meant to say that, but he couldn't stand the idea of what might happen to her if she stayed.

She shook off his hands. "No."

"Angel, it's not safe for you here. I mean, this asshole got to you with a set of guards watching the hotel."

"You think I'll be safer back in Philadelphia?" she said with a snort. "If this guy could get past all that security, what makes you think my pathetic apartment deadbolt is going to stop him from coming after me again? No," she repeated. "I'm staying with you, wherever you are. Work, home, wherever. I'm not leaving your side until this psycho is found."

"And then?"

Sean hadn't meant to say those words out loud. His embarrassment deepened as he realized Millan and the nurses were still standing around.

"Sean, I—"

Angellica's words were cut off when Millan's phone rang. And then Sean's phone rang. The two of them answered almost simultaneously. Millan took a few steps away to deal with his call.

"Sean!" Mags exclaimed through the line. "Did they get a hold of you yet about the girl they found?"

"Girl? What girl?"

"A blonde girl. It matches the description of your friend, Angellica."

Sean looked over at Angellica. "She's here with me. We're at the hospital. She's fine." He gave her hand a squeeze.

"Oh, thank God! I was so worried when I heard them describe her—blonde hair, green eyes, about my height. I thought I heard the officer say she was dead, but I must have misheard. I'm so glad she's okay."

Sean felt a thread of ice creep up his spine. Angellica's eyes were blue, not green. "Mags. What girl did they find?"

"She was in a TravelAmerica building. Some offshoot that was being renovated. The medical examiner chick asked me to call you and have you get down there. I figured she'd be with you."

Renovated? The building we took Angellica from was set to be demolished. And where is *Charlotte?* Sean vaguely remembered Charlotte following him to the hospital and sitting in the waiting room with Millan, but he couldn't remember her leaving. She must have gotten a call at some point.

A ball of lead seemed to plunk into his stomach. There was another girl.

"Mags, the call you got, it wasn't about Angellica. It was about a different victim."

A pause. "But I thought you said Angellica was the next target? Didn't she fit the clues?"

Sean looked at his ex-fiancée, her eyes clouded with confusion, waiting for him to tell her what was going on.

"Yes, she did. But apparently this other woman fit the clues, too. Is Doctor Salla still at the crime scene?"

"I'm not sure."

Sean saw Millan hang up his phone and signal that he needed to talk.

"I think Millan's going to fill me in. I'll talk to you later."

He hung up and looked at his sergeant.

"They found a body," Millan told him. "We're needed at the crime scene."

33

March 15th
5 a.m.

Sean parked his car in front of a "TravelAmerica—Coming Soon!" sign in a parking lot. The building the sign referred to appeared half-built, overflowing with large, blue tarps that flapped in the wind. The building sat next to Henderson Elementary School and Sean felt grateful it was too early for children to be in class.

Sean got out of his car, made a motion for Angellica to stay put in the front seat, and headed over to the crime scene. The scent of wet, freshly cut timber filled his nose as he approached Charlotte. She stood talking to Wilt and Tay, her white lab coat fluttering in the breeze.

The body was already bagged and on a stretcher, headed towards the medical examiner's van.

"Who is she?" Sean asked. His words came out clipped, his fists in tight balls. He was completely pissed at himself. He'd been so convinced Angellica had been the target, he never stopped to think she could have been a diversion to keep him away from the real victim. Spider now seemed to control Sean's moves, like a twisted puppeteer, and he'd completely followed the false trail. And now this girl was dead.

The medical examiner stood from her hunched-over position. "Her ID says she is Brina Colt from northern Boston. Her work badge says that she is an employee of Travel-America. And from my preliminary assessment, I would speculate she was poisoned."

Sean felt his insides turn cold.

"Of course, nothing is conclusive until I perform a complete autopsy."

Sean creased his forehead in anger. "You know what happened," he snapped at Charlotte. "I blew it. And now some other husband or boyfriend or friend has to find out that my personal feelings got in the way and their loved one is gone."

"You are blaming yourself for a result that is not your fault."

Sean shook his head. "How can you say that? This *is* my fault."

Charlotte gestured to the body. "This woman did not die because you did anything wrong. You did your job thoroughly and found Angellica. She matched the clues Spider left for you. There was no indication of another girl who worked for TravelAmerica in an abandoned TravelAmerica building. And if it had been the other way around, you would have concluded your search with Brina and not found Angellica."

"You're just trying to make me feel better," he grumbled.

She flipped her braid over her shoulder. "I would never say anything simply to make a person feel better. I say things because they are the truth. If you feel better because of what I said, I am glad, but it was not my reason for telling you."

Sean felt some of his tension melt away. "You're good, Doc. Really good."

The tweak of a smile touched her lips. "Thank you. But it is still true. Spider knows that to complete these deaths, he must distract you or make the puzzle harder. This says something about the situation."

"What's that?"

The medical examiner narrowed her dark eyes as they sparkled in the remaining moonlight. "That he is *losing*, Detective Trann."

Sean glanced back over at the body as it was loaded into the van. "Tell that to her."

Charlotte removed her gloves. "Tell me how you could possibly have saved her and I will join your pity party. I will even wear a party hat."

He turned toward her in surprise. "Did you just joke at my expense?"

She paused, as if actually debating the theory. "Perhaps I have been hanging around bad influences," she teased.

Millan left the forensics team and strolled up to the

medical examiner. "Poison?" he asked.

"I will have to do a full autopsy, but yes, that seems to be the general consensus," Charlotte replied.

"Damn," he muttered, shaking his head. "Spider is good. He knew we'd stop looking when we found one or the other. Now he's using decoys."

"If you will both excuse me," Charlotte said, nodding to each of them in turn, "I have some work to do. I will let you know my results as soon as I have them."

"Thanks." Sean turned toward his boss. "What do you want to do now?"

"You are going to go back to your place with Angellica and are going to take a couple days off." He held up a hand to block Sean's protests. "You need it. Don't argue. You have been through a lot tonight—both of you have."

Sean wanted to argue, wanted to do something more, but he'd been running ragged for days and knew the Sergeant was right. "I thought you said us being together was a mistake?"

Millan shrugged as he rubbed his hand across his stubble. "A woman's been through this kind of trauma and she's not rushing to call a hubby and wants to stay with you? I say take this moment while you have it. What happens after this ordeal is over. . ." he trailed off, holding his hands up in front of him, and backing away toward his own car.

"You'll call me with the results though?" Sean asked after him.

"Of course, kid. Now go home."

34

March 19th
8 a.m.

The Book tells of a woman who will be the messiah to us all. She will be known by several factors:

The first is that she will be marked across her body at birth, but the mark will fade, as she represents the true beauty that lies underneath imperfection.

The second is that she will be isolated from others, as her intellectual superiority and sense of rationality becomes a source of envy.

The third is that she will be one with death—as comfortable with it as life itself.

Which means I've found her.

After all these years of searching, I've found her.

The one whose childhood fits the prophecy.

The one who can continue my work.

My replacement.

Espresso-colored fingers gently traced a picture that lay on the table. They lingered for a moment along the soft curve of the woman's face, trailing down her neck.

Dr. Charlotte Salla.

So beautiful.

So perfect.

The chosen one.

35

March 19th
8:45 a.m.

Charlotte absentmindedly rubbed at the corner of her eye as she walked into the morgue. She may be a bit early for her 9 a.m. shift, but liked being the first to arrive. She usually used the time to review her notes from the previous day, recheck that all the instruments had been sterilized and returned, and cross-check the labels and storage security of each body.

Plus, she loved something about the smell of a sterile, clean laboratory that had yet to be used—fresh and ready for discovery. It may have been a little odd that she didn't mind the smell of formaldehyde, but she couldn't help it. She'd been around it so often it reminded her of her work, which she treasured.

Shortly before nine, she prepped herself to re-examine the drawer containing Spider's latest victim, Brina Colt. She'd already discovered the abnormality on the woman's body and had reported it to Sergeant Millan the afternoon after the murder, which had been four days ago. She also called Detective Trann and told him directly, since he'd seemed so distraught when they found the body, but he did not answer his phone. She shouldn't have been surprised, seeing as he was most likely taking the day off to spend with his female friend who'd been through quite an ordeal the night before, but for some reason it made her feel. . .off-put. Not in a serious, jealous sort of way, but just. . .a twinge. Although that twinge grew each day he didn't return her call. Not that he really needed to—she hadn't asked him to call her back—but she just. . .

She just what?

Charlotte paused in her thoughts.

Why *did* she care? The more she thought about it, the more she came to realize she enjoyed Sean's company. Not necessarily in a romantic sense, but she'd gotten used to thinking of them as—as a team.

She rebraided her hair after some strands had come loose and put on new gloves as she pondered the word. Team. The word never really applied to her before. Sure, she'd had lab partners in school and technicians she worked with on projects, but in the end, they'd always been assigned to her. She never would have chosen to work with any of them. In fact, she could think of a few times she would have rather worked on her own. But she found she *liked* this pairing between her and the Detective.

"That is impractical," she said out loud, pulling her purple glove tight over her slender hand.

"What's impractical?"

Charlotte nearly fell off her stool in surprise at the voice.

"I'm sorry," Sean said with a grin. "I didn't mean to startle you. This place is open right now, right?"

Charlotte glanced up at the clock and was stunned at the time—9:15. Then she looked at the door, which was normally locked and needed a keycard to open it, and noticed it had gotten propped open by a lab coat on the floor. She must have knocked it off the counter when she came in and it got stuck in the entryway.

"Of course," she said, composing herself. "The building has been open since nine." She grabbed the coat and returned it to the counter. The door closed with a *thwick* behind her.

"I thought I would come check in," Sean said. He stuffed his hands in his pockets. Charlotte assumed it was so he wouldn't touch anything by mistake since he didn't have gloves on.

"My message stated that the victim was indeed poisoned. There has been no new information. Sergeant Millan has the full report."

"I know," he said with a shrug. "Very official. I just wanted to follow up."

She nodded, knowingly. "You are bored."

Sean let out a huge sigh and swung his leg over a stool to

sit down. "Am I ever. It is *infuriating* to have to wait out an entire week before we know what's going to happen next. And I just thought that maybe, somehow..."

"Seeing the body would make you feel as though you are continuing to work on the case instead of feeling useless."

"Don't sugar coat it or anything, Doc."

"Why would I—"? Charlotte's comment was cut short as a young, blonde woman knocked on the glass door. Sean let her into the room. She entered, her eyes wide, her nose crinkled.

"Are there really dead bodies in here?" she asked, eyeing the morgue drawers warily.

Charlotte blinked. Then she recognized the woman from the hospital.

"Yes," she answered Angellica. "Some of these drawers contain cadavers."

"Creepy," Angellica replied with a shiver.

"Do you mind if she's in here?" Sean asked. "I know she's a civilian and all, but after what happened, I don't really want to leave her alone."

Charlotte watched as Angellica tiptoed behind Sean and put her chin on his shoulder.

"I don't really *want* to be here," Angellica grumbled.

Sean rubbed the side of Angellica's face with his hand without looking at her and smiled. "Just for a minute. I'm going stir crazy in my apartment."

"Never could sit still with a juicy open case on your lap," she said softly while she stood up straight. "You were at the hospital the other night," she said, speaking to Charlotte.

Charlotte was startled by the change in subject. "Yes. I followed you and Detective Trann."

"But you deal with dead people. I wasn't dead."

"Not at that point, no. But we were unsure of your future condition."

Angellica tucked her hair behind her ears. "No offense, but I'm glad you didn't have to work that night."

"Unfortunately I *did* have to work that night, though thankfully for your sake, not because of you."

Angellica sobered up. "That's right. That other girl died."

Charlotte paused, looking at Sean. She didn't want to seem rude, but. . ."I really cannot allow her to view the remains," she said. "Policy."

"Ugh, no problem," Angellica replied. "I gotta use the bathroom anyway."

Charlotte explained where the restroom was and after Angellica had left, pulled open the latest victim's drawer.

"She seems more reserved than at the hospital," Charlotte said, commenting on Angellica's mood.

"She's putting on a front. She's really terrified."

Charlotte thought for a moment. "I have never understood the need to lie about one's state of being."

Sean looked at her, incredulous. "Haven't you ever felt like you had to pretend to be tough? To impress someone you were around?"

Charlotte handed Sean a pair of gloves. "If I need to impress an individual by pretending I do not have normal emotional reactions to stressful situations, then that person is not worthy of my respect." She pulled back as much of the bag as she could without spilling any of the body's fluids. "Besides, Angellica has no need to impress me."

Charlotte started at Sean's bark of a laugh. "It's not you she was trying to impress, Doc."

She blinked in surprise. "You cannot possibly mean she thought she needed to impress *you*? Whatever for?"

Sean stopped looking at the body and stared with disbelief at Charlotte. "Have you never *looked* at yourself in a mirror?"

"Of course I have."

"Then you must realize how insanely gorgeous you are. *Any* woman, no matter how convinced she is that the guy she is with cares about her, would be jealous of you. So she wanted to keep up with you on your level, because all of this stuff is related to my work and she knows how much I love it. And she sees you, calm and collected, and thinks of that as a threat."

Charlotte glanced at the door. "Humans are strange creatures."

" *Women* are strange creatures." Sean snorted.

The medical examiner turned her eyes back toward Sean. "Really, Detective? Are you telling me you have never retracted your abdomen or flexed your muscles in front of your significant other when another male who was in better shape than you entered the vicinity?"

"Of course not," he said jokingly, contracting his biceps so they bulged. "What guy is in better shape than me?"

Charlotte felt a smile tug at the corners of her mouth, but the smile faded as they turned toward the body. They spent several minutes examining it, Charlotte telling Sean what she'd determined, until Sean shook his head.

"It's no good," he told her, indicating she should close up the bag. "There's nothing for me here. Not that I thought there would be, but. . ." He shrugged.

"I understand," Charlotte answered, sliding the drawer closed. "I have often found that doing something is better than doing nothing, even if that something turns out to be fruitless."

"We definitely agree on that," he said as he stripped off his gloves and threw them into the biohazard waste receptacle.

"By the way," Sean continued, "I never got the chance to thank you for helping me the other night."

She paused, trying to recall what he meant. "I am not sure I understand."

Sean looked at the door, his body posture seemingly nervous.

Why would he be nervous? Charlotte thought.

"I was pretty messed up when I'd gone out to the car— when I thought Angellica had been taken or left me. And you helped get me back on the case."

Charlotte nodded in remembrance. "We needed you. I thought my direct route would be the best way to pull you from your reverie."

"I just. . ." Sean paused to find the right words. "You did it well. Thanks. Thanks for bringing me back."

"You are welcome, Sean."

The silence was palpable. Charlotte felt she wanted to say something else, something to convey that she was merely doing her job, helping him to stop a murderer, but she couldn't say it. Because it wasn't the whole truth. She *liked* that she'd been the one who reached through and pulled him back onto the case.

And that was very unlike her.

Charlotte removed her own gloves when Angellica returned, her face pale.

"Are you all right?" Sean asked after he'd let her in.

"I'm so embarrassed," she mumbled, more toward Charlotte than to Sean. "I thought I'd be okay with all this dead body stuff, but I guess my stomach wasn't in agreement."

"No need for embarrassment," Charlotte told her. She saw Sean make a small gesture with his hand that Angellica couldn't see, encouraging her to say more.

"Ah. . .yes," Charlotte continued. "You should keep in mind that I have been working with cadavers, especially those of violent crimes, for quite some time. I have developed a way to change what I see to facts instead of people, but believe me, before I can make the transition, there is always that moment when I first see the individual, really see them. Try as I might, the feeling of sickness never truly goes away. But I believe it keeps me in touch with my humanity."

Angellica looked relieved at the reassurance, but Sean's eyes held a look that Charlotte didn't quite understand. Curiosity? Sympathy?

"Is there anything else you need, Detective?"

Sean eyed Angellica, who was attempting to put on a brave face, and seemed to be failing miserably.

"Nah," he answered. "Guess it's back to being stir crazy."

"Do you not have any pending cases to keep you busy?"

"Millan had me off for a few days so my few cases got reassigned. Nothing came up today yet."

"Well I assure you that if anything new develops with this case, I will contact you."

Sean put his hands on Angellica's hips and guided her toward the door. "I know, Doc," he called over his shoulder. "And thanks."

"Bye!" Angellica called out.

"And please do not slam the. . .

SLAM!

. . .door," Charlotte finished, wincing at the noise. She turned toward her laptop to make more notes about the situation. Several minutes later, she looked at the clock and realized Technician Knottes should be arriving soon. His shift was scheduled to start at 10 a.m.

Good. He can help me sort through some of this data. As long as he is actually on time for once.

Almost as if on cue, Charlotte heard the hiss of the door opening.

"I am glad you are here, Knottes," she said. She snapped her laptop closed, grabbed it, and turned toward the door. Her body jumped when she realized it wasn't Knottes.

"You startled me," she told the woman.

"I'm sorry," the woman answered, her voice low and sultry. She took a few steps into the room, reattaching her ID badge to her white lab coat, her pale brown eyes liquid and alive. "Are you Doctor Charlotte Salla?"

Charlotte switched her laptop to her other hand and tucked it under her arm. "Yes, I am. How can I help you?"

The woman walked toward her, purposefully, her dark cheeks slightly flushed, her springy and tightly curled hair bouncing with each step. She stuck out her hand.

Charlotte reached out and took it, shaking it firmly. She found herself enraptured by this woman's features. She was exquisite-looking. Her high cheekbones and full lips accentuated her slightly almond-shaped eyes and arched eyebrows. Her skin was creamy and dark, as if made of chocolate silk. She *smelled* of chocolate, too. Mixed with coffee beans.

Charlotte had never seen anyone so stunning.

"My name is Truth," the woman told her, squeezing the medical examiner's hand a little harder.

Charlotte felt something bite into her palm. She cried out and pulled her hand away. She stared at it as the tiny red circle on her palm slipped in and out of focus.

"Wha. . .?" she asked, her tongue thick in her mouth. Her knees weakened and she fell back into the wall before sliding to the floor.

The woman leaned closer as Charlotte swam in and out of consciousness.

"My name is Truth," the woman repeated, her eyes glowing. "But you know me better as Spider."

Charlotte felt an icy fist of terror clench her heart before oblivion took her.

36

March 19th
10:15 a.m.

"You sure you want to wait here?"

Angellica glanced over at Sean from the passenger seat of his car. Then she swept her gaze over toward the medical examiner's building. "Yeah," she answered, "I'm sure. That Doctor Sanna was nice and all, but the place gives me the creeps."

"It's *Salla*, actually. And I wouldn't have come back here if I hadn't thought—."

"You'd dropped your wallet," Angellica finished with a grin. "I know. It's not in the car and we haven't been anywhere else today—except the café we went to for breakfast, but obviously you had it when we left because you paid the bill."

Sean grabbed her hand and gave it a squeeze. "I will be back in two minutes. Lock the doors when I leave." He hesitated.

"Go!" she said, half teasing. "I'll be okay. Just hurry back. I'm ready to go back to the apartment."

Sean smiled and got out of the car. He walked into the building, looking at the tiled floor for his wallet, and retraced his steps to the basement. He walked into the morgue where he'd left Charlotte, but the door was propped wide open with a stool.

"Hello?" he called out, looking around. "Doctor Salla?" *Maybe she's in the bathroom?* he rationalized, though he couldn't imagine her leaving the door open. He almost turned to look for her when he saw his wallet lying underneath one of the sterile, metal tables in the center of the room. *Must have slipped out when I sat down on that stool to look at the body.*

Reaching down, he grabbed the wallet, and started at the voice behind him.

"Can I help you?" it asked, the voice thick, low, and accented.

"Ah, no," Sean said, straightening up quickly. "Found what I was looking for," he continued, flapping his wallet in the air.

"This section is off limits to civilians." The man peered at Sean with disdain, his pursed lips white against his olive-toned skin. He wore a long white lab coat that hung loosely on his skinny body, his thin arms crossed against his chest. His eyebrows were sharply arched in an expression of surprise, but the wary look in his pale blue eyes made Sean realize the technician wasn't pleased.

Man, this guy isn't going to give an inch, is he?

"I'm not a civilian," Sean explained, flipping open his ID. "I'm a detective with the Boston P.D. I was here earlier working on a case with Doctor Salla and realized I dropped my wallet so I came back."

The tech uncrossed his arms. His face softened, although his dark eyebrows remained arched. "How did you get in?"

"Through the door." Sean was trying to get a look at the man's badge for a name, since he hadn't introduced himself, but it was located on a key ring on his belt loop and was partially covered by his coat.

"It was open?" the man asked in surprise.

"Yeah. I figured the doc was in here, but maybe she went to the bathroom?"

The assistant shook his head. "No, she would have closed the door. It automatically locks behind you. You need a key card to open it," he explained, pulling his from his belt loop.

"Maybe she forgot her key card so she left the door open?" He got a glance at the name. Dr. Lenard Knottes— Chief Laboratory Technician.

Dr. Knottes snorted. "You *obviously* don't know Doctor Salla that well. She would never leave this area open if she wasn't here, even if she *had* lost her key card. She would have left and closed the door and found someone to let her back in."

Sean wasn't sure why, but he felt an urge to tell this guy

that he *did* know Doctor Salla, *Charlotte*, quite well actually, and that just a short while ago she'd slept over at his place after baring her problems to him while drinking heavily.

But then the non-asshole part of him realized that he'd just make her look bad.

Not to mention it didn't matter since he was with Angellica again.

And *that* didn't matter because nothing happened between him and Charlotte in the first place.

"So what you're saying," Sean asked, bringing himself back to the subject at hand, "is that she's still in this room?" He did a slow turn. "I don't see her, so *obviously* she left." He didn't hold back on drenching the word in sarcasm.

"I don't know," Knottes said with a shrug. "I just know she wouldn't have left the door open."

"Was anyone else scheduled to work down here today?"

"Well, we could check the key card log and see who swiped in last."

Sean nodded and followed the tech as he made his way to the office. The area felt cramped, with three desks crammed inside where there was only space for two. Knottes sat down at one of the computers, pushing aside a mountain of papers attached to clipboards, and pulled up the recent key-in scan information.

"It shows Doctor Salla entering the morgue at about eight thirty this morning."

"Okay. I came in a little after nine and left about a half hour after that. But I remember distinctly that the door closed behind. . .us." Sean blinked. "Oh, crap. Hold on. I'll be right back."

Sean heard the tech call out as he bolted from the room and ran out of the building. He got to his car and found Angellica sitting peacefully in the passenger seat, the sun slanting onto her face through the windshield. Her eyes widened at his expression.

"What's wrong?" she asked as she opened the door and stepped out.

"Nothing," he said, embarrassed that he'd completely forgotten he'd left her in the car. "I just need to check something out and I didn't want to leave you here waiting by yourself."

"Is everything okay?" she asked as they walked back into the building. "Is it about your wallet?"

"Huh? No, that's fine. I found that," Sean replied, patting his back pocket. "But there's an inconsistency Doctor Knottes and I are trying to figure out."

"Who's Doctor Knottes?"

"The lab tech."

"'Cause *that* answers my question," she said under her breath as she trotted to keep up with him.

The two of them entered the office.

"Find anything else?" Sean asked Knottes.

"Actually, yes." Knottes pointed at the screen. "There is something of a discrepancy at nine forty-nine. It says 'access granted,' but there is no card number listed."

"What does that mean?"

Knottes looked at him and shrugged. "I have no idea. A glitch in the system? Someone's card didn't scan right?"

"But you are saying for sure that someone entered the morgue that had card access?"

"That's what the computer says."

"And it wasn't you?"

He shook his head. "I just got here. I only went to the morgue and found you there."

"Hmm. . ." His sense of 'something wrong' started to crawl through his insides, like a centipede in slow motion. Sean pulled out his cell and started dialing Charlotte's number.

"You have her number memorized?" Angellica asked.

"Unfortunately I've had to deal with her a lot lately."

The look of concern fell from Angellica's face. "Oh, yeah. I almost forgot the reason you two know each other."

Sean hung up when it reached voicemail. "Does she have a specific work number?"

"No," Knottes said, shaking his head. "She lives off her cell. The only time I've seen her not answer was when her arms were elbow deep in—"

"Excuse me," Angellica mumbled before she bolted from the room, her hand over her mouth.

"Not in our line of work, huh?"

Sean laughed. "Not quite." The inkling of doubt inside his stomach spread faster. "Doctor, can you find out if she's still in the building?"

"I can page her over the PA. If she's here, she should hear it."

"Okay. I'm going to have someone drop by her place real quick. . .uh. . .can you look up her address for me?"

"Four twenty-two Hancock Street." As soon as he'd said it, Knottes blushed. "I, um, got to drive her home once. Her car got plowed into while parked and had to be towed."

Suddenly, Dr. Lenard Knottes didn't seem like such a bad guy.

"All right. We'll wait and see if she responds to the page and then I'm going to have an officer cruise by her place and see if she's home."

Knottes' forehead wrinkled in worry. "You think something happened to her?"

"I don't know. But the serial killer we've been dealing with has changed the rules too many times for my liking. I want to err on the side of caution."

Angellica walked in as Knottes started the building-wide page.

"How are you feeling?" Sean asked her.

"Wishing we hadn't eaten yet," she said with a weak smile. "So what's going on and when can I get out of this place? I'm acquainted a little too well with the plumbing."

"We're waiting for Doctor Salla to check in. Things aren't quite adding up. I just want to make sure she's all right."

The two of them waited and heard the page go off for the second time. About five minutes after that, Knottes walked back into the office, rubbing his hands together.

"If she were here, she would have checked in by now."

Sean was on his phone in an instant calling Millan.

"I'll send someone to go check out her place," Millan replied after Sean's explanation. "Normally I would say it's too soon to be worried, but this asshole already kidnapped

Angellica just to throw you off. I wouldn't put it past him to bring other players into the mix as well."

"Let me know as soon as the officer reports in. And tell everyone else to watch their backs. If they are involved in this case, they can now be a target."

"Will do. Sit tight. Maybe she'll show up."

Sean hung up and redialed Charlotte's number.

Ring.

"Come on."

Ring.

"Come on!"

Ring. . . This is Doctor Salla. Please leave a message. . ."

37

March 19th
11:30 a.m.

"He is persistent, isn't he?"

Charlotte inclined her head towards her phone. "If he has realized I am missing, he will not stop in his attempt to contact me."

The woman called Truth held Charlotte's phone in her hand. She slid her dark-toned fingers over its surface, turning it this way and that between her palms.

"He is a fascinating creature," she said as the phone rang again. Sean's number appeared on the caller ID. "His determination is admirable."

"I would have to agree with that statement," Charlotte

answered.

"Of course you would. That's why you have been chosen to replace me."

Charlotte had been captive for less than an hour and, if she had to be perfectly honest, it had been one of the best hours of her life. Of course, this excluded the fact someone drugged her and she wasn't allowed to leave, but otherwise she found herself in complete contentment.

She currently sat in the plushest, softest, most comfortable chair she'd ever sat in in her life. She didn't know the fabric, only that it felt amazingly soft against her bare skin. Because, in point of fact, she was naked.

Granted, a blanket covered her, made of the same material as the chair, which felt like a cross between satin and mink, if that combination were possible, but otherwise, she was completely void of clothing.

When she'd woken, she found herself lying in a bed about the size of her entire apartment bedroom. Layer after layer, fold after fold of the slinkiest, softest, smoothest fabric she'd ever touched enveloped her. Even though she felt frightened by her surroundings, somehow a sense of safety swathed her as well under the multitude of blankets. She had been neither hot nor cold—perfectly at ease on a mattress which held her like a dense cloud.

Minutes after she woke, Truth entered the room and asked Charlotte to follow her. At that moment she realized two things simultaneously. The first, Truth was naked. The second, so was she. But since her captor didn't seem to have a problem with it, Charlotte merely slipped from under the covers and followed her, chin held high, body bared to the world. She had no intention of letting her captor make her feel uncomfortable.

She was led into a bathroom the size of a small studio apartment. The bathtub, or small pool, sat filled to the brim with lavish bubbles. Several small cascades of water fell into the tub at different levels to keep the bubble level high. A scent floated in the air that Charlotte couldn't place—almost like a flower, almost like a fruit, almost like freshly cut grass, almost like the breeze after a storm. All scents that she thought should overwhelm her if put together, but somehow they mixed perfectly.

Charlotte slipped into the bath, pleasantly surprised by the texture of the liquid she submerged herself into. It felt thicker than water, like milk, but warm and clingy as honey. She tried to see what it looked like, but the bubbles were everywhere, making it impossible.

Her hair became washed, her body scrubbed, her shoulders massaged. Truth's touch was soft, delicate, and gentle, and yet completely non-sexual. It seemed more like a mother bathing a daughter or a girl playing with her doll. Once again, Charlotte knew she should feel uncomfortable, but somehow, she didn't. She felt safe, loved, and pampered. She wondered if this could be a side-effect of the drug they'd given her to make her complacent, and she resolved to stay focused and alert.

After the bath she was dried with towels that felt like feathers mixed with silk. Her long, dark hair hung in thick waves as it dried naturally and fell to the middle of her back.

After she got to choose a blanket to wrap herself in, which she currently had draped around her body, Truth brought her to what she could only describe as a sitting room. It seemed to have no other function than two chairs which faced each other in front of a large fireplace. A high-vaulted ceiling stretched above, holding a uniquely shaped chandelier—it spiraled down, giving the impression of a spiral staircase, with teardrop-shaped crystal lights hanging from each end.

She held in her hand a goblet that seemed to be glass, but shone multi-faceted as if made of diamond. In it was some sort of dark brown drink, and although tempted to sate her thirst, Charlotte didn't want to try it. She believed she wasn't going to be harmed, but the fact that up until now she hadn't had any choice in anything, refusing the drink gave her some measure of control.

"You mentioned that before," Charlotte told her captor, continuing the conversation, "that I was your replacement. What precisely do you mean by that?"

"I mean that all of this," Truth answered, indicating their surroundings with a circular gesture, "everything you see, this complete perfection, belongs to you when I pass."

"Are you implying your death will occur in the near future?"

Truth swirled her drink in her glass, the dark liquid sparkling against the crystal surface. "If that's the way things are set, then that's what will become of me. I don't know what my exact future holds, only this moment, this point in my existence. And each point in my life led me to you."

"To replace you."

"Yes."

Charlotte immediately wanted to decline the invitation, but she felt terrified about what would happen if she denied this woman. So far it seemed the only reason she lived was because she had value in taking Truth's place. The longer Truth believed that was a possibility, the longer Charlotte may survive. "What do you do that needs replacing?"

"I have been given the task of weeding out imperfection in the world. Humans have decided evolution doesn't apply to them anymore. We force our environment to fit to us. We allow those with faulty genetics to remain—allowing them to spread, keeping them alive in our human gene pool. We keep ourselves weak as a species by allowing these weaknesses. This must end."

Charlotte thought about the woman's statements, trying to keep her horror at the callousness in Truth's words about these murders at bay. They weren't exactly untrue. But then again, the ravings of most sadistic individuals often have some notion of truth embedded in them. And just because they were true, didn't mean they were right.

"I cannot argue against what you say," Charlotte began, weaving her words to subdue her captor, "but your methods of extermination are extravagant and unnecessary. You have not simply removed the genes from the gene pool by killing an individual, you have tortured them to death. Why?"

The ebony goddess delicately placed the goblet on the small end table next to Charlotte's phone, which for the moment had stopped ringing.

"Yes," she began, "the torture. It does seem like that,

doesn't it? But it's not really that simple."

"Explain it to me then."

Truth nodded. "Of course. You see, I am not alone."

Charlotte's eyes widened. "What do you mean?"

"I make up a third of a Triad. As it is with the male propagated-version—God, his son, and the Holy Spirit—it is with us. However we have been around much longer than Judeo-Christian viewpoints of a male-dominated overlord.

"I am the supremacy," Truth went on. "The judge who judges the next guilty party—who chooses who must fall. Our Second is the jury—she must decide how the transgressors are to be punished. And our Third is the executioner—she carries out the sentence."

"You are all women?"

"Of course. Only those who can bring life into the world will be allowed to remove it."

"And these other two women—you have no say in how they decide to punish their victims?"

"That is correct."

"So you feel no guilt about what has been done to these people?"

"It is not my job to punish, simply determine guilt, as will be yours."

Charlotte couldn't speak. How could Truth calmly talk about this like she was passing along an antique ring heirloom? With measured breaths, she focused on how to get as much information as she could before she had to start telling this woman that there was no way in *hell* she was going to decide which people should be sentenced to death because of a variation in their DNA.

Charlotte continued. "So who is responsible for the notes to the police department? And why send them at all?"

"Ah," Truth answered, once again picking up the phone as it began to ring. She seemed fascinated that the phone kept ringing. Charlotte felt torn—comforted by the fact that Sean kept trying to call her, tormented by the fact that even if she could answer the phone, she couldn't tell him where she was.

"That became a project of the Second," Truth went on. "She became interested in testing those who have been given power over men. If they could thwart us, then perhaps we weren't right in what we were doing. Obviously, we have not yet failed."

"Only because you changed the rules."

Truth's hands stilled and the tiniest semblance of a frown touched her full lips. "Explain."

Aha, Charlotte thought, *so this woman does not know everything that goes on with her Second and Third.*

"The pattern of the game has changed because of Detective Trann."

"The one who keeps calling?"

"Yes," Charlotte said. "He almost bested your Third a year ago. It stopped your executions until last month. Now the deaths come every week to make up for it. Your Third even kidnapped a personal friend of Detective Trann to throw him off the trail, most likely because she knew he would figure things out otherwise."

Truth's dark porcelain skin flushed. "They stopped killing for a year?"

Charlotte nodded, wondering why that bit of information worried Truth more than the change in the game. Regardless, she pushed it, trying to find a wedge she could shove between this woman and her associates.

"Yes. Last year Detective Trann found a victim still alive, before time had expired. After that, the killer, or I should say your Third, stopped her executions for twelve months."

Truth stood up abruptly. "If you'll excuse me. I must attend to something. I will be back shortly." With those remarks, she left Charlotte alone.

A twinge of hope rippled through her as she glanced over at the table, but no such luck. Truth had taken the phone with her.

Her body trembled as the terror of the situation hit her. There was a good possibility she wouldn't leave here alive. Though shaking, she wrapped the blanket tightly around herself and stood, determined to keep focused. "Let's see if I can learn something else about this place while she's gone."

38

March 19th
Noon

"What do you mean 'she's not home?' Where the hell is she?" Sean was nearly yelling into his phone as he raced over to the police department. The officer he spoke with was trying to explain that he'd entered the premises with the landlord's help and that Dr. Salla was nowhere inside.

"Damnit!" he yelled, hanging up his phone. He immediately dialed Charlotte's number. It rang. It went to voicemail.

"Sean," Angellica said tentatively, next to him in the car. "What are we going to do? What if she has her?"

"She? She who?"

"Spider."

Sean slammed on the brakes, swerved hard to the right, and pulled off the road. He whipped his head over to Angellica who shrieked at the sudden movement.

"Wait. Are you saying Spider is a *woman*?"

Angellica released her grip on her seat. "Yes," she said as she caught her breath. "At least, the person who held me captive had a woman's voice."

"Why didn't you say that before?" he snapped.

Angellica's face hardened. "I don't know! I didn't think about it. And maybe because I didn't care about who the hell she was, just that I had gotten away without being killed," she snapped back.

Sean let out a deep breath. "You're right. I'm sorry I yelled. I didn't even think about it. You just said you didn't remember anything until you were locked in that room and then Spider sent you down some food." He patted her knee and checked over his shoulder to pull back into traffic. "Let's head back to the station and we'll go through everything again—if you feel up to it?"

Angellica nodded.

"Right. I'll give Millan a call and let him know we're on our way."

Thirty minutes later, and four more failed phone calls to Charlotte—not that he expected her to answer, but he couldn't stop trying—Sean and Angellica arrived at the precinct. They sat down with Millan and Angellica retold her story. She told them everything from waking up groggy and disoriented, to the conditions of the room, to the description of Spider's voice and demeanor. They pressed her for every little detail, from the size of the bed to the type of food in the packet.

"And you don't remember anything about how you got there?" Millan asked.

Angellica shook her head. "Nothing. I just remember waking up in the room. My head felt stuffy though, like it was full of cotton, so I think maybe I was drugged."

"That still doesn't help us with how Spider got you in and out of the hotel, especially if you were unconscious," Sean said. "Our posted officers would have noticed something like that."

Millan chimed in. "Oh yeah, I forgot to tell you. I finally tracked down Holden, the guard at your place, Sean, during the day when Spider left his. . .I mean *her* note. He said the only people who went in and out of the apartment on his shift were you leaving for work and Angellica stopping by that morning. He assured me no one else came in and out, but I don't understand how that's possible."

Angellica's brow furrowed. "I don't remember going to Sean's that morning. I knew he'd be at work."

"Holden said you stopped by, said you needed your purse because you'd left it inside. He said you had the spare key and everything."

"I didn't—I wasn't. . ." Angellica's face twisted as she tried to remember. "I never went into Sean's apartment without him in it." She rubbed the tips of her fingers against her forehead. "At least, I don't think. . ."

"Maybe the drugs they gave you messed up your memory for the whole day?" Sean suggested. "You said you don't really remember much except for going to the hotel the night before and then waking up in the basement of the TravelAmerica building. We all just assumed you'd been taken in the morning, but what if she took you later in the day? What if you'd been up for a while in the hotel, but when you got drugged, you don't remember any of that?"

"So you have no memory of going to Sean's?" Millan asked.

"No."

"You have no recollection of speaking to the guard or picking up your purse?"

"No," she said emphatically. "I don't remember anything except waking up in that horrible place."

Millan glanced at Sean with a knowing look.

"No," Sean denied Millan's insinuation immediately. "No way!" Millan couldn't possibly think. . .

"What?" Angellica asked. "What is it?"

"Millan thinks *you* planted the note in my apartment."

"What?" Angellica asked, defensive. "What are you talking about? That's crazy! Why would I plant a note from a serial killer?"

"You said it yourself," Millan began slowly, "you don't remember going to Sean's place, but the guards remember you going in. The three of us were the only people who went in that day. If it wasn't Sean and it wasn't me. . ."

"And then, what?" Sean said, shaking with anger. "She locked *herself* in the basement? She fed *herself* through a grate in the ceiling?"

"Of course not."

"Then what *exactly* are you saying?"

Millan set his jaw. "I'm not saying anything specific. I'm just saying this is the first inconsistency we can put a face to. It is our *job*," he said, emphasizing the word, "to check out everything and everyone. Don't make it personal. We just need to figure out what's going on. Maybe Spider forced her to go in and plant the note because she knew Angellica could get past the guards and knew the drugs would erase that memory. I don't know, Sean. But it's up to us to figure it out."

Sean let out a shaky breath. "You're right, man, you're right. It's just. . ." He looked over at Angellica.

"I wish I knew what happened," she said, taking his hand and squeezing it. "I wish I could remember."

"We'll figure it out," he said, reassuring her. He turned his attention back to Millan. "I'm not letting this psycho woman hurt anyone else. We are going to find Charlotte. We are not going to let anyone else die."

"Uh. . .who's Charlotte?" Millan questioned.

"What?" Sean asked.

"You said we are going to find Charlotte. Who's Charlotte?"

"Oh. Right. Sorry. Doctor Salla."

"You're on a first name basis with the Ice Queen?" the Sergeant asked as his eyebrow rose.

Is he serious? Sean thought. *He's bringing up this shit in front of Angellica? What an asshole!* "She *does* have a first name, you know. And unfortunately I have been working with her a lot lately."

"I thought you *liked* working with her?" Angellica asked.

Oh my God! Seriously? Her, too?

"Of course I like working with her," Sean answered. "I meant unfortunately because of all the dead bodies that have been showing up lately."

"Right," Millan said.

"Look, let's just focus on finding her. No matter what I call her, she's still missing." He threw a scathing look at Millan as Angellica looked down at her empty coffee cup. Millan was trying very hard not to laugh.

"So did anything I tell you help?" Angellica asked, bringing them back to the point. She placed the empty cup on the desk. "Or should I stop talking before I incriminate myself some more?"

"You were definitely helpful," Millan reassured her, "and now we have some extra things to look into, not to mention we now know Spider is a woman." He turned toward Sean. "I'll ask Wilt and Tay to find out the exact time Angellica went to your place, how long she was there, if the guards saw anyone else with her or another vehicle, etcetera." Millan turned toward Angellica. "You mind if I talk with the kid here for a minute?"

"Sure," she replied. "I'll just grab a soda from the vending machine. Be back in a few." She gave Sean a quick peck on the cheek and walked out of Millan's office.

"What's up?" Sean asked, once Angellica was out of earshot.

Millan took a seat behind his desk and laced his hands in

front of him. His dark brown eyes looked tired, his face heavy.

"Sean," he began, tentatively, "I know how personal this case is for you. You've been targeted specifically by Spider, who has brought in your old flame, then kidnapped her, and now maybe has taken Doctor Salla as well. I understand how your brain must be completely fucked up by all this.

"However," Millan went on, "I need you to be an officer of the law. I need you to stay as professional as possible."

Sean felt his muscles tense with defensiveness. "I feel like I *have* been professional, considering the circumstances," he said, trying to keep the attitude from his voice.

"And up until now, you have."

"What do you mean, 'up until now?'"

Millan let out a sigh and looked out into the lobby to make sure Angellica wasn't on her way back. "Angellica is the prime and sole suspect right now in this case."

Sean clenched his jaw. "I know that things look *bad* for her—"

Millan held up his hand. "Stop right there. Take Angellica out of the picture and put in anyone else. Now tell me what you think."

This is so dumb, he thought. *Just because the only person who had access to and entered my room when notes were left by Spider, and the only person to make it out alive and relatively unharmed by Spider, and the only person who could keep my head muddled enough that I wouldn't stay professional. . .*

"Damnit," Sean muttered. He rubbed his temples with his fingertips.

"You see the problem."

"Yeah. I can't exactly be one of the main detectives on this case and be involved with our prime suspect."

"I know," Millan said softly. "So we have two options. One, you remove yourself from this case or two, we put Angellica in a holding cell until all this is over. It would keep her contained, out of harm's way, and remove her from being a suspect if notes and bodies keep turning up."

"I am *not* liking either of those options," Sean said through a clenched jaw.

"Trust me, neither am I. I like the girl and I don't want to think she's involved. But you can't be with her and work on this."

"I know. I *know*!" Sean kicked at the desk leg in front of him.

"Is it too soon for me to come back?"

Sean swiveled around in the chair and saw Angellica standing in the doorway, a bottle of cola in her hand.

"Come on in," Millan said, gesturing. "We might as well tell you what's going on."

"That sounds ominous," she said, taking a seat.

"We have a problem," Millan continued.

"Are you going to arrest me?" she asked, her eyes wide.

"No. We don't have any evidence that you did anything wrong. The only thing we know is you went into Sean's place—"

"Which I don't remember."

"—during which time the note may have been left for Sean. So what we want to do is take you out of the equation."

She raised her eyebrows. "Meaning?"

"He wants to put you in a holding cell until all this blows over," Sean answered, barely containing his anger.

"You—you want to put me in jail?" The words came out screechy toward the end.

"No. A holding cell. It will be much more comfortable and you will be by yourself. I promise."

"What about the hotel room? What if I *swear* not to even *think* about leaving it?" Her fingernails dug into the arms of her chair. Sean realized she was panicking. He'd forgotten how claustrophobic she was. Being stuck inside a holding cell would be torture for her.

"You have already managed to get taken from or leave the hotel room without our guards knowing. We can't risk that again."

"Then get better guards," she snapped. "Tell them to keep their eyes open so that I don't get kidnapped and drugged again! You want to arrest someone, arrest the assholes who let me get taken in the first place. Are they under suspicion, too? Do they get to stay in a cozy fucking holding cell?"

"Angel—" Sean began.

"Don't 'Angel' me. This is *bullshit*!" She stood, gesturing frantically with her hands. "I get dragged into this by some psychopathic bitch, have to confront the man I left at the altar, get kidnapped while under supposed guard, and now I need to stay in jail because *I'm* a suspect! This is ridiculous!"

"She's right," Sean said to Millan, his own anger bubbling over. "This isn't fair to her."

"Sean," Millan warned. "Don't do this. We need you on the case. You know it's the right thing to do."

"No. She's been through enough. I'm not putting her in a holding cell. Period."

Millan's face was completely emotionless, except for the faintest twinge of sadness. "Then you're off the case. And to make sure you don't do anything stupid, you're temporarily suspended and ordered to stay in your apartment with Angellica."

Sean started. "What?"

"Badge and gun," was Millan's reply.

"You're serious."

"I told you, kid. There are only two options here. Either she goes in a cell or you're off the case. It has to be this way."

"Sean," Angellica said softly.

"You know I'm right," Millan said, keeping his gaze locked onto Sean's.

Sean roughly reached for his sidearm and unloaded it before placing it on the desk.

"Sean, no," Angellica went on, reaching for his arm.

He shook her off and removed his badge, throwing it down in front of Millan.

"Let's go, Angel."

Sean whipped around and stormed out of the office, Angellica trailing behind him. Right before he reached the building's door he heard Millan call out.

"Guess Doctor Salla's life is less important than a few nights behind bars for your girlfriend! I'll be sure to tell her that if I ever see her alive again!"

Sean slammed the door so hard behind Angellica that one of the windows shattered. He stopped and let out an inhuman sounding yell.

Everyone in the area turned to look, stopping whatever they were doing. Sean ignored them and sank down onto the curb.

Angellica sat down next to him, her hand on his knee.

"Sean," she said, "I'm sorry."

Sean barely heard her. His mind was a chaotic jumble of darkness, anger, and noise. He felt sick to his stomach, furious with Millan for forcing the situation. He even felt resentful that Angellica was there because it meant he had to take care of her first, instead of doing his job. And terror coiled its way through his chest at the thought that Charlotte might be the next person to die in some horribly painful way and he'd done nothing to stop it. In fact, by taking himself off the case, he'd probably just let Spider win.

Sean may be the only person who could beat this woman. And she knew it. She knew it so well she'd twisted everything and everyone around him so that he'd step away from the case. So that he'd quit.

And that's exactly what just happened.

Sean's eyes cleared and he came back to the present. He could feel the chilly springtime air blowing through his hair. He could smell the freshly mowed lawn on either side of the building. He could feel the gentle pressure of Angellica's hand on his knee.

He looked over at the love of his life and saw—

—a distraction.

The woman sitting next to him was everything he thought he wanted. Everything he thought he'd dreamed of. And then she left him just when they were about to start their lives together without any word, any reason, anything at all.

Now she was back, by his side, loving him. . .or was she? They'd never discussed their feelings toward one another. They never talked about what would happen when all this ended. It had only been moment to moment, never a thought about anything but themselves at that point in time.

And that summed up their entire previous relationship. Sean had proposed to her a year and a half ago, not because he couldn't imagine a future without her, but because it was what he wanted at the moment. They'd never talked about anything dealing with the future. Even their wedding had been thrown together in haste.

When he thought about having her next to him in the years to come, growing old together, spending all their time talking about nothing except for getting coffee every morning and what to have for lunch, it made him apathetic. There was no growth, no challenge, no drive to be better together. It was . . .a boring future.

She was everything he wanted—right now. But after that. . .

"Sean?" Angellica asked, breaking his thoughts. "Should we be going?"

She looked so beautiful. He wanted to take her away from everything and keep her safe and secure and—

And he wished he could love her the way he wanted to love someone.

But he didn't.

What is wrong with me? Why am I thinking about this stuff right now? I just turned in my badge and gun, Charlotte is still missing, and Angellica is sitting next to me free as a bird when—

When she shouldn't be.

"I'm sorry," he said. "We can't go anywhere. Or, actually, *you* can't go anywhere."

"I—what do you mean *I* can't go anywhere?"

Sean took her hands in his. "I need you to stay in a holding cell. Just for a few days."

Her face became stony. "Are you serious? You can't be serious. You just told your boss you wouldn't let him do that to me."

"Angellica, I *have* to be on this case. And the only way for us to be sure you aren't a part of anything is if I'm with you all the time or if you're in a holding cell. I can't be with you and be on the case at the same time."

"I figured that out when you turned over your gun and badge," she snapped. "Or was that just for show? What am I, a yo-yo? You can't just pull me in one direction then throw me in a different one."

"Listen, I know you're scared—"

Angellica roughly pulled her hands away. "You have no *idea* how I feel," she told him, the words full of venom. "I didn't want to come to this stupid city in the first place. I didn't want to ever see *you* again. I should have just thrown away that note as soon as I'd gotten it."

"Grow the fuck up."

Angellica's expression was that of someone who'd just

been slapped across the face.

Sean continued. "*You* didn't want to come here. *You* didn't want to see me. You think I wanted to see you? And look at us! What are we even doing? Sleeping together? Rekindling the old flame? What a joke! We haven't changed. I'm still a detective and you still don't want to be with one." Sean had never talked to her this way. In all the time they were together, he'd been so focused on being with her, he never saw how incompatible they really were as a couple.

Angellica's words came fast and breathy. "You can't talk to me that way. I've been through hell since I got here!"

"You think this is easy for any of us?" he challenged her. "My Sergeant was responsible for having a man ripped into pieces. The medical examiner I'm working with is missing. My ex-fiancée who stood me up at the altar is the prime suspect in the investigation. And I seem to be the only person who can solve this fucked-up case and because of that, this crazy, serial-killing bitch is fucking with everyone in my life so that I'm so messed up I end up off the case. And look what just happened! Just because you can't spend two or three days in a freaking holding cell."

Angellica's eyes became storms of thunderclouds. "Don't trivialize it. You know I'm claustrophobic, Sean. I can't stand the idea of being locked in a small room. I will go crazy. It's not that I don't want to help, but I can't do it!" Her anger melted into fear.

"Then we will get you some sedatives or have someone stand outside your cell twenty-four hours a day to talk to you or we'll let you out every hour to walk down the hall. I don't know! But we'll think of something."

He turned on the curb to face her, the cement scratching against his pants. "Angellica, I *know* you can do this."

Sean took her gently by the shoulders.

"Please," he told her, his tone softer. "We need to stop this killer. I can't do it without your help."

Sean could see a battle taking place inside her. Her face paled, her brow broke out in sweat, her hands twisted and wrung in her lap.

Angellica swallowed against a lump in her throat. "I'll try," she whispered.

He gathered her up in his arms. "Thank you," he said into her hair.

The two of them stood.

"I really thought we might work out this time." Her blue eyes were moist with tears.

"Yeah. Me too."

39

March 19th
1:30 p.m.

It had been over an hour since Truth left Charlotte alone in the sitting room. Charlotte used that time to search for anything to help her escape. Her thin fingertips ran over the beautiful brick work. Or wood work. Or tile. She really couldn't tell what the walls were made of—some sort of seamless blend she couldn't place. Regardless, she didn't find any cracks, flaws, or chinks she could exploit.

Not that she really expected to find anything wrong with this place. So far everything had seemed completely, well, perfect. But she tried anyway.

The whole situation left her feeling homesick. Sort of.

Not actually her home. For her work. She found herself longing for the sterile walls of the lab, the meticulous way she organized her instruments, the sharp smell of industrial cleaning products.

What is wrong with me? she thought. *Why on Earth would I be missing those things? Is my life really so empty that I seek comfort in a dead environment? Have I detached myself so completely from the world around me that I miss the barren life I lead?*

She paused in her search of the room's walls at these thoughts. She'd never thought of herself as lonely before. *Alone*, yes, but not lonely.

So what had changed? She was still in the same field of study. She still lived in the same apartment. Her job as Chief Medical Examiner was fairly new, but it wasn't much different from being simply a Medical Examiner.

So what had changed?

The thought lingered there, touching the edges of her mind with tiny finger-like wisps, but an answer didn't come.

She slowly finished her second round of the room, gripping the blanket she held wrapped around her slender body while she knelt to check the edges of the fireplace, when she heard the door behind her open.

With a quick movement, she straightened up as Truth walked into the room, her dark hair cascading over her shoulders.

"Looking for a way out?" the ebony goddess asked.

"Of course," Charlotte answered truthfully. She settled herself back into one of the chairs when Truth gestured for her to do so.

"Thank you for being honest with me," Truth told her. "I despise dishonesty."

"I can relate."

"The need to lie seems like such a waste of time. I don't understand why humans do it, and so frequently."

Charlotte thought of her last encounter with Sean and Angellica. "Perhaps because they are afraid of what might happen if they told the truth."

"Ah. . .fear. Yes, that is a strong motivator."

A few moments of silence passed.

Charlotte tried to think of something to say, but her thoughts kept coming back to their previous conversation— to the notion she would be Truth's replacement. She didn't want to talk about it, and yet she found herself curious to know more. In one way, she was flattered. There must be something special about her to be considered for Truth's position, though a bit morbid of a thought. And yet Charlotte felt afraid to ask.

What if she *wanted* the job?

The notion was absurd. Of course she didn't want to decide if others should live or die.

But this woman carried an allure about her. She spoke in a way that made sense, and if Charlotte had any flaws, it was following logic.

Still, despite her fear, she needed to know.

"Truth," Charlotte began, "why did you choose me to replace you?"

Truth's smile appeared soft and gentle. "I didn't choose

you. You were *chosen*."

"Chosen? How do you mean?"

"I have something I want to show you." Truth left the room and returned a few minutes later holding a large, elaborately-bound book in her hands. The binding was stunning, a combination of leather, ivory, and gold. The markings on the front were unfamiliar to Charlotte, who was fluent in twelve languages, but she found herself craning her neck to see the symbols anyway.

"It's beautiful, isn't it?" Truth asked, her dark eyes shining.

"Remarkable. What language is it? It looks like cuneiform writing, but the symbols seem wrong for Sumerian."

"It's pre-Sumerian. It technically doesn't have a name."

"Pre-Sumerian?" Charlotte asked, stunned. "That is impossible. There are no known pre-Sumerian written languages."

"Not known to the scientific world, no, but they are known. This," Truth said, her fingertips dancing over the cover, "is one of them."

Forgetting for a moment she was being held captive against her will, Charlotte found herself completely engrossed by the tome. "It is quite breathtaking. The indentations are exceedingly intricate."

"Yes, the language is remarkably detailed. This Book is actually over six thousand years old. It's the oldest Book in existence that has yet been found, although we have several others within the same thousand-year period."

Charlotte pulled her wavy tresses into a loose bun behind

her head. "It is in extraordinary condition for its age."

"It's only brought out once every ten years, when a new Triad is chosen. Of course, you are an exception. It has not been a full ten years since my Triad has been in place."

Every ten years? How long have these people been killing?

Truth moved the glasses on the table and gently placed the book next to them. She opened the cover and withdrew her long fingers. Charlotte could hardly believe she would touch the book with bare hands instead of being gloved, but though the text appeared worn, it did not look damaged.

"When a new Triad is called into play, the Book is re-authenticated," Truth said.

"What do you mean, re-authenticated?"

Truth crossed her silken legs, her blanket sliding up around her thighs. She seemed unconcerned, and in fact, Charlotte guessed that the only reason she wore a covering at all was to make the medical examiner more comfortable.

"My position is unique. We are usually hand-picked, but never forced into joining the Triad, unlike the other two positions. Although your circumstances are a bit different, I don't expect you to enter into this arrangement without your full consent. It's forbidden to trick or trap you into your future position. The Second and the Third yes, but not you."

Charlotte wondered about that statement, but left it alone for now.

"You must come of your own accord," Truth went on, "understand the reasons, and be completely devoted to the task at hand. Because of this, you are allowed to explore what you are told. You will be allowed to confer with any two persons—one to determine the authenticity of the language and one to confirm the age and validity of this book. We can provide you with someone on staff or you may choose to bring anyone in from the outside. The only restriction is they must be women."

"If this text has been analyzed so many times, how can the scientific community be unaware of this find?"

"Because those who are brought in are either killed or kept on to help us in our own tasks."

Charlotte let out a noise of disbelief. "You are joking."

Truth's silent response confirmed her seriousness.

Charlotte shook her head violently. "I will not have someone validate this book only to be killed or kept here as a slave against her will."

"They are not kept as slaves. If they don't wish to stay here, *then* they are executed." Truth said this as if is talking about a child who hadn't cleaned his room and so had to be grounded as a punishment.

Charlotte tried to control her horror as she spoke. "As a scientist, I cannot dismiss there may be languages, peoples, and items that existed prior to what we have previously documented. And so I would not be able to choose a person to validate them and therefore forfeit her life."

"But if they work for us, then they can live. And most people in that field think of it as an opportunity to study the texts we have. They would never have the chance to do so otherwise. In fact, most of the scientists have opted to work with the texts."

"With death as their alternative, that does not leave them with much choice."

Truth shook her head and smiled. "You misunderstand. They are not told their alternative is death."

Charlotte couldn't keep the look of shock from her face. "What? You mean they are unaware that if they do not choose to work with you, they will die?"

"How can we know if they can be trusted if their only motivation is to save their own lives? It's the same as using torture to retrieve information—one can never be sure if the information is actually true or if they are just saying something to make the pain stop."

Logically, it made sense, although somehow it felt more deceptive than lying. Still, she couldn't find fault with Truth's reasoning. As barbaric as it seemed, it was true, from Truth's perspective.

"Truth, these individuals I choose to authenticate the text, how long do they have to determine its accuracy?"

"Seven days."

"What if I choose someone who doesn't have enough experience or can't authenticate it in that amount of time?"

"Then they die and you choose someone else. The next individual also has seven days."

"And if I refuse to choose anyone at all?"

"We will choose for you and they will be killed at the end of seven days, without the option of working for us."

Hm. . .this may be harder than I thought. Charlotte would have to think carefully. There must be a loophole somewhere, she knew it, but she just hadn't found it yet.

In the meantime, Charlotte wanted to learn as much as she could about these people and their beliefs. Anything to gain more knowledge to help her escape.

"If," Charlotte began, "as you say, this Book is six thousand years old, how was it determined that I am chosen to replace you?"

Truth's eyes grew wide with joy. "You, Charlotte, are what we have been waiting for, for these six thousand years. The Book has foretold your coming. You are not just *my* replacement. You are here to replace the heads of *all* the Triads. For you see, *you* are our messiah.

"You will be the savior of humankind."

40

March 19th
3 p.m.

Sean sat in a bathroom stall in the men's room at the police station, his head resting in his hands. He stared at the checkered-patterned tile floor through his laced fingers. He'd already come back in, apologized to Millan, got reinstated, and convinced Angellica to leave with the officers for her holding cell. He told her he'd be by later to visit.

After he chatted with the Sergeant about what they were going to do about finding Dr. Salla. They hadn't come up with anything constructive, especially since they couldn't find a note. The good news was they were fairly certain Charlotte was not the next intended victim, and so in all probability, wouldn't be harmed, just like Angellica hadn't. The bad news was they had a missing medical examiner with no clue how to find her and in one day there would be a real victim with 24 hours to live.

Since the good news hung on "hopes" and "probablys" and the bad news was a certainty, Sean found himself with a whopper of a headache. He told Millan he needed some air, but he didn't want to go back outside, where he'd just realized he didn't really love Angellica, whom he'd believed was the love of his life.

He thought if he could just get away from everything for a little while and think, that *somehow* things would unravel themselves and he would figure them out. But the longer he sat, the worse his head ached, and the further away he felt from any solution. Not to mention that the men's bathroom wasn't the best place to get "fresh air."

What the hell am I going to do? I've got nothing to go on. Absolutely nothing.

Sean took a deep breath in through his nose, ignoring the smell of urinal cakes and poorly distributed flowery air freshener, and blew it out through his lips.

Calm down, he told himself. *This isn't going to figure itself out. You have to help it along. So do what you always do. Start with what you know.*

He felt like he didn't know anything.

That's bull. You know plenty. You know Angellica is a suspect. Why? Because she was seen at your apartment the day she disappeared and so it's assumed she left the note for Spider. So start there. Go back and talk to the officer who was on duty. Ask him to go over everything again. See if he missed something.

Sean's headache ebbed. Slowly, but surely. It wasn't much of a plan, but it was better than sitting on a toilet doing nothing.

41

March 19th
4 p.m.

With help from Millan, Sean tracked down the guard that had been on duty the day Angellica disappeared from the hotel. He was working traffic at the intersection of Tremont and Beacon, where a streetlight had been knocked over after being run into by a semi. The crossroad wasn't even a mile away from the police department, but Sean still drove. He pulled over, ignoring the meter, and ran out into the middle of the intersection.

"Holden," Sean called out to the cop. "Officer Holden. I need to have a word with you."

"I'm a little busy," Holden hollered back, twirling his

right arm to let a few pedestrians walk across the road. His blonde hair was shorn so short that the late afternoon sun gleamed off his skull, reflecting into Sean's eyes. "My relief comes in a couple of hours. Can we talk then?"

Yes.

"No," Sean said out loud. "It'll just take a minute."

Holden held up his right hand toward the eastbound traffic and allowed the northbound/southbound traffic to move forward. "What is it?"

"You were on duty the day Angellica went into my apartment, right?"

Holden stepped away for a moment, stopping a car from nearly plowing into another one that was turning left. "Jesus, people! Can't you see my hand? It means STOP. Yes, sir," Holden continued, addressing Sean, "I was there. I made a report and everything."

"I know. I read it. I want to go over a few things again."

The whistle was in Holden's mouth, issuing a high-pitched screech. "Get back in the crosswalk until I tell you to go," he yelled at some pedestrians.

You're going to get someone killed. This guy needs to concentrate on what he's doing. Every panicked twinge in his body made him want to stay, but he realized he needed to wait. "Listen, Holden, I'll catch up with you on your break. I didn't realize how bad it was at this intersection."

"Thanks, man. As you can see, it's been a big mess." Holden nodded at the snapped-in-half traffic signal which still lay partway in the road. "I called a maintenance truck over an hour ago and that thing is still there."

Sean took a quick glance around and saw a pub halfway up the street. "Let's meet there. Dinner will be on me."

"Can do. I'm off at seven."

Sean jogged toward his car, feeling dejected, but he couldn't risk screwing things up just because he felt anxious about Charlotte. That's what Spider would want.

42

March 19th
4:30 p.m.

"Me. I am your messiah."

"Yes."

Charlotte laughed. She couldn't help it. It was the most preposterous thing she'd ever heard. She may be excellent at her job, but she wasn't anyone's savior, much less for a group of megalomaniacs determined to systematically remove all genetic distortions from the human race. It was an impossibility regardless. Even if these women killed one person a month for the next 1,000 years, it wouldn't have the slightest effect on the overall population. How could they think they were making any difference?

And why on Earth would they think *she* should run it?

After the bomb of a statement, Truth had left Charlotte to her own thoughts. At some point, another woman entered, wearing a robe and soft boots, and carrying a tray of food. The woman appeared so plain in comparison to Truth she almost looked ugly, although she would most likely be considered beautiful otherwise. Her dark brown hair sat on top of her head in an elaborately braided bun, her cheeks flushed, and her eyes stayed lowered.

Charlotte thanked the woman, who only blushed harder.

"What is your name?" Charlotte asked.

The woman lifted her eyes, gave one of the most luminous smiles Charlotte had ever seen, and then hurried from the room. The encounter may have been short, but it let her know other people worked inside this place. And some wore clothing. Perhaps a classist-type significance? Or just personal preference?

The medical examiner briefly thought about over-powering the server and escaping, but after hearing about the scale of Truth and her operation, she changed her mind. First, she had no idea where she was. The room could be inside a massive bunker, or rigged to explode if she tried to escape. These women could have tracking devices planted inside her body, thermal scanners, or cameras everywhere. Until she knew more, she couldn't risk trying to leave.

So she ate the food, dozed in the chair, and awoke when Truth returned, continuing their conversation as if they hadn't parted a minute in the past couple hours.

Truth smiled at Charlotte's laughter and waited a moment before she spoke. "It may seem farfetched, but I can guarantee you are the chosen one. You shall lead the Triads and restore balance to our sick world."

"Triads?" Charlotte perked up. "Are you insinuating that there are multiple groups?"

Truth delicately shifted one of her short, springy curls off her forehead as she spoke. "Of course. You don't think we'd make any difference genetically if there was only one group of us killing one person a month, do you?"

Pinpricks of fear trickled through her belly. "How many Triads are there?"

"Currently there are five hundred thousand."

Charlotte's mouth hung open, aghast. She did the math in her head—if each group killed one person a month or 12 in a year. . .

"You are responsible for six *million* deaths a year!"

Truth nodded, completely unphased. "That's correct. Almost ten percent of all deaths in the world are attributed to us."

This is insane. How can this possibly be? How can these groups function and continue without anyone knowing? Six million *deaths a year.*

Tears welled up in Charlotte's eyes. She was shocked, angry, and totally without words. Trying to comprehend the magnitude of what this woman just told her was impossible. She sat there, hands trembling in her lap, as the tears slid down her cheeks. What had she been brought into?

Truth looked at her, sympathetic. "I understand how you feel."

"That seems unlikely. You have just informed me I will be in command of several hundred thousand groups which murder millions of people each year."

"Don't forget, I was exactly where you were three years ago. I, too, was subjected to these figures. I, too, was appalled at the number of deaths my predecessor spoke of in a casual manner, as if those people's lives didn't matter." Truth leaned forward, her blanket slipping off her shoulders and down to her waist. "But once I read the text, once I had it authenticated, once I realized the purpose of this cause, how could I sneer at the woman who taught me the truth?

"These people," Truth continued, waving a hand arbitrarily around her head, "they aren't supposed to be alive. And so they cannot be allowed to exist—or reproduce. We as a species have become too arrogant, too dependent on medical technology, too focused on creating, extending, and supporting life at any cost that we've broken the fundamental rules of evolution."

"Why not use some sort of sterilization process?" Charlotte asked, desperate for an alternate solution. "Surely with all your resources you can single out these individuals at birth and ensure they do not reproduce. You would not have to kill them."

"It's complicated. And it has to do with this," she said, patting the text. "The rules are specific. We can't deviate from them."

"Who is circumventing evolution now? This Book was written thousands of years ago. They did not have the technology to do these things. *You* do. You can prevent deaths.

You can allow these people to live their lives without passing on these genetic defects to their offspring."

Truth shook her head. "These people shouldn't be alive. Sterilization prevents reproduction, but it doesn't remove them from existence."

Charlotte ran her fingers through her hair in frustration. How could she debate someone who believed so fiercely in the contents of this book? They could sit here for hours and nothing would come of it.

Truth had to know that Charlotte would want to refuse—or at least wonder what would happen if she did. She didn't feel as though she could get anything else from her captor.

"Truth, I must ask—"

"You want to know what will happen if you decline this offer."

Charlotte nodded. "You said I must join willingly. Since the ten years are not up and I am clearly an exception since I am categorized as your messiah, I cannot help but wonder what would happen if I refuse? You cannot simply choose another messiah as you would other Triad leaders, correct?"

"That is true."

"Then what happens if I decide not to join your cause."

Truth let out a sigh. "You will never leave this place again."

"You will not kill me?"

"We can't kill a messiah."

Charlotte paused, wondering about Truth's choice of words. "Wait, have you had this problem before?"

Truth nodded. "I shouldn't be telling you this, but I

believe you are our true messiah."

"Your *true* messiah."

"Yes. There have been. . .others."

"What happened to them?"

"They were thought to be true, they even accepted their calling, but were found unable to handle the responsibility and so were deemed unworthy."

Charlotte closed her eyes for a moment. "Unworthy?"

"Yes. If the messiah doesn't want to join or is unable to perform the required tasks, they are considered unworthy for our cause and are kept until they expire."

"Why not simply kill them?"

Truth looked stunned. "The Book has strict rules against it. We are not murderers."

Charlotte couldn't believe this woman just said that. Was she so deluded that she really believed killing people wasn't murder?

Yes, she does. She does not think she is a murderer at all. She thinks she is helping *by ridding individuals that would harm humanity as a whole.*

"And you cannot simply let these messiahs—the ones that do not conform to your goals—go?" Charlotte asked.

"We can't let a false messiah back out into the world. If they fit all the criteria, but are not the messiah, then they must not be allowed to leave. They may alert others of our presence and start a rebellion."

Charlotte sat, absorbing this new information. She couldn't see any way out. If she refused, she would stay here until she died. There was nothing to indicate anyone had ever come close to discovering these Triads. And who knew if Detective Trann would ever find her? Now that Truth knew that the Second and Third had changed the rules without her knowledge, there was no guarantee they would continue sending notes. And if there were no notes, there would be no way to track these women down.

And she would be lost here forever.

Charlotte felt her composure waver. She'd always been able to get herself out of any situation, but now she felt completely helpless. There was nothing she could do. She couldn't go along with Truth. Although it was ironic in a way. This woman wasn't crazy. She was using logic as her weapon. Facts were always what Charlotte relied on. No matter the emotional component, the mechanics, or the circumstances, logic could make everything right.

Truth's facts were sound. But they weren't right.

Charlotte could picture Sean saying "The Ice Queen has melted!"

A smile touched the corner of her mouth at the thought. She felt lighter, calmer, safer. She would get out of here, even if it meant a lifetime of Sean teasing her about her horrible nicknames.

Breath filled her lungs through a deep inhale. She could do this. The air left her body slowly. For the first time in her life, even though she was on her own, she didn't feel alone.

A plan began to form inside Charlotte's mind. Her shoulders relaxed, her posture straightened, and her hands stilled. She wasn't sure if she could pull it off and it might put more people in danger, but she knew what she had to do.

43

March 19th
7 p.m.

Sean ordered a Bacon & Blue burger and told Officer Holden to get whatever he wanted—it was on him. They sat at Emmet's Irish Pub, down the block from where Holden had been directing traffic. Holden ordered the Old-Fashioned Rueben and downed his glass of water as they waited for their food.

"It's a mess out there," he said, wiping his brow. It wasn't that warm out, but sweat dripped down his neck into his uniform in thick streaks regardless. "The maintenance truck finally showed up and moved the traffic light, but insisted on blocking half the intersection to do so, even though it could have fit alongside one lane." He raised his glass at a nearby waitress, signaling for a refill. The ice cubes clinked against each other as he shook the cup.

"Sorry," Sean said lamely. He knew he shouldn't be so impatient, but right now he didn't care if this guy's head was on fire. He wanted answers.

After Holden chugged half of his second cup of water, he set the glass down on the wooden table with a bang and leaned back in his chair. "You wanted to ask me something about my report on your apartment?"

"I just want you to go over what you saw that day. Your report says Angellica went into my apartment. Was anyone with her?"

"Not that I can remember."

"Did she say anything about someone else? Was she on the phone? Did she seem nervous?"

Holden drummed his fingers on the table top. The restaurant was starting to fill with people, so Holden raised his voice to compensate. "She wasn't on the phone or nothing 'cause she spoke to me." Holden paused as his sandwich was laid in front of him. He took a huge bite, sauerkraut dripping from the end of the bun, and Sean waited in agony as he chewed the portion the recommended 32 times.

Holden swallowed. "I wouldn't say she was nervous either, sir. In fact, she seemed angry."

"Angry? Why do you say that?" Sean's burger had arrived as well, but he hadn't touched it yet. Then the smell of bacon and bleu cheese hit him and he realized how ravenous he was. He hadn't eaten anything all day.

"She was abrupt with me," Holden continued. "When I asked her for ID she rolled her eyes and said I knew who she was. Then she said obviously she couldn't show it to me since it was in her purse, which she came to the apartment to get."

Sean sunk his teeth into the burger, the mixture of grease, ripe cheese, and bacon filling his mouth. He took a moment to savor the juicy flavors and then swallowed, his stomach happy with the addition to his body. "You didn't put that in your report."

"Honeshly?" Holden said through a mouthful of runny cheese and meat. "I din wan to write tha your gillfriend was acting like a bish."

Sean paused while bringing his burger up for another bite. *Did he just call Angellica a bitch?* Sean held his temper. "I appreciate that," he said through clenched teeth.

"Don't mention it," Holden said as he wiped his mouth on the sleeve of his uniform. "I mean, she's hot, so I get it."

Sean blinked, not expecting the comment. "Excuse me?"

Holden crammed another portion of sandwich into his mouth. He said something that sounded like "I'd hit that too!"

Sean hadn't even realized he'd stood. He was unaware how he'd gotten over the table. And he had no idea why Holden was lying on the ground and his own hand felt like it had hit a brick wall.

"Out!" called a voice behind him. Sean spun around to face the manager of the pub. A squat man, face purple with rage, pointed to the door, his hand shaking. "Get out!"

Holden pulled himself up and grunted at the restaurant

owner. "It's okay, man, we're cops."

Sean glanced around at the other patrons and inwardly groaned. Several held up their phones, recording the incident.

"I don't care if you're the president," the owner shouted. "No fighting in my restaurant. Out!"

Oh, man, Sean thought as he backed away from the table. *This is* not *good.*

44

March 19th
8 p.m.

"You hit him." It was a statement, not a question.

Sean squirmed in his seat under the Sergeant's glare. He was in Millan's office, sitting across from him at his desk. Sean had never seen his boss work so hard to restrain his anger. "Yes, sir," Sean answered.

"In the middle of a restaurant."

"Yes, sir."

"Because he said he'd also 'hit that' about Angellica?"

Sean nodded.

Millan rubbed his thumb against the spot between his eyebrows and exhaled forcefully through his nose. "I should suspend you. You were completely out of line." He paused and looked upwards, as if saying a silent prayer. "I *can't* suspend you because I need you on this case. But from now on you are *not* allowed to interrogate anyone, see anyone, touch anyone, or do ANYTHING without someone else with you. Is that clear?"

"Crystal."

"You are lucky Holden isn't pressing charges," Millan grumbled. "As for any press. . .we will deal with it later. Right now we need to focus, and I mean fast. Tomorrow is when Spider will take his—I mean *her*—next victim. So far the notes have been delivered to your apartment somehow. With Angellica in a holding cell, if the note still gets delivered, then she's off the hook. If not—"

"Then she's a pretty damn good suspect," Sean finished for his superior.

"This is a pretty fucked-up situation to hope that you still get a note tomorrow."

"I know."

Millan leaned back in his chair. "I take it there's still nothing from Doctor Salla?"

It was Sean's turn to sigh. "It just rings and then goes to voicemail. My only hope is since it's still ringing the battery isn't dead and maybe someone will hear it and answer. I'll keep trying."

"Well there's nothing else you can really do for tonight. Go visit Angellica and then try to get some rest. Hopefully Spider will still stick the note in your apartment and we'll catch her."

"I'm worried about that, Sergeant."

"How so?"

Sean collected his thoughts before he spoke. "This time around, Spider has been changing things. I wonder, with Angellica in a holding cell, if she won't just skip the note because then she'll know Angellica will remain the prime suspect."

"I've considered that, but what else are we supposed to do?" Sean shrugged in defeat.

"Well if you think of anything, let me know." Millan looked up at the addition to the room. "Ah, Officer Eth. I think Detective Trann is ready to leave."

The officer strode into the office and threw out his hand to Sean. "Pleasure to meet you, Detective Trann. Looking forward to working with you."

Sean eyed the tall officer with disdain. He already hated his overly large smile, his pale skin with rosy cheeks, and the twinkle in the man's blue eyes. He looked like he was about sixteen years old and ready for his first babysitting adventure.

"You're kidding," Sean said to Millan. "An escort to the holding cells?"

"I told you—you don't do anything without someone else around. You are under too much pressure—not that I blame you—but it's gotten out of hand. I can't have you jeopardize your job any more over this situation."

Guilt and anger battled for a moment inside Sean. Guilt won. "You're right. Let's just get this over with." As Sean left, Officer Eth rambling cheerfully behind him, he dialed Charlotte's number again.

"*Ring. . .Ring. . .This is Doctor Salla. . .please leave a message. . .*"

45

March 19th
8:30 p.m.

Anya blinked her eyes and they adjusted to unfamiliar surroundings.

Something was wrong. She wasn't where she was supposed to be. How had this happened? How could she have screwed up so badly and ended up here?

Anya sat up in the bed. She was used to waking up in strange places, but never in a place like this.

Oh, no. I'm in trouble.

46

March 19th
9 p.m.

Sean walked up to the cell, its bars smooth and shiny where they'd been rubbed by numerous hands. He'd left his car in the precinct lot and Officer Eth drove them to the building where Angellica was being held. After they entered, Officer Eth stayed at the reception desk so Sean could have some privacy.

Angellica was pacing.

She must really be having a tough time cooped up in there. "Hey."

She looked up, surprised. "Oh, hey." She walked over to the bars. "How are you?"

He let out a sigh and ran his fingers through his hair, wincing at the tightness he still felt in his hand from punching Officer Holden in the jaw. "Exhausted. Frustrated. Angry. Pretty much the same as last time you saw me. How are things for you?"

"Wishing I wasn't in here," she said with a smile.

"I don't blame you. But hopefully after tomorrow you'll be cleared and we can get you out of here."

"Tomorrow, huh? That doesn't sound too bad."

"I know you're trying to put on a brave face. Your anxiety must be overwhelming right now. You don't have to pretend with me."

Her face blanked for a moment. "Yeah. . .I guess it's not as bad as I thought it would be."

Sean raised his eyebrows. "Really? That's great."

She smiled without showing any teeth. "Yeah." There was a pause. "So. . .anything else new since the last time we talked?"

"Not really." He shifted uncomfortably from one foot to the other. He didn't really know what to say, how to talk after they'd split up again. "I still haven't been able to get a hold of Doctor Salla," he said, averting the topic from them to the case. "Still no answer on her cell."

"That's too bad."

That's too bad? The phrase seemed a bit callous. "I suppose so, yes."

Angellica must have realized how crass she sounded. Her shoulders drooped. "I'm sorry. I guess I just don't know what to say. And I'm pretty freaked out still."

Sean softened. "It's okay. I understand. It's a pretty messed up situation."

"Yeah."

Seconds clicked by in silence.

"Well, if you feel like you're doing okay. . .?" he started.

"Of course. If you need to go. . ."

"I mean, I can stay for a while if you want?"

"No, no. It's fine. I mean, I'm sure you have stuff you need to do. Busy time for you right now."

"It is."

Another awkward pause.

"Well, have a good night," Sean said. "If you need to get a hold of me or if you remember anything else, tell the guard to call me."

"I will. I promise." Angellica leaned her face against the bars for a kiss.

Sean hesitated. It seemed an odd thing for her to do after their conversation. *Maybe she just wants comfort?* Sean leaned in and kissed her quickly.

"I'll miss you," she said with a purr. "See you tomorrow then?"

"Uh—yeah. See you tomorrow."

"Goodnight."

"Goodnight."

47

March 19th
10 p.m.

"Maybe Angellica was more nervous than she wanted to let on?" Officer Eth said as they drove to Sean's apartment. He took a turn onto Westland Avenue. The wheel of the police car squeaked every time it spun, which somehow cut through Eth's constant babble, irritating Sean like nails on a chalkboard. "I mean, my sister's husband always tries to pretend he isn't freaking out about something. He said sometimes if he didn't voice it, it wasn't as bad. Like he could contain it better if no one knew what he was really going through."

"I guess so." Sean stared out the window, the objects

outside the car a blur of green and gray as his focus drifted. He tried his best to ignore the baby-faced officer, but he couldn't seem to tune him out. He already regretted mentioning how he thought Angellica had been acting oddly in the holding cell.

"Not that I think that's the best route to take. I've always found that if people voice what's going on inside them it actually helps. Suppressing is a coping mechanism, but it's not a permanent solution."

"Hm," Sean said, noncommittal.

"Anxiety is a strange thing. With those who can't control it, it makes a person jump at shadows that aren't there, and they can't seem to stop the 'what ifs' from cycling over and over inside their heads, but you, Detective Trann. . ."

Sean noticed the lack of talking and turned his head. "What? What were you going to say?"

"Just that. . ." Eth trailed off.

"*What?*"

"Maybe you're jumping at shadows because over the past several weeks those shadows have been real. And terrifying. It makes sense that any out-of-the-ordinary behavior, no matter how small, is going to go off as an alarm inside your head. And any out-of-the-ordinary reaction from Angellica is probably triggering something in you."

Sean kept silent.

"I mean think about it," Eth continued as he took a left turn onto Sean's block. "This 'Spider' character has you a complete mess. She's screwed with your personal life, she's upped the amount of murders, and she makes you feel guilty by saying it's your fault she's done these things. This woman has turned you around so many times your compass is still spinning. How can you trust anything or anyone around you?"

The officer had a point. A good point. "Still," Sean replied, "I'm a good detective. I can tell the difference between shadows and reality."

"Then what do you think is the truth? Regardless of who you know, what you've been told, and who's back in your life. What do *you* think is going on?"

Sean grunted and looked back out the window as they pulled up to his apartment. He didn't want to think about it. All he'd been doing was thinking about it. And he didn't like the direction things pointed.

Eth turned off the engine. "You know I'm right."

"And how did you become all-knowing?"

The two of them exited the vehicle. "Well, I *am* the department's psychologist."

Sean started. "You're the *what*?"

Eth smiled. "It's true. I am an officer, but I was recently promoted to counselor."

"Millan sent a shrink to truck me around all over the place?"

"I volunteered, actually."

Sean flung his arms into the air. "Great! So you think I'm crazy!"

"Why does everyone think you need to be crazy to talk to a psychologist?" Eth stopped and leaned against the vehicle. "Detective Trann, you are NOT crazy. But you are involved in some serious stuff. Any person would have difficulty dealing with this. I volunteered to see how you were doing. Just to check in. And, to be honest, you are doing quite well considering the circumstances."

"Thanks." Sarcasm oozed off the word as he stalked away from the cruiser. He didn't want to hear any more from Officer Eth or Counselor Eth or Babysitter Eth. He just wanted to go to bed.

The two officers on guard outside his apartment building nodded at Sean as he entered.

"I'm just saying," Eth called out. "Regardless of what Spider is putting you through, you already know the truth. Just trust yourself."

Sean ignored him and slammed his apartment building's door behind him. He stomped up the stairs, his fists clenched in rage.

Where does that jerk get off thinking he can give me advice? We've only been around each other for about an hour, most of which I was with Angellica in the holding cell. What a quack. "You already know the truth." What kind of nonsense is that?

Sean walked into his apartment, kicked off his shoes, and shrugged out of his jacket, which he let fall to the floor. He made his way to the kitchen and opened the fridge.

I mean, seriously, what does that even mean? I don't know anything more than I did yesterday or the day before that. What the hell truth do I know?

Sean sighed and shut the fridge. Even though his stomach growled since it had nothing in it since the single bite of burger three hours previously, nothing looked appealing.

And now I'm supposed to sit back and wait for Spider to somehow get past my guards again, which she already did once, except how could she when Millan, Angellica, and I were the only ones to come into my apart—

Sean stopped mid-thought. There really wasn't any other explanation.

"Fuck," he said out loud. "Angellica must be involved somehow." Sean picked up his cell phone to dial the jail and cursed again at the static that hissed through the receiver. He went to his landline and placed the call.

You can't really be thinking this, he thought as the phone rang on the other end. *You can't be about to accuse your ex-fiancée of being involved with a serial killer. You can't. You can't!*

But Sean couldn't hang up the phone. Officer Eth, or Counselor Eth, or whatever the hell his title was, was right. The truth had been right there in front of him. If the note had been delivered that day and the only three people who'd been in his place were himself, Millan—who'd been with him the whole time—and Angellica—who'd entered on her own— then she must have planted the note.

"Thank you for calling the Suffolk County Sherriff's Department. How can I help you?"

"This is Detective Trann. I'm calling about Angellica Neros who is in the holding cell there."

"Hold please. . .uh, yes. She has been checked out."

Sean blinked. "Checked out?"

"Yes, sir. She was released about. . .fifteen minutes ago.

Officer Let signed her out."

Sean closed his eyes, trying to place the name to a face. "Officer Let? Who is that?"

He could picture the receptionist shrugging. "Beats me," he answered. "She had transfer papers for Miss Neros. Everything seemed in order, so I released her."

"Wait. . .Officer Let is a *she*?"

"Yes, sir."

"Shit!" Sean depressed the phone tab to disconnect the line and punched in the numbers for Millan's phone when he heard the dial tone.

"Come on, come on!" he said to the ringing as he tried to reach his shoes with his foot. The phone cord stretched beyond its limit.

"Hel—"

Millan got cut off as the phone fell off the table, hit the carpet, and the cable to the receiver pulled out of the jack—by the wires.

"Fuck!" Sean yelled, holding up the now useless cord.

"*DON'T START UP THERE! I'M WATCHING* WHEEL OF FORTUNE*!*"

"*Pipe down, Gerald! There's cops outside the building!*"

"*GOOD! THEY CAN TELL THIS RIFF-RAFF THAT I'M SICK AND TIRED OF ALL THE GOD-DAMN NOISE UP THERE!*"

Sean slammed his feet into his shoes. "Shut UP!" he screamed at the floor. "My ex-fiancée may be a serial killer! SHUT THE FUCK UP!"

To Sean's amazement, they were quiet below him.

"Thank GOD!" Sean tore open his door and slammed it shut behind him. He raced down the stairs so he could get reception on his cell phone, but as he passed his lower neighbors, he heard a blood-curdling scream that stopped him in his tracks.

"Help! Someone help me!"

Sean changed course and went to the door of their apartment. He pounded on it.

"It's me, Sean, from upstairs. Open up!"

Nell was still shrieking, but Sean could hear her work the bolt on the other side. The door swung open and Sean went in, struck immediately by the smell of over-flowery air freshener and something rancid. Their living room looked like the inside of a log cabin, with brown paneled walls, wooden furniture, and sporting a giant mounted 10-point buck head on the wall above the TV.

"What's wrong?" Sean asked.

She pointed a veiny hand to her husband, who was hunched over in a pile of his own vomit.

Oh, God, he thought. *Spider has killed my neighbor.* The thought was ridiculous—there were too many things that didn't fit Spider's pattern, but Sean was no longer in the realm of rational. He was in the area of "my whole life is a fucking mess so why the hell not?"

"Call an ambulance," he instructed Nell. Nell quieted and picked up the phone. She pressed the plastic receiver up underneath the curlers that hung around her head. Sean could hear her talking to 911 as he checked out her husband.

"Gerald," he said softly to the shaking man. "Gerald, can

you hear me?"

Nell covered the receiver. "You'll have to speak louder. He's deaf in one ear—probably deaf in the other one, too."

"I can hear just fine," Gerald grumbled through a wheeze. The wheeze deepened and turned into a cough, which brought up a bout of bile.

Sean ran to the bathroom, decorated in pinks and yellows, and moistened a hand towel. The faded rose pattern darkened with the moisture.

I bet Nell picked these out. I wonder what kind of towels Charlotte has. Most definitely not flowers.

He smiled at the thought, then shook his head. Why on Earth was he thinking about Charlotte's towel collection?

I must really be losing it.

He also realized he hadn't tried her phone in several hours, or thought about her during that time. Guilt flared up inside him as he returned to Geriatric Hell's living room. He placed the cool, wet towel across Gerald's head, which was burning up.

Nell hung up the phone and wrung her hands as she stared at her husband.

"Is he going to be alright?" she whispered.

"He'll be fine," Sean reassured her, having no idea if Gerald was going to be okay. The man looked so frail, his olive-toned skin pale and sallow, his eyes bloodshot from the force of his heaving. Sean didn't even know how old Gerald was. Had this ever happened before? Was he prone to vomiting? Was he going to die?

"Is the ambulance on the way?" Sean asked.

Nell nodded, her curlers bouncing.

Sean looked back at the elderly man. *You are not going to die. I can't handle another death so this isn't going to happen.*

"You're going to be fine," Sean whispered, desperate for the words to be true. "I promise."

A knock at the door made him jump.

"Who is it?" Nell called out.

Oh, God. It's Spider! Sean didn't even have time to warn Nell before she'd flung open the door, not waiting for the other side to answer.

Relief flooded Sean. It was one of the officers from downstairs. He needed to get it together. Eth was right—he was jumping at shadows.

"I heard the call over the radio—thought I could help..." he trailed off as he saw Gerald. "Jesus, man. What happened?"

"I don't know," Sean said, wiping the back of his hand across his upper lip. He regretted the movement instantly— his hand smelled of puke. "I found him this way. But I need to get to the station."

Nell screeched. "Please don't leave me here!"

Sean smiled in what he hoped was a reassuring way. "Okay, don't worry, I'll stay until the paramedics arrive." Sean stood and gripped the officer's arm. "You have to call it in that Angellica is no longer in her holding cell. Call Sergeant Millan and let him know."

The officer looked at Nell. "This woman is supposed to be in a holding cell?"

"No," Sean answered, frustrated. "This is Nell, Gerald's

wife."

The guard's confusion increased. "Oh, okay. Then who isn't in her holding cell?"

"Angellica Neros!" Sean yelled. "She was supposed to be in a holding cell and she got out."

"So is she, like, related to these people?"

Sean grabbed the officer by his bony shoulders, digging his fingers into the thin flesh. "Listen to me very carefully and don't ask questions. Call Sergeant Millan and tell him Angellica is gone. He'll understand. Tell him to call me at. . ." Sean whipped his head around. "What's the number here?"

"555-0318," Nell replied.

"You heard her."

The officer got on his radio and notified his partner of the situation. Sean could hear the woman's tinny voice reply. Her response was overshadowed however when Gerald threw up again. The officer went into the hallway to hear better.

"Where is that ambulance?" Sean said as he readjusted the cloth on Gerald's head. "I don't have time for this!"

"Please don't leave!" Nell cried out. "I don't. . .I can't—"

"It's okay," he told her. He closed his eyes and took a deep breath. Before he could exhale, the phone rang.

Sean sprinted and answered it before Nell could.

"Millan?"

"Who?" An elderly woman asked. "Nell? NELL? IS THAT YOU?"

Sean hung up.

"Who was it?" Nell asked.

"Wrong number," Sean lied. He didn't want the phone

line tied up. He had no idea if call waiting existed in Geriatric Hell and he couldn't take the chance he'd miss the Sergeant's call.

The phone rang again.

"Sergeant?"

"Yeah, it's me. What's going on?"

Sean let out a sigh of relief as he filled Millan in on the details.

"We've got video surveillance at the jail. I'll contact them to get footage of this 'Officer Let.' She may be who we've been looking for."

"There's more," Sean started. Now that he had Millan on the phone, the words were reluctant to come.

"Such as?" Millan prompted.

"Angellica must be involved."

Millan paused. "You're sure?"

Sean closed his eyes, thinking about how Officer Holden said Angellica had been rude to him, how she acted different in the jail cell. "It's what the facts tell me, it's what makes sense, and my gut is screaming it, even though every other part of me wants to deny it."

"You don't think this Officer Let sprung her from the holding cell to throw you off the scent? Or maybe Angellica is the next victim?"

"It's before midnight. Spider wouldn't have taken Angellica until tomorrow if she were going to be a victim."

"But she took the medical examiner before midnight."

"True, but I don't think Char—Doctor Salla is involved."

"But what about—"

"No. No 'buts.' I don't know how or why, but Angellica is a part of this. And now we've lost her."

"We'll get her back." There was a moment of silence. "How are things by you?"

Sean looked back at his neighbors. "It looks like food poisoning maybe, but I can't be sure. The ambulance should be here any minute, but I told the wife I'd stay here until they arrive."

"Okay. How do you want me to contact you when I get the video? I know your cell doesn't work in your building. You going to be at this number still?"

Sean ran his fingers through his hair and then regretted it, wondering if they had vomit on them. "Probably not. Gerald will have to go to the hospital. I won't stay here after they leave. Maybe I could meet you somewhere?"

"How about the jail? I'm headed there right now."

"Sounds good."

Knock, knock, knock!

'That'll be the EMT. I'll head over to the jail with Officer Eth and call you when I'm on my way."

48

March 20th
12:30 a.m.

"They were just loading up Gerald onto the stretcher when I left," Sean told Millan through the phone as he drove. Rain drizzled on his windshield. His wipers squeaked each time they cleared his view. "Some intern EMT came in first, nearly passed out at the sight of the puke on the floor, and then left. The two official techs came in after and dealt with everything. Gerald should be all right." He glanced at the street sign as he drove through an intersection. "I'm almost to the jail."

"You sure you don't want to be at home? The note is supposed to come sometime today."

"I've already been there while the note was delivered. In fact, Charlotte was even there once—"

"That's right. Doctor Salla was at your place overnight."

Sean scrunched up his face. "It wasn't—it wasn't like that."

"Sure, kid, sure."

"Look," Sean said as he took a corner, "we can talk about it some other time when the good Doc isn't missing anymore and my ex-fiancé is found and there are no more dead bodies or notes or Spiders. Deal?"

"She's not your girlfriend anymore, huh?"

Sean blinked a few times. "What?"

"Angellica. You referred to her as your girlfriend before and now she's back to 'ex-fiancé.' Was this before or after you thought she was involved with a serial killer?"

"I don't. . .what? Look, who the hell cares what I call her? What is this? Have you been talking with Eth?" Sean turned and scowled at his passenger, who merely smiled back with rosy cheeks.

"No, nothing like that. I just noticed it."

"Well can we just focus on the case here and *not* what's going on in my love life?" he snapped.

"Sure thing, kid. Sorry."

Sean couldn't think about things between him and Angellica. Or things between him and Charlotte.

Sean took a deep breath. He had to stay focused. And if he didn't find Charlotte *or* Angellica, it didn't matter *what* they were to him. "I'm just about at the jail. I'll meet you inside." Sean hung up and pulled into the parking lot. He exited his car without bothering to wait for Officer Eth and trotted into the building, scrunching down into his jacket to avoid the rain. Once inside, Millan gestured him into the viewing room.

"The receptionist pulled up the video. We were just about to review it," Millan told him.

The two of them watched as a female officer with wisps of black, wavy hair peeking out from under her cap, walked in, flashed her identification, signed the log, and waited until Angellica was brought out. The two of them had a brief conversation with the receptionist, then left, the other woman never quite facing the camera.

Millan zoomed in on the face of this unknown Officer Let. "We're going to post this right away. She won't get far."

Sean looked at the paused video image of Angellica's blonde figure leaving the station. *Where is she? Is she an accomplice? Is she being forced to help this Officer Let? How can I find her?*

"I'm an idiot." Sean said abruptly. He pulled his phone from his jeans pocket. "I didn't even try to call her."

He dialed Angellica's number. The phone rang once and then—

—and then a phone rang behind the desk.

"What the...?"

The receptionist searched around for a moment and brought up a box of items. He scrounged in it and pulled out a cell phone.

Sean snatched it from him. "This is Angellica's phone." His voice was emotionless. "Why is her phone here?" The look he gave Millan was one of a child after finding out Santa Claus wasn't real—complete incredulity. He pawed through the rest of the items in the box.

"ID, wallet, purse, keys, watch, necklace. . .these are all her personal effects."

The receptionist nodded, wide-eyed. "Yes, detective. She left without them. I even asked her if she wanted to take them, but she um. . ." he paused, flushing, his orangey-fake-tanned skin turning a strange shade of tomatoey-carrot.

"She what?"

"She told me to use the money in her wallet to buy myself better fake tanning products," he mumbled.

"Wait . . .*Angellica* said that?" Sean was astounded. Angellica may be a bit superficial, but she would never insult someone directly like that. In fact, Sean had never heard her say a mean thing to anyone since he'd known her. What was going on?

"Yes, sir. The blonde woman. The officer with her just. . . laughed."

Millan looked at Sean. "Sean—"

"I know," Sean interrupted. "But I can't explain it. The Angellica I know wouldn't have done something like that. And if she's being coerced by this Officer Let, I can't see how insulting a receptionist could be part of the scheme. Which makes me think she's not being forced into anything." He sat, hard, onto the bench next to the desk. "I can't believe this. I just can't believe this." His whole world was falling apart around him. The woman he was once going to marry was involved with a serial killer who'd kidnapped Charlotte. And why? *WHY?* What could Angellica gain from helping this killer? Or was she a killer herself? And why take Charlotte? Just because Sean knew her? Was Angellica jealous and wanted to eliminate any competition?

Sean's head swirled with conflicting thoughts. He could feel himself breaking down. He couldn't handle this. He couldn't handle this. He couldn't—

"Sean. . ."

Sean looked up into Millan's dark eyes, full of sympathy. Next to him stood Eth, his brow furrowed in concern.

"I know," Millan continued. "I *know*. But right now, I need you in this. I need the detective in you to focus. Can you do that?"

"Sergeant, I don't' know if medically that's a good idea," Eth interjected.

Millan grunted. "Maybe not, but it doesn't matter. He needs to do this. And I know he can. Can't you?" he said, asking Sean.

Sean swallowed hard against the lump in his throat and nodded. He had to keep things together and concentrate. People's lives were at stake.

Millan slapped a meaty hand on Sean's shoulder. "We may still get a note from Spider and have another person to find by tomorrow."

"But if Angellica is involved, shouldn't we try to find her?"

"My concern right now is the innocent person that may die and Doctor Salla. Can you think of a way to track Angellica or this Officer Let?"

Sean shook his head. "They could be anywhere."

"Well then, we'll just take this one step at a time. We'll look at outside security cam footage and have the patrols keep their eyes open until the morning. Maybe we'll catch a lucky break. But for now, go home. You need sleep. Who knows? Maybe Spider or Officer Let or whoever will just skip this week?"

"The problem is," Sean said softly, "the only way to track them is to try to figure out the clues in the note. No note, no clues, no way to find them."

"Yeah," Millan said in a dark voice, "but a note also means another potential dead body."

49

March 20th
1 a.m.

Mags waved goodnight over her shoulder as she left the police department—the last bite of her sandwich, wedged inside her mouth, made it impossible to verbally bid her coworkers adieu. She was starving, as the remnants in her mouth were actually the remains of her lunch—not of a dinner she hadn't had time to get. But everyone in the precinct was in overdrive, which meant she'd been working at light speed and hadn't had time to eat.

Inundated with reports, files, searches, and research, Mags hadn't gotten much sleep the past few nights, much to her fiancé's dismay. He'd just recently taken a job working second shift in order to finish his degree in communications full-time during the day, so they rarely saw each other as it was. Her recent late nights and early mornings didn't make him very happy.

But she promised him that tonight, come rain, shine, or murder, she'd be home. And if she hurried, she'd be there about a half hour before his shift ended—and she could start a bath running for him to come home to—with her in it for company of course.

A smile bloomed across Mags' face as her body shivered with excitement. She could *definitely* use some stress relief. And her fiancé was very good at relieving her stress.

She hummed, wondering if she should pick up some fast food on her way to appease her grumbling stomach, when something sharp bite into her neck.

Mags slapped her hand at the pain and pulled out a thin dart from her skin. "Mother fuh. . ."

She stumbled, the dart dropping to the ground. Everything dimmed then refocused. Her legs wouldn't go. They seized up and she pitched forward onto the ground, cracking her jaw against the asphalt. She lay there, expecting the darkness of unconsciousness to consume her, but it didn't come. She could see with perfect clarity through her tilted glasses, feel her bashed jaw, sense the scrapes from the pavement where she'd sheared away skin.

Terror overtook her.

Oh my God, she thought. *I've been shot by Spider! Help! HELP!*

Mags tried to scream the words, but her vocal chords were as paralyzed as the rest of her body.

She heard approaching footsteps. Someone from the

police department *had* to have seen her fall. Even at this time of night.

Oh please! Please help me! she yelled inside her head.

"Do you remember her?" a woman's voice asked.

"Not really." The second voice, also female, bent close to Mags' face. She pushed away the dark bangs that had fallen across Mags' eyes.

Angellica? Mags asked. No words accompanied her attempt to speak.

Angellica stared back at Mags with a blank look.

"Nope," Angellica continued, "I don't know this girl at all. She sure doesn't *look* like a scientist." Angellica's gaze scrolled down Mags' body, taking in her ripped jeans, maryjane shoes, and black argyle-patterned sweater.

"It doesn't matter what she looks like," the first woman said, just out of Mags' sight. "Truth said she's the one we are supposed to take back to base."

The two women lifted Mags' limp body and carried her over to a nondescript gray van.

"Good thing we already dealt with the target tonight," Angellica said with a grunt. "And we still have another one of these scientists to pick up? I'm really getting a workout."

They threw Mags inside and she rolled onto a thin mattress in the back. Her arm was pinned awkwardly beneath her body as her face smashed into the side of the van.

"Easy!" the first woman said. "She's not a target. She's supposed to live."

"Don't worry, she'll live," Angellica said, under her breath. Mags felt a pinprick in her arm. "Sweet dreams, sweetheart."

Mags fought the sedative, desperate to remember every detail she could.

"Anya! Let's go! We still have another pick-up."

"I'm coming, I'm coming," Angellica grumbled. She tapped her fingers on Mags' forehead as her eyelids fluttered closed.

"No," Angellica said, "I don't recognize you at all."

50

March 20th
2 a.m.

Detective Juliette Tay's head dropped to her chest, her red hair framing her face. She lay in bed, reading another romance novel—something where Juan's loins were bursting from his tight leather pants at the sight of fair-haired, soft-skinned Brianna. Or had it been Alexander's loins pressing against his tight suede riding pants when he saw dark-haired, rosy-cheeked Olivia?

Either way, the loin segment had not been steamy enough to keep Juliette's attention and she nodded off in the middle of someone in tight pants lusting after someone else.

She hadn't realized she'd fallen asleep until she awoke to

the sound of voices in her room.

"That her?"

"Yes."

"She's pretty."

A sigh. "Yes."

Juliette's eyes snapped open. She stared at the two intruders—two women, one brunette with cinnamon-colored skin and a blonde. . .

"Angellica?" Juliette croaked.

The blonde threw her hands up in disgust. "God, *this* one knows me, too. What the hell have I been doing while I've been under?"

"Beats me," the brunette replied.

Juliette's body tightened with readiness. "Angellica, what's going on? Why are you here?"

"I wish everyone would stop calling me that. It's Anya, okay? My name is An-ya. Got it? I'm not that fucking spoiled little tanning freak who almost got *married* to that asshole Sean."

While Angellica, or Anya as she called herself, ranted, Juliette took the opportunity to reach under the pillow for her gun.

"Looking for this?" the brunette asked, holding up Juliette's 9mm. She pointed it at Juliette's head.

"I need you to come with us," the brunette told Juliette.

"Are you Spider?"

Anya snorted a laugh. "You guys are so pathetic."

"Be quiet," the brunette snapped.

Anya scowled, but remained silent.

The brunette cocked the weapon. "I won't say it again."

Juliette slowly pushed off the covers and stood.

"Move it. Downstairs."

"Can I get dressed?" Juliette asked, wearing only underwear and a tank top. Her multitude of freckles popped out against her pale skin.

"No."

Juliette walked behind Anya and in front of the brunette, who stayed far enough away that Juliette couldn't grab the gun. She tried to think of a way out of this situation, but nothing came to mind.

The three of them marched out of Juliette's duplex on Hillside Avenue, down the walkway, and toward a gray van. Juliette's eyes flickered from left to right, hoping a neighbor would be awake, but the houses were all dark.

Anya opened the back door. "Hop in."

Juliette gasped as she saw Mags, unconscious and tied to a mattress. A large red mark spread along her jaw line and she bled from several scrapes on her face. Juliette rushed over and felt for a pulse. It was there—strong. Juliette gave her a rough shake.

"Don't bother," Anya continued, following Juliette into the van. "She's out cold. Just be thankful you weren't our first pick-up."

"What do you mean?" Juliette asked.

"Truth was mighty pissed when she heard how rough we were with Miss Thing in the back here. She said you two weren't supposed to be harmed, but how the hell was I supposed to know—?"

"Shut it!" the brunette snapped at Anya through the side door. "Just sit down," she ordered Juliette, "and handcuff yourself to the back." She waved the gun in the direction of the shackles in the rear of the van. "Anya will secure them, so don't get any ideas." The brunette moved out of sight around the van.

Juliette did as she was told, still searching for a way out of this desperate situation. But even if she could escape, she couldn't leave Mags here vulnerable to these murderers.

Once cuffed, and the tightness of the cuffs checked, Anya reached into a bag and retrieved a syringe.

"Buenas noches, Señorita," she said to Juliette.

"You done yet back there?" the brunette called out from the driver's seat.

"Get off my back, Violet!" Anya yelled back. "It's not like I've never done this sort of thing before."

Juliette flinched as the needle entered, watched the contents of the syringe empty, and felt the effects of the sedative almost immediately. She thought about how these women were messing with the wrong police department. Their team had never been better.

Before sleep overtook her, Juliette smiled.

"What's so funny?" Anya asked. Her voice sounded far off, as though at the end of a tunnel.

"I'm just glad I'm going to be there."

"Be there for what?"

Juliette blinked heavily. Her words slurred, but she could tell by the scowl on Anya's face that she'd made sense.

"For when we nail your asses to the wall."

51

March 20th
3 a.m.

Sean's eyes felt like he'd planted himself face first into a vat of sand. Blinking repeatedly, he gave a half-hearted wave to the guards outside his apartment building and went inside. He trudged up the stairs, his head pounding.

He walked past Geriatric Hell—the place silent. Most likely they were still at the hospital. Gerald wasn't exactly a young enough man to have repeatedly puked his guts out onto the floor. The doctors would probably keep him overnight.

Fine with me. I can leave the TV on all night, open my fridge—hell, I can even walk around my own place without him screaming!

The thought, although meant to amuse himself, got nothing more than a lifeless snort. He would rather have the old geezer screaming at him from below than have him tucked in some hospital bed.

Sean jammed his apartment key into the door next to the keyhole before he re-aimed and hit the mark. He tried to turn it to the side, but it wouldn't budge.

What the. . .?

Sean turned the knob and the door swung open. *I must have forgotten to lock it when I left earlier. I was in such a rush to tell someone about Angellica being involved. . .*

Angellica.

Sean stumbled into the unit. He still couldn't believe she was a part of all this—even though his guts told him so, even though logic dictated it, even though he'd seen it with his own eyes on video. He still couldn't believe the woman he almost married was some sort of serial killer. Or at least a serial killer's accomplice.

Sean's eyes screamed at him from being so tired. They were gritty, dry, and red. Sean walked into his bathroom and turned on the shower. He stripped off his shoes, pants, shirt, boxers, and climbed in. The water ran over his face and he snorted short breaths, letting his eyes clear. He then scrubbed down—he wished he had a Brillo pad. He felt dirty, contaminated, tainted.

I slept with Angellica, again. I fell for her and her lies. She used me. She betrayed me. She helped kill people and stood by laughing as I blundered through. How could I have been so stupid!

Sean slammed his fist into the shower wall, all his anger

surging through his arm and into his balled-up hand. The months of never knowing why she left him, the days of believing she might care again, the anguish at being made a fool once more. The tiles cracked under the pressure of his fist. His hand shot alarms of pain through his nerves to his brain, but he didn't care. He punched again and again. He screamed into the steaming water. Bloodied the tiles. He let his rage force its way through his vocal chords.

Abruptly, Sean sat down into the tub. The water streamed over him. He started to sob.

Oh, God. I'm cracking up. Here it is. I've broken.

The sobs turned into laughter. Sean grasped his side with his good hand, his wet skin slipping through his fingers, but the peals continued. He couldn't breathe. He was going to die naked in his shower, laughing hysterically like a madman.

The thought brought more laughter and Sean curled slightly fetal onto his side, wheezing for breath.

Little by little the laughter turned to hitches for air. He got to his knees, sliding, and placed his bad hand on the edge of the tub to push himself up. A shriek of pain erupted from his lips. He fell to one knee, holding his damaged hand to his chest.

He got up slowly, pulled the curtain, and noticed the steam in the room.

Really? The landlord finally fixed the hot water? He hadn't even noticed.

Sean fought the laughter that threatened to bubble up again. He grabbed a towel from the rack, dried off the best he could, and wrapped it awkwardly around his injured fist. Shaking water from his hair, he walked out of the bathroom.

"MotherfuckingpieceofshitgodDAMMIT!!" he screamed as he stubbed his toe on the corner of his bed. He sat down on its edge, rubbing his toes into the carpet, as water dripped from his hair into his eyes.

He needed a vacation.

He needed a shot of whiskey.

He needed to sleep for a month.

The pain in his hand worsened, indicating injury beyond what a towel-wrapping could fix. He mentally scolded himself. He didn't need the delay of going to the hospital to check out his hand, but he had no choice. The throbbing amplified, with jagged stabs of pain increasing while he sat.

Sean let out a long breath and closed his eyes. He didn't want to leave his apartment, but with the guards outside, there was no reason for him to stay. Still, he felt like if he left, Spider—or *Angellica*—would somehow find her way inside.

But he had to get his hand looked at.

Sean opened his eyes.

He cocked his head to the side and stared into his bathroom toward his clothes on the floor, the steam clearing away now that the door was open.

His gaze drifted and paused on the mirror.

"You've got to be fucking kidding me."

Through the doorway to the bathroom Sean could see words on the shiny surface, streaked in the leftover steam.

"*12:20 A.M. THIS IS GETTING TIRESOME. YOU CAN'T BEAT ME.*"

52

March 20th
4 a.m.

"Jesus, kid."

Sean cringed with embarrassment. "Yeah, it looks pretty bad, huh?"

Millan and Sean sat in the waiting room at the hospital. Sean's hand had swollen about twice its normal size and blood smeared his knuckles. He attempted to wipe off as much as he could, but the dry paper towels merely spread the red fluid around.

"What happened?"

Sean shook his head, shifting on the metallic, waiting area benches. "I thought I could win a fight against my bathroom wall."

Millan snorted and rubbed his left hand over his right knuckles. "Been there."

Sean smiled. "Is there anything you *haven't* done first?"

"Probably not."

A nurse approached the two men. "Mister Trann?" Dark circles rimmed her brown eyes.

"Yes?"

"The doctor will see you now. Please follow me." She led Sean through a few corridors into a small, white, sterile room. He sat for several minutes on a hard, plastic chair next to a tiny desk. His gaze drifted toward the bed-like contraption on the other side of the room—covered in a long white paper sheet. It looked out of place, half-hazardly shoved to the side. Worn metallic stirrups stuck out of the end of the table. Sean always felt a little uncomfortable looking at those.

A few minutes later a doctor entered.

"Hello, Sean," the doctor spoke, her smile large and friendly. "I'm Doctor Cain." She looked down at his hand. "Lose a fight?"

"With a shower wall."

Dr. Cain took his hand softly in hers, her plump dark fingers gentle, yet precise. "We'll have to take an x-ray, but it's probably safe to say it's fractured." She picked off a piece of bathroom tile. "Let's clean it off first and then we'll move you to where you need to go."

"Thanks, Doctor."

Sean waited close to an hour, angry at himself for being

stupid enough to break his hand against his wall, pissed at Charlotte for not answering her phone, (although the anger merely shielded his true fear that she wasn't coming back alive), and infuriated at Angellica for deceiving him. He sat, ignoring Millan's futile attempts to start a conversation, and repeatedly hit redial on his phone. Charlotte's voicemail picked up every time. His emotions crescendoed. On top of it all, the note in his bathroom meant there was another victim plus Charlotte missing on top of Angellica's betrayal on top of his stupid fucking broken hand!

Millan tried several times to get Sean to think about the clue in the note Spider left, but Sean kept shrugging him off. His anger throbbed inside his head, but he didn't have the strength to do anything about it. He couldn't deal with this shit anymore. His hand pulsed with pain, even with it elevated and iced. The painkillers they'd offered didn't seem to make a difference for his hand or the migraine that threatened to explode his head from inside. He felt tired, sore, emotionally beaten, mentally drained, and soul-sucked.

Sean watched the hospital workers scurry to and fro in their appointed tasks. Each one dressed in scrubs or white jackets. Each one with a specific destination in mind and a hundred other things inside their heads.

Sean's gaze floated around the waiting room, noting the pastel-colored paintings and out-of-date décor. He watched, detached, as a team of EMTs brought in a woman on a gurney, an oxygen mask over her face. The EMTs shouted orders to the nurses, who promptly took the wounded individual to the ICU. The pair of technicians took a moment to catch their breath before they headed back out onto the streets.

The ICU, Sean thought. *I wonder if that's where they took Gerald. I should go check to see if he's okay. But the ambulance arrived pretty fast. I'm sure he's fine. It's not like the EMTs didn't know what they were doing. Well, the intern didn't seem to, but the other two—*

Sean stopped, mid-thought. The female intern. The one who'd arrived first.

A strange sense of calm settled over him. "Millan?"

"Yeah, kid?"

Sean tugged at his bottom lip with his good hand. "Something wasn't right."

Millan waited, as if expecting more from Sean, then piped in, "Something wasn't right about what?"

"About earlier."

"Earlier?"

Sean nodded, still unaware that his remarks, though coherent in his own head, didn't make sense to Millan.

"What—happened—earlier?"

Sean came out of his daze. "I was thinking about when the EMTs came to get Gerald. Three of them showed up— one right away, a female intern, who left. And then two other women. The women didn't seem to know what was going on. I had to repeat the situation to them when they arrived. It was as if the intern hadn't told them anything."

Sean's eyes came into focus. "Oh my God."

"What?"

Sean remembered the image of the woman with

Angellica at the jail. On the footage, Officer Let had dark, wavy black hair, tucked under her hat. The EMT intern wore hers down and had glasses, but. . . "It was her. She was there."

Millan rubbed his tired eyes. "Who was where? Sean you aren't making any sense."

Sean grabbed Millan's arm. "The first EMT who came in—she wasn't really an EMT. It was the woman from the video. It was Officer Let. That's how she got into my apartment and left the note. She posed as a paramedic to gain access to the building."

"Are you saying you didn't notice she seemed out of place?"

Anger flared up inside Sean. "She just poked her head in then covered her face, acting like she was going to faint. It went so fast, I didn't really think about it."

Millan held up his hands in defense. "Easy. So what do we do about it?"

"We—well if we—and she could—how about if. . .?" Sean laughed. The sounds were sharp like barks. Several nurses turned in his direction, concerned at the sudden outbreak. "I have no idea," Sean hiccupped between gasps of air.

A nurse in a pair of pink scrubs approached the two detectives.

"Mister Trann?" she asked.

"Yes."

"I'm here to take you down to x-ray."

"How long will this take?" Millan asked.

"'Bout half an hour."

The Sergeant nodded. "Sean, the note was left at 12:30 this morning. I'm going back to the office to see what I can do to help. You think you'll be able to make it in after your x-rays?" Millan's worry was evident—not about the physical problem, but about Sean's emotional state of mind.

Sean couldn't blame him. He was worried about his own sanity as well.

Keep it together.

"Yeah," Sean said, "I'll be there."

53

March 20th
6:30 a.m.

Sean left the x-ray area after being told he had a compression fracture in his hand. They fitted him with a temporary brace and referred him to an orthopedic surgeon for a checkup. They gave him a prescription for some strong ibuprofen for the pain and inflammation and shooed him on his way.

When Sean walked back through the hospital lobby headed to his car, he was greeted by the smiling, rosy-cheeked, baby face of Officer/Counselor Eth. He did *not* feel like dealing with a shrink right now.

"How bad is it?" Eth asked about Sean's injury.

"What are you doing here?" Sean's tone came out harsh.

Eth's smile faltered for a moment. "Millan ordered an escort for you at all times. In fact, you disobeyed orders when you drove yourself to the hospital."

Irritated, Sean pushed past his babysitter and left through the sliding doors. "In case you didn't realize it, we are in the emergency room. As in, it was an *emergency.* I didn't have time to call you." Sean knew he was being an asshole, but he didn't care. He really wanted to go home, get wasted, and sleep for the rest of his life.

But no.

He had to go to the station and figure out Spider's newest note so someone else wouldn't die in less than 18 hours.

He had to find Angellica.

He had to find Officer Let.

He had to find Charlotte.

Sean ignored Officer Eth as they approached Sean's Jaguar. He looked at the car with disgust, remembering it was a present from Angellica's father. Did her parents know who she really was? Did they realize they'd raised a woman capable of roasting people alive and bleeding them out for 24 hours while leading the cops on a wild goose chase?

Sean wanted to smash the windows, break the headlights, slash the leather seats, tear out the stereo system, and crack the dashboard.

His hand throbbed as if to remind him of the last time he'd battled an inanimate object.

Not that it mattered. He felt too tired. The anger inside

him subsided as quickly as it came. He didn't have anything left.

Sean let Officer Eth drive. He'd been able to drive to the hospital, albeit painfully, but with the brace now on his right hand, shifting would be even harder. Eth didn't live too far from the hospital, so he'd walked. The counselor kept babbling as he drove, but Sean's attention was focused on the blurry images as the outdoors flew by. He wanted time to think, to slow down, to take a few minutes and relax. But they arrived at the police department too soon. Even though fifteen minutes had gone by, they were there too soon.

Officer Eth turned off the car and rotated his body toward Sean.

"Don't," Sean said before Eth could speak.

"Don't what?"

"Don't say whatever you are about to say. I don't want to hear it. I don't want a pep talk. I don't want to be coddled. I don't want to hear it's all going to be okay or that I'll make it through this. I just want quiet."

"Sure."

Sean stared at the outside of the precinct. His eyes took in the red brick and yellow door with the BOSTON POLICE lettering across the top. He knew what waited inside for him once he entered the building.

The hustle and bustle would begin again.

Demands would be made.

Scurrying would ensue.

Expectations would commence.

"I can't do this."

Officer Eth remained silent.

Sean closed his eyes. He pressed his forehead against the glass, the pane cool against his warm skin. The temporary relief on his head just made his hand throb more. "I just can't do this."

Eth waited a few beats. "Can't do what?"

"I can't go in there and face all those people and have them expect from me what I can't give them."

"And what can't you give them?"

Sean opened his eyes and looked at the building. It had always been a place where he knew what his goals were. Every time he entered, he had a sense of purpose. He was going in to solve a puzzle, to catch a bad guy, to save the day.

But he didn't know if he could deliver on any of those if he walked through those doors right now. Fear prickled across his skin. He was afraid he would let everyone down. He'd already lost Angellica. He hadn't protected Charlotte. And now this new victim depended on him to be rescued.

"A hero. I can't give them a hero. And that's what they want. That's what they need." The words were quiet. Sean closed his eyes again. He couldn't look at the building anymore. He felt so ashamed. Embarrassed. Guilty.

Why wasn't he getting out of the car? Why wasn't he *trying* to help? How could he just sit here and wallow in his own pity party when there were people out there who needed him?

But no matter how he scolded himself, no matter how he bullied, he couldn't make his good hand open the door.

Sean started as the engine revved. He whipped his head

over toward the driver.

"What are you doing?"

Officer Eth turned his head to check his blind spot. "I'm taking you back to your apartment."

"What? Why?"

"Honestly?" Eth continued, turning on his blinker to pull away from the curb. "Because I'm exhausted. You don't have the easiest babysitting hours, you know? It's tiresome."

Officer Eth peeled away from the curb, the Jag's tires squealing.

The noise was like electricity in Sean's head.

"What did you just say?" he asked Eth.

"I said I'm taking you home because I'm exhausted."

"Right. Right. You said it's 'tiresome.'"

Officer Eth stopped at the red light at the end of the street. "Yeah. So?"

"Tires." A tiny flicker of motivation popped inside Sean's chest.

"What about them?"

"A tire salesman. The clue. 'This is getting tiresome.' I wonder if they thought of that?" The flicker grew into a flame.

"You wonder if *who* thought of that?"

"Everyone. Anyone. Millan. Wilt. Tay. Whoever." Sean opened the door to get out of the car, even though the light had turned green. Luckily, no one was behind them to complain.

"I thought you were giving up?" Eth asked as Sean exited the vehicle.

"Guess the universe doesn't want me to yet." He swung his arm in a circular motion. "Go around the block and park. I'm headed inside." He jogged back up the block and ran into the precinct. He made his way to Sergeant Millan's office and burst inside.

The crowded room hummed with multiple conversations. Millan looked up, surrounded by several other officers. He motioned for Sean to make his way over to the desk.

Detective Wilt caught him halfway through the room.

"Trann! Nice battle wound." Wilt grinned as he sucked on his toothpick.

"Yeah," Sean replied, embarrassed. "Only wish it hadn't been my shooting hand." He paused. "Can you do me a favor?"

"What do you need?"

"Can you ask Mags to meet us in here? I think she said she was coming in early so she should be around. I need her to help with a search."

"Sure thing."

Sean patted Wilt on the back as he left and approached Millan's desk.

"Nice to have you here, kid."

"Nice to be here," Sean said. "Almost didn't happen."

"I wondered. You got something?"

"Yeah. Do you have tire salesmen on your list?"

Millan scanned the room. "Uh. . .where's Wilt? He's got the damn list."

"He's getting Mags for me."

Wilt stuck his head in the room and called Sean's name.

"I can't find Mags," he said. "She's not at her desk."

"Well it is only seven," Millan replied. "She didn't leave last night until one in the morning."

Sean shook his head. "She said she was coming in early," he repeated to his boss. "She wouldn't have even gone home last night except she said she had plans she couldn't blow off." He pulled up the directory and found her cell number. The phone rang and went to her voicemail.

"Maybe she overslept?" Wilt asked.

"I guess. She's usually pretty prompt, though."

"Well, Detective Tay isn't in yet either," Wilt went on as Millan grabbed the list of possible victim professions from him. "I can give her a call and ask her to swing by and check on Mags if you want?"

"Thanks, Wilt. That would be great." Sean yelled out one last thing as Wilt turned to leave. "Have Mags call me as soon as Tay picks her up."

"Will do!"

Sean turned his attention back to Millan. "So how's the list shaping up?"

"We've managed to get a few job ideas based off the words 'tiresome' and 'beaten.' Different professions from sleep study monitors to musicians who keep a beat. Nothing about tire salesmen. I'll add that to the list."

"All right. Now as soon as Mags gets here she can do her speedy-search-thing and find us some people with bad medical conditions. We have a lot of time left." Sean grinned, the expression tugging at his tight muscles. "I think we might make it on this one."

Millan smiled back. "It's good to see that on your face."

"It's good to have it." He paused. "I know it's not everything—Charlotte is still gone, Angellica is still out there, this 'Officer Let' woman is still trying to kill, but it's some kind of progress. If we can stop these women—just once— like last time, we can catch another break. Maybe they'll return Charlotte if they see we found this victim beforehand. Maybe they'll give up completely."

"I hope so, kid. I really do."

"Hey, guys. . ."

Sean and Millan looked toward the door. Wilt stood there, tucking his oily hair behind his ears.

"They on their way?" Sean asked.

"Uh. . .actually? I can't get a hold of them."

Sean's brow furrowed. "What do you mean?"

"Detective Tay isn't answering her cell. And when I looked up Mags' home number, her fiancé answered. He said they were supposed to meet last night, but his car died on the way home from work. He'd called to say he was going to be late, but no answer so he left a message. By the time AAA came, towed his car, gave him a rental, and he made it back home, it was five a.m. He assumed she'd left for work. She'd said she was going in early and he figured she was pissed he hadn't been home. They had been planning that night for a week."

Sean gripped the edge of Millan's desk with his good hand. His knuckles turned white as he clung to the wood, knowing it was the only thing keeping him steady as his knees wobbled.

"You don't think. . .?" Wilt trailed off, unable to finish the thought out loud.

Sean was glad. He didn't know what he'd do if Wilt had finished by saying Spider had taken both women.

Tay and Mags.

Both gone.

Both part of Sean's life.

Just like Charlotte.

Gone.

Millan's dark face was as pale as when he'd realized he'd been responsible for the last victim's death. "Please, God, no."

The whole room fell silent.

"Sean?" Millan asked softly.

"Yeah." It was an acknowledgement. The word caught in his throat. He hated the sound. He hated the cowardice in it. The fear. The paralyzing guttural noise that comes from someone else dictating your life.

He thought of Detective Tay—her fiery hair always pulled back tightly into a bun. She never took shit from anyone.

Mags—spunky through and through with a love of everything technology. She never cared what anyone thought of her.

And Charlotte. The only thing Charlotte wanted was to do her job better than everyone else. And once in a while vent to a friend.

He thought of those three women—strong, independent. They would never give up.

Sean's grip loosened. His shoulders relaxed. His breath slowed.

He wasn't going to let anyone, *anyone,* hurt the people he cared about. He wasn't going to let Angellica or her partner or whoever steer his life anymore.

He was going to give Tay shit again about the trashy novels she read.

He was going to allow Mags to criticize him for not knowing the newest cell phone model.

He was going to listen to Charlotte vent about anything she wanted for the rest of her life.

"Yeah," he repeated to Millan, determination in his voice. "I'm here."

54

March 20th
7:30 a.m.

Charlotte did her best to remain as calm as possible during the evening. She ate her dinner—a meal of warmed, dense, dark bread, creamy green curry sauce, and a bright, strawberry salad. She read books offered to her—everything from classic English literature to Japanese poetry to world newspapers. She laid in the bed provided for her to rest—its silken sheets now a deep russet with cream-colored blankets.

But she couldn't sleep.

Instead she thought. And thought some more. She tried not to, but the notions came in fast-paced waves regardless of her desire for them to leave.

She tried not to think about her desperate situation.

She tried not to think about Sean and how much, surprising even to herself, she missed him.

But mostly she tried not to think about the fact that she might have signed the death warrants for Sean's receptionist and fellow detective. With limited options, she logically knew she'd made the best choice. She couldn't bring in two scientists who might be killed because they didn't know what was happening. In this regard, at least Mags and Detective Tay had an edge. And hopefully, Charlotte would be allowed to speak with them and explain the situation.

This thought stung at the front of her mind. If Truth refused to allow her to see them, the entire plan Charlotte envisioned would be moot.

If she could call it a plan—more like a frantic attempt to stop three women bent on dealing out death.

The medical examiner heard her door open. Truth entered, nude this time, and crossed the room. She approached the closed, heavily embroidered curtains and opened them. A blast of light flooded the room, though Charlotte couldn't be sure it was actually the sun.

"Good morning," Truth said. "I hope you slept well."

"I did not sleep at all," Charlotte replied. The medical examiner also spent most of the previous night thinking about how to speak to Truth. As an intellect, Charlotte wondered how long her lies would hold up under any scrutiny. So she decided to tell the truth unless absolutely necessary.

A tiny wrinkle on her forehead indicated Truth's concern. "It pains me to hear that. Was something wrong with the bed?"

"No, the accommodations were fine. I have simply had a lot of thoughts in my head. They made it difficult to rest."

Truth nodded. "Understandable. I was surprised how quickly you chose the individuals to validate the Book's origins."

Charlotte hesitated a moment. "Once I thought about the situation, it was not a hard decision."

Truth sat on the edge of the bed. "Would you care for some breakfast?"

"Please."

Truth led the way out of the bedroom, down a long, high-ceilinged corridor. The mirrored walls gleamed with shine. Charlotte watched her reflection, folded into the layers of the rich blanket, which trailed behind her. Her hair fell loose, and it bounced softly on the bare skin of her back.

As the two of them left the hallway and turned through a set of doors, Charlotte couldn't stop the involuntary gasp from her mouth. The room was twice the size of the bedroom. A domed ceiling curved above with thin braided branches of greens and silvers, some metallic, others matte. The thin lines converged down the sides of the walls, accumulating into thicker trunks. Along the bottom edges of the rounded room the roots crept along, connecting each trunk to the next, and spilling out into a silvery-green pattern on the carpet. The plush carpet was a darker shade of green. The center of the room had no carpet, just a round, white, tiled floor, which sparkled as if studded with shards of diamond. In the center of the circle stood a single circular table with two chairs. The glassed top was covered with a spread of fruits, cheeses, and baked goods.

"Please," Truth said, motioning toward the table. "Have a seat."

The two of them sat and Charlotte began to eat. Just like dinner, the food tasted exceptional. The fruit flavors burst in her mouth; the cheeses were soft and sweet, the breads warm and flaky. Everything tasted as if she ate the absolute best of each type of food.

"I have to ask," Charlotte said after swallowing a bit of kiwi. "The food here has been delicious. Where do you obtain it?"

Truth smiled. "Trade secret, so to speak. Although once you lead us, you will know everything we know."

Charlotte decided to play up Truth's desire to have her take over this whole operation. "What about the other individuals who work for us? Are they privy to the same knowledge? For instance, I am not sure where we are. I assume that once I lead, I will be able to exit and see the exterior. Is that the same for everyone else?"

Truth hesitated. "I'm not really supposed to tell you these things."

Charlotte allowed herself a pouty frown. "Why not? I would think the more enticement the better."

"The problem is you aren't supposed to be enticed at all. You're supposed to make this decision based on the Book, its contents, and the scientific proof of its origins."

"Then why bring me here at all? You must have known this room would appeal to me."

Truth's answer came, hesitant. "I wanted to have breakfast with you." She picked at a loaf of bread with her delicate fingers. "I mean, there's nothing wrong with wanting a bit of company. We have other women who work here besides ourselves and the scientists—sometimes previous Triad members stay on to help—but the total number is quite small."

Charlotte did her best to hide her realization—Truth wasn't just interested in her because she was going to be the next leader. Truth felt lonely.

Truth popped a piece of bread into her mouth. "My position is often one of isolation. I truly am one of the only people here that is always aware of everything." Her gaze drifted down toward the table, her words soft. "Second and Third—they are conditioned. We find matches for the personality type we want and then with chemical stimulants and behavioral modifications, they are transformed into the vessel we need them to be."

Charlotte processed this information as fast as she could. "So they are not aware of what has been done to them? They are brainwashed to become killers?"

Truth gave her head a little shake. "You don't understand. These women already *are* killers. They are born that way. I reprogram them to live in society without the urge or desire to kill for several years—detailed backgrounds are established, relationships are created, false families, friends, everything. I take them *off* the radar. Then I trigger their false identities to turn off and they report for duty. Since most deaths occur quickly, it isn't strange for them to be gone during that short period of time. In fact, most often they can accomplish their goals during normal business hours. Second can do most of her planning from her desk. Third needs only a few hours to kill someone."

Charlotte felt the last few pieces click into place. "Except your Second and Third seem to no longer be under your control."

Truth let out a snort of disgust. "That is an impossibility. Individual body chemistry, brain functions, and movements are tracked daily. Both Second and Third are within normal parameters."

Charlotte furrowed her brow as she sat back in her chair, finished with breakfast. "And there is no way around your system? Your Second and Third have both instituted massive changes: Third's notes to the police department, Second's extensive murder scenarios, and both of their personal vendettas against Detective Trann."

"I monitor their bodily functions myself. And every decade the passwords and access codes are changed so that only the current First can use the program. No one else can get into the system." Truth's words came out strong, but the tone of her voice lacked conviction.

Charlotte pushed the wedge further. "You are a woman of logic. Look at the facts. These two women are out of control. They have increased death rates to every week without your knowledge or consent, they are allowing personal feelings to get in the way, and they are disregarding your orders."

"No," Truth denied. "They are making up for lost time.

Those individuals were always on my list. Second and Third just got behind and—"

"What happened during those months when they were supposed to be killing?" Charlotte interrupted. "Where were they? Were they in their own personalities or their pretend ones? What did they do during that time? And why come back? It was not out of guilt. Or loyalty. They never told you they stopped killing. Your reports went out and they confirmed them, month after month. Truth, they *lied* to you. Do you really think you have them under your control?"

"I—," Truth stammered.

"And do you think," Charlotte pressed, "that they will listen to me when I take over? They have tasted power. Do you think they will give that up?"

"The Book. . .the Book says. . .they have to listen to the Book."

"The Book is ancient! You said so yourself. The world will adapt and evolve. These women are adapting their own interpretations. How long will they continue to follow blindly? Are the other Triads still under its influence? Have they taken matters into their own hands as well?"

Truth reached across the table and clutched Charlotte's hands, chocolate surrounding golden beige. "But that's why we need you!" she hissed. "Don't you see? You need to bring back order." Tears rimmed her beautiful light brown eyes. "I'm afraid, Charlotte. I'm afraid the world has progressed further than we can save it. If that's the case, then why do we even bother?" Tears slid down her dark cheeks. "I feel as though I've lost my faith," she whispered.

"I hate to hear that."

Charlotte and Truth both turned their heads toward the new voice. Two women entered the room. The first, who had spoken, walked straight and proud. Her short, black hair was tucked behind her ears. Her cinnamon-colored skin glowed under the ceiling's golden lights.

The second woman, tall, thin, pale, swaggered in behind, her big blue eyes taking in the large room. She ran her fingers through her blonde, curly hair and let out a low whistle.

"Nice digs."

Charlotte's mouth dropped. "Angellica?"

The blonde woman looked at Charlotte. "Oh great, another person who knows me." She threw her arms up in frustration. "Seriously, Violet, why did you keep popping me in and out so much?"

"So it's true," Truth chimed in. She'd stood from her seat, her posture tall. "You have stayed in your original personalities."

"Just me," Violet replied. "I've been triggering Anya into Angellica when I needed to throw Detective Trann off our scent. Unfortunately, things went too far so I've pulled her out for good."

"You can't do this," Truth continued, hands on the back of her chair for support. "You can't change the rules to fit your own personal whims."

Violet narrowed her eyes. "Actually, Truth, I can. And it's about time, too. Your methods are outdated. The Book is what I follow—but the world *has* changed." She indicated Charlotte. "Your pathetic 'chosen one' knows at least that much. But I don't believe she *is* our chosen one. And I'll prove it to you."

Violet squared her body with Charlotte's.

"The Book says we can't kill any chosen one, even if they aren't the real messiah. So if she really is who you say she is—"

A flash of silver glinted in the light, flitting through the air.

A *thud* issued from Charlotte's chest.

"—then she won't die."

The medical examiner dropped her eyes, unable to comprehend why the tail end of a knife protruded from her chest.

"Oh."

She fell backwards out of her chair, her head cracking against the tiled circle.

She heard Truth scream.

She heard Angellica laugh.

Charlotte's eyelids fluttered.

The ceiling's light narrowed to a tunnel until blackness engulfed her.

55

March 20th
9 a.m.

Sean held the faces of Charlotte, Mags, and Detective Tay in his mind every time he felt fatigued. Every time another tire shop told him no one was missing. Every time traffic slowed him down.

He would save the victim. He would save his friends. He would save the day.

Sean currently drove a borrowed police cruiser since he couldn't shift his Jag with his hand in a brace. They had as many people helping as possible, so Millan told Sean Officer Eth didn't have to accompany him. Although he wished he could have taken his own car since the police vehicle smelled of french fries and cloying perfume, its normal occupants off duty for the day. But spring felt like being nice to him today, so he drove with windows rolled down and the fresh air helped keep him awake.

Without Mags' assistance and her amazing hacking skills to get into medical record databases, the police department was back to random searches of places which might fit with the clue. Sean chose tire dealerships since that had been his suggestion. Only a couple of hours had passed since he left the station, but he felt good about his chances.

The one only worry gnawing at his mind was that Angellica knew he, Charlotte, and the police department had discovered the genetic abnormality connection between the victims.

Maybe that's why they kidnapped Mags? To keep her from helping us research medical records.

But why Detective Tay? She'd barely gotten back from her vacation. She was hardly involved in this case. What would be the purpose in taking her?

Sean shook his head to clear his thoughts as he took a right, the street curving ahead of him. To be honest, all Detective Tay needed to be was someone who knew Sean.

I should just stop talking to anyone with ovaries.

Sean grunted a laugh—though the joke was crude, it was the only remnants of humor he could muster.

He veered off Broadway to enter the parking lot of South Boston Tire and Auto Repairs when his phone rang. He spun the steering wheel with his good hand and pulled into a spot next to the blue-trimmed, white building. With the car stopped, he turned on his phone and stuck it to his ear, hoping it was Millan with good news.

"Detective Trann," he answered, peering through the windshield at the building. The place was small, so hopefully their employee roster was small, too.

"Hello, Detective. This is Truth. I am in charge of the women you collectively know as Spider."

The sound of Sean accidentally leaning onto the horn of the car brought him out of his shock. A couple walking into the store looked at him briefly, trying to see if the horn honk was meant to get their attention. Sean waved them away impatiently and looked at his caller ID—the call was from Charlotte's phone.

56

March 20th
9:30 a.m.

"Where's Charlotte!"

"I don't have much time," Truth replied to the detective, her tone hushed. She sat crouched in the sitting room where she'd first brought the Book to Charlotte. After Violet had thrown the knife into Charlotte's chest, Truth ducked out through a passageway behind one of the walls in the tree-patterned room. It led to a hallway, which she closed off with a sealed door, then sprinted down into the sitting room. She felt guilty for leaving the medical examiner there, but she'd had no choice. She was no match for the Second and Third's skills.

Especially now they'd gone rogue.

"Charlotte has been wounded—I fear fatally," Truth whispered to the detective. She reached underneath the table in the center of the room where the Book lay and opened a small, hidden compartment. She fumbled inside and pulled out a gun, her hand shaking.

"Charlotte's hurt?" the detective questioned. "What happened?"

Truth peeked her head out of the sitting room, weapon in her free hand. The hallway remained empty, although it wouldn't take Second and Third long to get through the sealed door. She closed the regular door to the sitting room, turned off the lights, and crouched hidden behind one of the chairs. "It was not of my doing, but of the Second. She and the Third have altered their paths against my will. I can't control them anymore."

"Second and Third?" Sean asked. His voice sounded desperate and confused. "Who are they? Is that what you call Angellica and that fake police officer? Officer Let? What paths?"

"I don't have time to explain." Truth heard the hiss of the airtight, sealed door at the end of the corridor. "They are coming. Soldiers and Sailors. Press inside the wreath. One-two-two-seven-four. Find Charlotte. She must save us."

Truth hung up the phone. She cocked her 22A S&W pistol. She'd never actually used the gun before. It had been a present from her father before she'd become First.

It was strange to think of him at the end.

The door to the sitting room swung open fast, slamming

into the wall.

Truth fired three shots into the lit doorway.

She heard Anya's voice from the other end. "Miss!"

Truth heard the screech of moving ceiling panels above her. She swung her gun above her head, but the impact of a body falling on her forestalled any shots. In an instant, her gun hand twisted behind her body, her chest facing the silhouetted Angellica.

She gasped. Cold steel slid across the front of her throat. Blood sprayed from her wound, coating her bare breasts.

"Hit." The word came as a whisper in Truth's ear. It was Violet.

Truth garbled a response as her knees buckled. She fell to the floor, red fluid drenching the beautiful wood panels. Her fingers twitched, once, twice, before oblivion devoured her.

57

March 20th
9:45 a.m.

"No, no, no, no, NO!" Sean called Charlotte's number, his fingers trembling—no answer. "Oh God, please pick up. Pleasepleaseplease."

No answer.

Sean closed his eyes and repeated Truth's last words to him. "Soldiers and Sailors. Press inside the wreath. One-two-two-seven-four."

Sean grabbed the cruiser's radio and called dispatch. "All available units and nearest EMT drivers—meet me at 139 Tremont Street." He dialed Millan's cell number and tucked the phone onto his shoulder so he could start up the car.

"Trann?" Millan answered.

"Yeah."

"What's all this about meeting at the Soldiers and Sailors statue?"

Sean swerved a sharp U-turn to leave the parking lot. He flicked on the vehicle's siren. "Truth—I mean Spider—or one of them just called me. She said Charlotte—ugh! Doctor Salla is injured. Critically. We gotta get there and stop them."

Millan hesitated. "What makes you think she was telling the truth?"

"I don't know. I just do," Sean said over the cruiser's wails.

"But we still have another victim out there. I can't give you everyone to look into this."

"Well I have to go. I *have* to, Millan." Sean sped through the red light at the T-intersection as he took a left onto Congress Street. Traffic was minimal, but it would still take him another ten minutes to get there. And Charlotte could be dead by then.

"I get it," Millan acknowledged, "but I need everyone to keep searching for the victim. I can't take manpower off that."

"Fine," Sean said, frustrated. "Then send me one EMT crew and I'll go myself!" Sean hung up and tossed the phone onto the passenger seat. He swerved in and out of traffic, nearly colliding with a large semi on the bridge across the channel, and ran several red lights. Pedestrians jumped out of his way as he drove through the Boston Common Baseball Field. He drove up to the side of the Soldiers and Sailors statue and parked. Leaving the vehicle, he looked around, but the ambulance wasn't there yet.

There was one other car there, though—Officer Eth stood at the base of the statue's steps, staring upwards at the female AMERICA figure at the apex of the 126-foot structure.

"Officer Eth?" Sean called out.

The lean figure turned around. "Hello, Detective."

"You know Millan gave me permission to move around without you."

"Oh, I know," Eth replied. He pointed across the park. "I was actually right over there checking someone else out as our potential victim. No luck. Then I heard the call from dispatch. So now I'm here." He waved around. "Anyone else coming?"

"We're it." Sean began to circle the statue. "Millan couldn't take anyone else away from finding the other victim. He sent us an EMT crew though. They should be here soon."

"So why are we here in the first place?"

"A woman claiming to be one of the women responsible for the murders called me from Doctor Salla's phone."

Eth looked confused. "The medical examiner?"

Sean nodded. "She disappeared yesterday." He paused. "God, was that only yesterday?"

"So this woman is responsible for Doctor Salla's disappearance then?"

"Apparently so. She said she'd been injured." Sean looked up at the statue, concentrating on remembering the exact words. "She said the Second and Third have altered their paths and she can't control them anymore. I'm not sure what

302

that means, but then she said they were coming, gave me a reference to this statue, and told me to press inside the wreath."

"Oh, man." Eth stood next to Sean. He gestured to the circular rings set on each of the four, short, square pillars around the statue. "So I'm guessing these are the wreaths she meant? But some are single and some are two entwined. Did she tell you which ones to push?"

"No. Guess we'll try them all." He nodded to his left. "You go that way. We'll meet on the other side."

They both started on the north end, pressing on the inside of their respective wreaths. Sean went around to the right. He wanted to rush, but he worried he wouldn't push hard enough or the right way, so he took his time, pressing inside each wreath deliberately, with different levels of pressure.

Sean made it all the way around to the southern end with no success. Eth finished his side and joined Sean.

"Well, last one."

Sean took a deep breath and pushed inside the wreath. The white granite gave ever so slightly under his hand. The marble tiling at the base of the steps retracted underneath the statue, revealing a slim staircase.

"After you," Eth gestured.

Sean pulled out his weapon and led with it down the stairs, his braced hand held underneath for balance. The flight of steps was steep and curled downwards. The only light came from the sky behind them and as soon as Eth was below the surface, the tiles above them closed. Blackness surrounded them.

"Now what?" Eth whispered.

"We go until the stairs stop."

The two of them continued, Eth's hand on Sean's shoulder.

"Do you know how to get back out of here?"

"No idea."

Eth snorted. "Great."

Down, down, down. They must have gone down at least two hundred stairs.

What would that be? Sean thought. *Let's say twenty steps per floor. . .so at least ten floors down. And this has been hidden underneath the statue this whole time.*

Eth gripped Sean's shoulder, hard.

"Trann!" he whispered harshly.

"What?" Sean panicked. A dozen things rushed through his head at once.

"What about the ambulance?" Eth asked. "They are never going to find us down here. And if Doctor Salla is hurt. . ."

Sean closed his eyes, which gave no alternate impression since everything was still pitch-black. He paused to think. "We should go back up and. . .but we don't even know how to get out of here. And if Charlotte needs help. . ."

"Why don't I go back up?" Eth offered. "I'll try to figure out a way to open up the top or I'll yell until someone can press inside the wreath. You keep going. Hopefully you'll find Doctor Salla."

"Okay, yeah. That sounds good." He paused again. "We probably shouldn't split up."

"What choice do we have? The EMTs are never going to find us down here. And if Doctor Salla needs medical assistance, time is of the essence."

"Okay. We split up then. Good luck."

"You, too."

Sean felt Eth's hand pat his shoulder and then his touch was gone. As Sean continued downward, he heard Eth's footsteps for several minutes heading back up the staircase before they faded away.

After about a hundred more stairs, Sean stepped onto flat ground. He groped around with his good hand, which still held the gun, until he found what felt like a lamp. He struggled for a moment, deciding finally to holster his gun, and fumbled for the switch.

The lamp flickered once, then brightened—its soft rose-colored light spread radially outward along the wall, which was smooth and carved from what appeared to be the same type of granite as the statue above. The hallway stretched out in front of him—so long he couldn't see the end, until the light came up to full. It then triggered the next light, and the next in a series of five lights on either side of the walls. Each light was tinged a different color so the corridor lit up as a rainbow path that led to a solid steel door at the end.

He had a vague memory of watching The Wizard of Oz with his mom as a kid and was reminded of the moment when Dorothy stepped out of black and white into color. He pulled his gun back out and with a tight grip, he made his way down the hall, checking around him for cameras, sensor devices, anything that might alert others to his presence. He couldn't see anything overt, but that didn't mean he hadn't been detected. Regardless, he had to keep going. If Charlotte was behind that door and wounded, he had to find her and help her if he could.

58

March 20th
10 a.m.

"Where the hell are we?" Mags wrapped her hands around her head in an attempt to stop the pounding. She'd just woken up from being sedated by Angellica. No—*Anya.* But she no longer lay on a mattress in the back of the van. Instead she was inside a windowless room, lying on the cold, cement floor. Someone squatted beside her.

"A room," the other prisoner answered, handing over her glasses. "That's all I've got. A room."

Mags recognized the clipped, British accent. She sat up, put on her glasses, and turned her attention to the voice.

"Juliette?" Mags asked. The slim, ruby-haired, freckled

woman came into view—completely naked.

Detective Juliette Tay put her hand on Mags' bare knee. That was when Mags realized she was nude as well.

"Yes, it's me. How are you feeling?"

Mags scrunched up her face and then widened her eyes to shake off the remaining effects of the drugs. "Besides indecently exposed? I'm trying to remember the number of the bus that hit me." She tucked her legs into her chest and held her knees as she looked around the room. Juliette had been accurate in her description. It was definitely a room. And there wasn't much else about it to tell them otherwise. The walls were white and blank. A single light bulb hung from a socket above them, shining down harsh, bright light that hurt Mags' eyes. Only a single door—steel from the looks of it—indicated a way out.

"How did we get here?" Mags asked.

"Angellica, or I should say Anya, which is apparently her real name, and a second woman called Violet abducted us last night."

Flashes of hitting the asphalt in the parking lot outside the police department mere feet from her car popped into Mags' mind. She didn't remember anything else after being thrown into the back of the van except that Anya said she didn't look like a scientist.

"I take it they nabbed you after me?" Mags asked.

Juliette nodded. "Apparently I was lucky to be second." She gingerly reached up and touched Mags' jaw. Mags winced at the pain.

"They said someone named Truth was mad you'd been

hurt," Juliette continued. "I guess they weren't supposed to injure us."

Mags touched her own face gently. "I got hit with a paralytic agent and crash-landed face-first into the parking lot." Mags felt her neck where the shot had hit her. She craned her head and got a glimpse of her bare shoulder—it was covered with a spiderweb pattern.

"Wait a minute," she exclaimed, indicating her skin. "If this was the paralytic Spider is using, shouldn't we be in some sort of torture device with twenty-four hours to live?"

"A dark-skinned woman who introduced herself as Truth injected you with something that would counteract both the paralytic and the sedative. She apologized for the way we'd been treated and said she would return shortly with clothes, food, and bring us to better quarters. I'd estimate that was close to three hours ago." Juliette looked at the door. "I have a horrible feeling something has gone wrong. I don't think she's coming back."

Mags remembered Anya referencing Truth. "I got the feeling this Truth woman is in charge."

"That was my impression as well. She also seemed concerned with our wellbeing. If something has happened to her, I fear we may be in danger."

Mags motioned to their surroundings. "*May* be in danger?"

Juliette rubbed her hands together. The room wasn't terribly cold, but it was chilly without clothing on. "The two women who took us, Anya and Violet, had no problem hurting us. In fact, they damaged you more than they were supposed to. If Truth wants us undamaged, I'd say she's the only one. If she hasn't returned and something has happened to her, I doubt our kidnappers will care as much about our state of being."

Mags shivered—the reaction having nothing to do with her body's temperature. "I can't believe Angellica is. . . It's just incredible." She paused. "Poor Sean."

Juliette stood. "Sean is the least of my concerns right now." She walked to the door. "We need to figure a way out of here."

Mags followed her. She ran her hands across the smooth surface. "I don't see what we can do until someone opens this from the outside." She tapped her knuckles on the metal. "Seems pretty solid."

Juliette sighed. "Wish I had my bloody gun."

Mags' eyes narrowed, her mind calculating. "I don't think that would help. A bullet might dent the surface, but I don't think it would get us out of here. If I'm not mistaken, I think this door is magnetically sealed. I can't see any bolts or locks in the gap between the door and the wall."

"Sean is always talking about how good you are with computers. Can you short circuit it or something?" Juliette asked.

"Unfortunately, no. Not unless I had access to the panel outside. And that would mean the door was already open." She looked around the empty room. "There isn't anything here we could use, either." Glancing up, she caught sight of the light bulb. She walked to the center of the room and stood underneath it.

"What?" Juliette asked.

"I may not be able to short circuit the door, but I might be able to get their attention enough to *open* the door."

"What do you have in mind?"

Mags smiled wryly and pushed her glasses higher onto the bridge of her nose. "Well, first we are going to do something that will make every frat boy across the country simultaneously feel like they are missing the coolest thing in the world—but won't know why."

Juliette raised an eyebrow. "Meaning?"

"Meaning for me to get to the light, I'll have to climb on your shoulders. And since clothing is non-existent, we'll both be naked while I do that."

"Riiiighhht." Juliette squatted to one knee. "Well, bottoms up."

Mags grabbed Juliette for balance and flung her leg over the detective's shoulder. "No pun intended."

59

March 20th
10:30 a.m.

Sean stared at the steel door—the remnants of the final lamp cast a shade of lavender light across it. It looked pretty solid. He couldn't see any sort of handle, but a sophisticated panel sat attached to the wall just to the right. It was a touchscreen with a number key code entry face.

"Here goes nothing," he whispered. He punched in the number sequence Truth had told him. 1-2-2-7-4. The panel lit up green under his fingertips with every touch. After the code was entered, the entire screen lit up. The door hissed and cracked open a few centimeters. With a deep breath, Sean pushed it open the rest of the way.

The door opened to another hallway, lined with more doors. The wood floors were oiled and sleek. The mirrored walls reflected his image—broken, tired, scared. He thought of Mags, Detective Tay, and Charlotte and watched his shoulders relax, his face turn from fearful to determined.

Sean crept down the corridor, testing each door handle. They were all locked. Each had its own panel like the outside door, but Sean didn't dare try the combination Truth had given him. He couldn't believe the inside locks would be the same and he worried that if he entered the wrong code, he might trigger an alarm.

God, I wish Mags was here.

He continued, desperately hoping one door would be open. But each one remained sealed. He'd gotten to the sixth door, still with no end in sight, when the lights went out.

What the hell? Did I trigger something?

Sean pressed himself against the wall in the blackness, concealing himself inside one of the door jambs. His eyes adjusted to the faint green glow let off from the door entry panel.

Sean heard a hiss. One of the doors opened a few meters away from him. He ducked to the floor as he heard voices.

". . .must have a short in the wiring. I'll flip the breaker. It'll just take a minute."

Sean could hear the woman walk away from him, her voice brisk. It wasn't the sultry voice he'd heard on the phone so this was someone other than Truth.

"Hurry up," a second woman called out, still inside the room. "I don't want to drag her body without being able to see where I'm going."

Sean bit the inside of his check to keep from yelling out. He recognized the second woman's voice.

It was Angellica.

60

March 20th
10:45 a.m.

"I don't think this did anything except plunge us into darkness," Juliette said to Mags.

The two women were crouched on the floor on either side of the door, waiting for it to open.

Mags ignored the sarcasm in Juliette's voice. "I never said it was a *good* idea, just an idea. And I never claimed they would look in on us while it's still dark. Maybe they need to check the circuit breaker first. Once they realize it's a short, they'll have to come find the source."

Mags' hands were coated in sweat, but she couldn't wipe them off on anything, since her naked skin felt just as clammy.

She tried against the wall, but it didn't help very much.

"Do you think they know we did this?"

Mags shook her head, then realized the futility of that action. "Probably not yet. They won't have any idea where the surge came from until they inspect the room. And that's what we want."

"I wish I had my bloody gun," Juliette repeated.

Mags didn't reply. She wished the detective had her gun, too. She wasn't really sure what two nude, sweaty, terrified women could do against these killers, but they had to do something. Or at least *try* to do something. Even if they failed, it was better than being locked in and forgotten or waiting around to be executed. And they hoped they still had the advantage of having their captors believe they were still sedated and unconscious from the abduction.

It also didn't hurt that Juliette was law enforcement. She may not have been trained for this specific situation, but she seemed very cool under the stress of it. Much calmer than Mags felt.

The door hissed open.

"This one is dark, too." A woman's voice filled the room, heavy with a southern drawl. There was hardly any light from the hallway—a faint green glow illuminated the short woman's silhouette.

Someone else yelled out from across the hall, but Mags couldn't make out the words.

"Give me the flashlight then," the woman called back. A beam of white light bounced down the hall.

"I don't know why we're botherin' to keep them in this

room. They should be upstairs by the Book, checkin' it out."

Mags heard the woman in the hall say something about how the scientists were no good until they woke up.

That's us. Good. They still think we're unconscious.

The flashlight preceded the woman and the beam swept over the room.

"Hey, Tera," the southern woman called out. "There's no one—"

Her sentence was cut short by a *thud.* Mags heard the body collapse. The flashlight spun out of control across the floor. Mags watched Juliette scramble to grab the light as Tera entered the room. Juliette and Tera trained their flashlights on one another.

"What the—?"

It was all the new woman got out. Mags reached out and grabbed the flashlight from the woman's grip. In one swift motion, she swung the device in an underarm swing and bashed the woman in the face with it. The sound of teeth cracking and a nose splintering were the only noises in the room until the body hit the ground.

Mags felt horror overwhelm her as she watched her own hand move the flashlight to the woman's face. Blood had sprayed across the wall and pooled at the edge of the woman's mouth—two teeth lay on the floor like shiny, white pebbles amidst the red fluid.

The woman wasn't breathing.

Mags stared, not comprehending why the woman lay so still.

"I didn't—I didn't hit her that hard," she pleaded to

Juliette.

Juliette felt for a pulse and shook her head. "I think you drove her nose into her brain."

Mags realized she had just killed someone. "I didn't mean to—" She turned her back and retched, although thankfully her stomach was fairly empty. Still the convulsions shuddered through her for a few moments before she could stand back up.

"Are you all right?" Juliette asked. She was checking for signs of life on the southern woman. Mags couldn't see any movement in her chest.

"Yeah. I think so. Let's just get the hell out of here, okay?"

"Sounds good to me." Juliette snatched the robe from the dead southern woman and handed it to Mags.

"I can't wear this."

Juliette pushed it toward her. "You have to. It's too cold. These women have no more use for them."

Mags hadn't realized her teeth chattered. The hallway was much cooler than their room. She shoved her arms into the sleeves and looked down to see a pair of boots lying by her feet. She pulled them on—they were a bit big—but not so much so that they would impede her ability to run, if need be. The warmth spread instantly through her body and she rubbed her arms inside the robe. The material clung to her like silk, but warmed her like fur. She shined the flashlight over onto Juliette, who wore a similar outfit, stripped from the second woman.

The one Mags had killed.

Don't think about it, she told herself as a new wave of nausea threatened her. *You can throw up later.*

Mags felt the wave subside. "So what's the plan?"

"We do whatever we have to do to get out of this place."

"Sounds like a plan to me."

61

March 20th
10:45 a.m.

Sean slid through the cracked door. He knew Angellica was in there somewhere, but the room was still pitch black. Soft carpet muffled his footsteps, which he knew would obscure her movements as well. He held his breath, listening for hers. He could hear it, but he had no idea exactly where in the room she was, not to mention any furniture or items that might stand between the two of them.

So he waited, gun raised in the direction of the continual inhales and exhales.

White light flooded the space as the power returned.

"Finally," she exclaimed. "Now I can—" She stopped.

"Detective Trann." Her eyes flitted between his face and the end of his gun. "A pleasure, as always."

"Angellica, you have the right to remain silent." The words came, forced.

Anya threw her head back and laughed. "First, it's Anya. Stop calling me that bitch's name. And second, I'll waive that right and I'll tell you why. If you try to arrest me, I'll fight back, which will waste precious time. And the last thing you want to do is waste time."

Her blue eyes, eyes Sean once loved, held none of the brightness Angellica's had. This woman's eyes were cold and hard.

Anya took a step to the side.

There was Charlotte, body splayed out on the tiled center of the floor, silver knife handle protruding from her chest. Her eyes were closed, her skin pasty. A pool of blood matted the hair around her head.

But her chest rose once—twice. It was slow, but steady, although Sean didn't know how much longer that could go on.

Sean took a step toward the medical examiner.

"Uh-uh," Anya said, blocking his view again.

Sean raised his gun level with Anya's face. "Get out of my way."

"You gonna kill me, Detective?" she asked, her voice thick and syrupy. She raised her arms slowly. "I'm not armed, sir. Please don't shoot, sir." She smiled, cold.

Sean's hand shook. No one would blame him for pulling the trigger. No one would even have to know. This woman was a killer. She was preventing him from saving Charlotte.

All he had to do was *squeeze.*

"She's still in here, you know."

"What? Who?"

"Angellica," Anya replied.

Sean's finger loosened a fraction on the trigger. "What are you talking about?"

"She's in here, somewhere." Anya made a loose circle with her finger around her face and chest.

"That's impossible. You made her up. She was pretend— a fake identity to keep me fooled."

"Not true," Anya said. "Not true at all. Angellica is very real. Just as real as you are. Everything you know about her— her hopes, dreams, habits, style—they are real. When she exists, I don't."

Sean shook his head. "You're just trying to confuse me. You're trying to delay me so I can't save Charlotte. Or so your partner has time to get back." At that thought, he looked over his shoulder, relieved that there wasn't anyone in the hall. He shut the door, so he'd at least hear the other woman enter the room.

"It doesn't matter *why* I'm telling you this, it's the truth." Anya moved her right arm slowly across her body and pointed at a spot underneath her other arm. "There is a small chip right below my tricep. If I activate it, Angellica will be here and I'll be gone."

Sean hesitated. This was a trap. Or a stall. It had to be. But when she was Angellica, she *did* seem like a different person. He had to know. "Explain. Fast."

"When I was recruited by Truth—she's the head of this operation by the way—she told me I'd be reprogrammed as someone else. During this 'down-time,' I would live my life as this other woman. When it was time for me to come back and assassinate someone, Truth would send a signal to my chip which would reverse the process."

"You said reprogram. So Angellica is some sort of personality construct?"

"Not at all. She's me—well, me without my sociopathic tendencies. You see, Detective, she is what I *would* have been if I didn't have the taste for killing that I do. That's why I was chosen. When Truth found me, I was in a psychiatric ward. I'd already killed my entire family. And to the state, I was *clearly* delusional." She rolled her eyes, as if the state was the ones with the issue. "So Truth gave me a choice: stay locked away on medication that would keep me a zombie for the rest of my life or give away a few years and then come back, be able to kill, and get away clean."

Could what this woman was saying be true? Could she really be both people and a mere signal to her brain decided the difference? Sean wanted to believe her, but the tale was so incredible.

Regardless, this woman had just admitted to several murders. He couldn't let her walk away free, no matter how many personalities she had inside her. "You have to be arrested for your crimes. I can't let you get away with what you've done. Move to the wall and place your hands against it."

Anya narrowed her eyes, rebellious, her fingers sliding

along the edge of her arm. "Then maybe I'll press it anyway. Then you'll have to put Angellica in jail for the rest of her life. Can you do that? Put her in a tiny cell with other murderers forever? Or maybe she'll get lucky and they'll just think she's crazy. Then she'll get wrapped in an extra long-sleeved white coat and given meds that will make her eyes glaze over as if she were always submerged underwater. She'll feel that way too, never quite part of the land of the living again."

Sean did everything he could to appear calm. But inside his stomach roiled, his head pounded. He could feel sweat begin to prickle under his arms. What could he do? Anya was right. If he shot her, Angellica would die, too. If he arrested her, she'd become Angellica, who would suffer what should be Anya's fate.

And all the while Charlotte lay on the floor, breathing what could be her last breath.

"There is an alternative." Anya tapped her arm. "I could be her again. I could be her for the rest of my life. All I have to do is trigger this chip and I would be yours. We could save Charlotte, we could stop Violet, or as you know her, Officer Let. Truth is already dead. She can't change me back. Angellica could live out the rest of her life with you."

"But you said you wouldn't exist. Wouldn't that be like suicide?"

Anya shrugged. "What are my options? At least I'll exist in some way. And it seems like you and she were happy. I mean, you *were* going to be married."

Sean's face darkened at the memory of him standing at the altar, grinning like an idiot, until his almost mother-in-law came up and told him Angellica wasn't coming.

A theory dawned on him. Maybe it hadn't been Angellica who'd stood him up at all. "*You* had something to do with her leaving me, didn't you? She mentioned something about blacking out. You took over and left me on my wedding day!" His finger was back on the trigger.

Anya laughed, almost hysterical. "This is GREAT! You think I had something to do with it. Oh no, sweetheart, that was totally little Miss Priss. She left you all on her own. I didn't resurface until after." She wiped away some tears. "Priceless."

"Shut up, shut UP!" The story was insane. He couldn't believe it. He couldn't!

"Either way, Romeo, the past is past. You must have had something with her, to be rekindled after all this time. So now you two can have a second chance. What do you say?" Anya nodded her head in Charlotte's direction. "Tick tock, Detective."

Sean felt sick. He didn't really love Angellica anymore. But this psycho would wait until she was in jail or committed and then release Angellica to suffer her fate. He couldn't let that happen. And Charlotte needed his help. *And* the other killer, Violet, was still at large.

He had no choice. "Deal. You become her and you disappear forever. As soon as we are out of here, I'm going to have that removed from her arm."

"I wish I could see how this all turns out." Anya pressed down on her arm. Her eyelids drooped and her eyes rolled into the back of her head. She collapsed to the floor as her knees buckled.

Sean ran over, gun still on her, and prodded her with his foot. He had to make sure before he could turn his back on her and check on Charlotte.

Hang in there, he mentally projected to the medical examiner. Her chest rose again and he brought his attention back to Anya.

Or Angellica.

Whoever she now was, she opened her eyes. She blinked several times before she registered the gun aimed at her face.

"Sean? Sean!" she exclaimed. She sat up and slid away from the weapon. "What's going on?" She whipped her head around. "Where am I? Why are you pointing your gun at me?" An edge of hysteria tinged her voice.

"How do I know it's you?"

She shook her head, confused. "What do you mean? It's me. Angellica. What the hell is going on? Stop pointing that thing at me!"

Sean lowered his weapon a touch but didn't holster it.

"Prove you're Angellica. Say something only she would know."

"Only. . .what? What are you—"

"Prove it!"

"God, God, okay. Um. . .only something I would know? I-I don't know," she stammered. She began to chew on her thumbnail.

She always chewed on her thumbnail when she was nervous.

There was no way Anya would know that, right? Anya

had probably never even *been* nervous.

It *had* to be Angellica.

Sean holstered his gun and held out his hand. Angellica looked at it warily.

"I didn't say anything."

"You don't have to. I know you."

She took his hand and he pulled her to her feet. There was an awkward moment before Angellica threw her arms around him in a hug. Surprised, he wrapped his good arm around her, patting her awkwardly on the back.

"What is going on?" she asked, her voice terrified.

"I promise I'll tell you," he said, "but we have to help Charlotte first."

"I don't think she's going to make it," Angellica said, close to his ear.

Sean felt a chill from the tone in her voice.

Suddenly blood, bone, and hair shot out of the back of her skull.

Someone behind Sean had just shot Angellica through the forehead.

Sean screamed as her head snapped back then ricocheted forward and hit his shoulder. Her teeth sunk through his shirt, breaking skin.

Oh my God, he panicked. *It's Violet. The door was locked. She is the only person who can access the room. She must have seen Anya change into Angellica and killed her.*

Sean jerked his head around, awkwardly holding the body as it buckled in his grasp. His bad arm, still immobile, was no help to reach for his gun.

He was unarmed and defenseless.

His eyes locked with the person in the doorway whose gun still smoldered from the shot.

It was Officer Eth.

62

March 20th
10:50 a.m.

Mags stood on tiptoe behind Juliette as the detective peered into the hallway.

"Anyone?" Mags asked in a whisper.

Juliette shook her head.

The two of them slid into the corridor—Juliette holding her flashlight up and alert to lead, Mags grabbing hers with both hands and swinging it wildly behind them.

Suddenly, the place lit up. Lightbulbs glowed from long, twisted chandeliers draping down from the ceiling to the ends of the hall, stopping just above the end doors.

The two of them clicked off their flashlights and blinked

in the sudden brightness.

Mags turned her head from left to right. "Any suggestions on which door to use?"

Juliette shrugged. There was nothing else in the corridor except smooth black walls that reflected the chandeliers' points of light. "Looks like this hallway was made only for this room. If I had to guess, I'd say each end door leads out, but to different parts of the complex."

"I'd say let's flip a coin, but I must have left it in my other stolen dead person's robe." Mags regretted the callous joke as soon as it left her lips, but she hadn't been able to help it. Humor was a defense mechanism for her.

They went right. When they reached the door, it wouldn't open.

"Another security panel," Mags said, smoothing her fingers over the glowing green face. "We won't be able to get through without a numerical code."

"Wish we hadn't killed both of them," Juliette muttered, glancing back at the cell they'd just left.

"It might be okay. . ." Mags trailed off. She flipped her flashlight around and bashed the underside of the panel.

"What are you doing?" Juliette whispered.

The bottom of the panel cracked open, exposing several wires.

"You're kidding."

"Nope," Mags replied.

"You mean everything Sean said was true?"

"Yep." Mags smiled at Juliette and knelt to the ground. "Hold the flashlight so I can see what I'm doing."

"I don't believe this," Juliette remarked as she bent to apply the light at the correct angle. "You can seriously unlock this door by hotwiring it? I was just making a joke before when I asked if you could do that."

"Actually. . ." Mags paused, stripping two wires with her teeth. She wrapped them together and the panel went black. "I can unlock *all* the doors."

"Brilliant!" Juliette exclaimed as she pushed and the door swung open. She grinned at Mags. "Maybe I should have gone to school to be a receptionist."

63

March 20th
11 a.m.

"NO!" Sean yelled. He let Angellica's lifeless body slide to the floor. He pulled out his gun and pointed it at Officer Eth. "You sonofabitch! Why? WHY? How can you be working with them?"

Eth let his weapon flip around on his finger and held his hands up. "Detective Trann, stop. Put the gun down."

Sean's head swam, confused. How had he not seen this coming? There were no clues, no indication that Eth was a part of this scheme. And yet there was no way he could have gotten in unless he knew the code to the door.

"Get down on the ground, NOW!" Sean screamed.

Eth kneeled, begging to explain.

"I don't want to hear it. You fucking piece of trash! How can you work for these women?"

It was Eth's turn to look confused. "What are you talking about? I don't work for these women. I'm on your side!"

"Then why? Why kill Angellica? She'd changed. She was herself again. She wasn't—"

Eth pointed to something on the ground. Sean turned slowly. A slim blade lay next to Angellica's hand.

No, *Anya's* hand.

She'd never changed back. He knew it. He'd heard it in her voice.

"I'm sorry, Trann," Eth pleaded. A sheen of sweat covered his young face. "She was about to kill you. You were blocking her body so I couldn't just injure her. I was scared if I yelled, she'd just plunge the knife into your back. I had no choice."

Sean's head throbbed. He turned back toward Eth. "How did you get in?"

"The doors are unlocked. All of them. I went back up the stairs, like we decided. I couldn't figure a way out. I pounded, but no one could hear me. My phone didn't have any bars. So I came back down to help you. I got to the rainbow-colored hallway when the lights went out. I waited by the door, staring at the green-lit panel. The lights came back on and after a bit, the panel went dark. When I tried the door, it opened. I heard you talking inside this room."

It made sense. But why were the doors unlocked? Why

had the lights gone off and on? These women seemed too well-organized for these types of glitches to happen.

"Trann," Eth said, bringing Sean back to the present. "What about Doctor Salla?"

Sean whipped his head around. "Charlotte." He sprinted across the springy carpet and onto the tiled center. He knelt down next to her. She still breathed, but it was labored. The knife protruded out of the right side of her chest, right below her breast.

Eth slid down on her other side. "What do we do? I have very limited medical training. All I know is do not remove the knife."

"We have to get her out of here, to a hospital."

"I agree, but how? She's in no condition to be moved. And I don't know how we'd carry her up all those stairs without causing more damage."

Sean looked around, frantic. "There has to be a phone or a communications device around here."

"Where?"

"Check the other rooms. There must be something somewhere."

Eth headed toward the door, his gun at the ready.

"And keep an eye out for Officer Let—Violet!" Sean called out.

Eth nodded and peeked out of the doorway before leaving.

Sean lifted Charlotte's head gingerly to check the wound on her scalp. Most of the blood had clotted and dried on the floor. He pushed her hair away from the gash—it looked shallow. He glanced at the table, which was covered with breakfast foods. He grabbed a napkin, dipped it in the pitcher of water, and wiped away what blood he could.

Sean lifted his gun at the door when it opened and lowered it as Eth popped his head back in the room. "I couldn't find anything—or anyone," Eth said, out of breath. "This place is wide open though. I opened the doors to each room. They seem to be mostly bedrooms—no phones or anything else that looked like communications. The other end of the hall leads down another flight of stairs. I don't know how far down this place goes. Do you want me to check around? Or do you think the top of the stairs might be unlocked now as well?"

Sean felt torn between helping Charlotte and finding Violet. He knew he couldn't do both. "You go up, I'll check down. If the way we came in is open, bring paramedics down here to Charlotte first, find me after. Hurry."

Eth took off down the corridor.

Sean returned his attention to Charlotte. "You are the toughest Vulcan I know. Do not give up on me. I have some serious shit I need to vent about." He brushed a strand of hair from her face and stood.

"I'll be right back," he told her. He jogged to the door and peered into the hall—it was empty. He ran the opposite way from Eth toward the other end of the corridor and opened the door.

Sean almost fired his gun into the face of Detective Tay.

"Sean!" Juliette cried out, her relief evident. Before he could speak, someone came from behind her and wrapped their arms around him, squeezing air from his lungs.

"Can't—breathe—"

"Oh, sorry." Mags let go, her face lit up with a huge grin.

"Are you two okay?" Sean asked, looking into each of their faces. Juliette's freckles jumped out at him from her pale skin and Mags' jawline sported a dark purple bruise. They were both dressed in thin robes and wore furry moccasins on their feet.

"We're fine," Juliette reassured him, her clipped accent taking on a professional tone. "We broke out of our containment cell and got past two—I guess you'd call them guards. Mags here shorted out the lights and then managed to turn off the security panels to the doors."

"So *that's* what happened. Have you seen any communications devices? Any way to contact outside? Our cell phones don't seem to work and Charlotte—Doctor Salla—needs a hospital. She took a knife to the side of her chest."

Mags' face paled, her eyes wide behind her smudged glasses. "Is she going to be okay?"

"Not if we don't get her out of here soon."

Juliette turned toward Mags. "Do you remember seeing anything that could help us?"

"No. How did you get in here?" she asked Sean.

"Under the Soldiers and Sailors statue. Truth told me how to get in. I had to push the inside of a wreath."

"Truth? She's the bad guy! Or, girl," Mags corrected herself. "Woman, actually. You know what I mean!"

"I know. But it's true. When Charlotte got hurt, Truth called me from Charlotte's phone and. . ." Sean's eyes widened. "She *called* me. There must be an area in this structure where phone signals can get through." He shook his head. "But every path leads farther down. That would only make it worse."

Mags lightly smacked Juliette in the arm. "Don't you remember? There was a door at the other end of our cell's hallway. One of the women said they should take us *upstairs* to look at some book. The door we chose led us straight here. Which means the other door must lead higher up!"

"We need to get you two out of here first. I'll show you where Officer Eth went and you can follow him out."

"Counselor Eth is here? How did *that* happen?" Juliette asked, surprised.

"It's a long story that starts with him being my babysitter and ends with him saving my life. I'll tell you all about it later. He went to see if the top of the stairs is open."

"It isn't."

Sean spun around. There she stood, Officer Let, *Violet.*

She stood directly behind Eth with a gun pointed at the back of his head.

Sean's gun immediately rose, his non-dominant hand unsteady.

"Put it down, Detective." Her dark eyes shone against her cinnamon-colored skin. "This hallway is too enclosed for you to risk taking a shot at me. Especially using your off-hand." She cocked the weapon. "Put it down."

"Don't do it, Sean," Eth said. "Fucking shoot through me to kill her if you have to."

Violet fired next to his head. The shot lodged in the door

frame above Mags. Mags let out a shriek as wooden splinters rained down around her and Juliette took a protective stance in front of her.

Violet pointed the gun back at Eth. He was cradling the side of his head, shocked from the blast next to his ear.

"I could kill you all," she said, her voice smooth and even. "But I don't want to risk getting injured. I simply want to leave. So put—it—down."

"Okay," Sean said, licking his lips. He didn't want to disarm himself so he tipped the gun upward toward the ceiling. "You're right. Just relax. You're in control here."

Violet smirked. "Idiot." She grabbed Eth by the back of his shirt collar as a human shield, then pulled the trigger. Eth's head exploded in front of them, a mess of blood and skull spattering the walls, their bodies, their faces.

Sean had no time for shock. He shoved Mags and Juliette through the door behind them, firing two shots blindly with his left hand toward Violet.

"No!" Violet screeched. The smirk on her face vanished.

"RUN!" Sean yelled.

He heard the other gun ring out. A hot mass hit him in his right arm, just above where his brace ended at his elbow. He was pushed forward from the impact and nearly fell down the stairs. His left arm smashed against the wall of the staircase and the gun flew from his hand. He sloppily shut the door and peered into the dimly-lit area. The two women were ahead of him, already at the bottom.

"Keep going!" he hollered. Sweat dripped in his eyes as pain like fire spread through his elbow. He didn't see his gun, though he could hear it clattering down the stairs in front of him.

He heard the door above them open. Violet was right there. So close.

Sean slid through the bottom door and closed it behind him. With great strides he sprinted through the hallway where Mags and Juliette had been kept prisoner, the shiny black walls reflecting a distorted image of their bodies. Both women were already to the other side and through another door.

Sean stumbled through this new doorframe as he heard another shot ring out. The bullet grazed his right side. Still running, he clamped his good hand against the gash, blood sliding through his fingers.

You're fine, he told himself. *It's just a scratch.* The absurdity of that statement made him bark a laugh, although the movement caused his side to inflame like a bonfire and caused a fresh stream of blood to spurt out.

Panic raced through him. His wound was probably worse than he thought.

Forget it! he told himself. *Just focus on running! Get yourself to safety first.*

They hit a set of stairs and ran up higher and higher on a twisting staircase. *Who built this place?* Sean wondered. *It makes no sense!* But it didn't matter. The circular structure made it impossible for Violet to get off a clear shot. *Unless she catches up.*

Sean heard the door open above him. "Go, go, go!" he screamed, using the last of his breath, which came in hitches.

His side burned. His arm blazed. And then he was there, in another hallway. This one tall with golden walls. Pearls of gold light dotted the ceiling above them.

Sean turned and shut the door, this one made of beautifully carved wood. He slid down and braced himself against it. He drew in gasps of air, his side protesting each breath. "Go until you find the room with Charlotte's phone and call for help."

Juliette sat next to him and planted her feet as well. "You can't hold the door by yourself. You've been shot."

"Twice," he said through a laugh. *Geez. I must have lost more blood than I thought.* Lightheadedness washed over him. *Get a grip! Stay awake!*

Bang! Bang!

Violet kicked the door, once, twice. It vibrated behind them, but didn't give.

Mags pulled her thin robe more tightly around herself.

"Go," Sean told Mags. "Call Millan. Tell him about the statue. Tell him to push inside the southern-most wreath. Say we need paramedics."

Mags froze, torn. Sean could tell she didn't want to leave them, but there was no time.

Two shots hit the door from the other side. They splintered through the wood a few feet above them.

"GO!"

Mags took off, checking briefly inside each room. She got to the end of the hall and peered through a large, metallic door. She glanced at the two of them. "You *better* be alive by the time I get back." With that command, Mags ducked out of sight.

Juliette turned to Sean. "How long until she gets through?"

"I have no idea."

Violet's voice came through one of the holes. "There isn't anything you can use to block the door. Which means you are using yourselves. Which means. . ."

A third shot.

Juliette screamed. Blood sprayed the side of Sean's face.

"Juliette!" he yelled as he slid further to the ground. Violet had aimed lower and the bullet came through the door at the height of their heads.

Juliette clamped her hand to the side of her face. She rolled away from the door.

"You fucking *bitch*!" she screamed. "You shot off my ear!"

Violet kicked the door again. This time it popped open an inch before Sean slammed it back closed with his body.

"Go," he told Juliette. "She'll just keep shooting until she hits something vital."

"She'll kill you," Juliette said. "I can't leave you here alone."

Bang! Bang! Bang!

"You can get behind that door," he said, indicating the door at the end of the hall. "It looks sturdier. She probably won't be able to shoot through it."

"You're coming with me."

He shook his head—big mistake as the corridor spun. "I don't think I can stand."

"Bollocks. All you need is extra time." Juliette stood,

blood pouring freely from the side of her head. She gripped the door handle, flung open the door, and kicked.

Violet, caught off guard, took the blow to her chest. She stumbled backwards, one gun flying from her hand, another firing randomly. Her knees buckled and she fell back down the stairs a few steps.

Juliette slammed the door shut, hooked her hand under Sean's good arm, and heaved him upward.

"Move," she told him.

The floor had somehow become the ceiling. Sean closed his eyes, ignoring the upside-down world, and moved, keeping in step with Juliette. They stumbled through the airtight door and closed it behind them.

Sean fell, disoriented. He pushed himself up with his good arm and watched as Juliette sank to the ground to hold the door closed.

"Find—Mags—" she gasped. "Get—paramedics—".

"Juliette?" Sean asked.

Juliette smiled, her teeth stained pink with blood.

That random shot. It had hit her.

"Where?" Sean asked. "Where are you hit?"

"Sean?" Mags called out at the end of the short hallway. "Sean! They're coming! I found the phone. Next to this big book. They're on their way,"

Sean grabbed Juliette's hand. "You hear that?"

Bang! Violet was back, kicking.

Sean closed his eyes. He opened them, determined. "They're coming," he said to Juliette. "The cavalry is on their way. You are going to be just fine."

A shot rang out, but it didn't break through the metal door. Curses from Violet followed by more loud bangs. The door slid open a little further each time. They couldn't hold it closed. They couldn't keep Violet out. They didn't have enough time.

Mags was next to him, pulling on his arm, trying to get him away from the door. To get him to come with her to the other room.

Violet will be through any second now. She'll follow us to the last room and put a bullet through each of our heads. Then she'll figure out some way to escape and no one will ever find her and we'll all be dead.

Sean thought of Charlotte, pale and beautiful on the floor.

Bang!

He thought of Officer Eth—he had never even learned the man's first name for Christ's sake.

BANG!

Now Juliette and Mags.

"No," Sean whispered. "No more." He pulled Mags down against the door. "Hold this door. Do NOT let her through. I will be right back."

"Where are you—?"

"I will be—right—back."

Sean stumbled along the hall to the open door, using the wall for support, bloody fingers leaving smears along the way. He walked inside and looked around. A dead, naked woman lay face down on the floor, her throat slit. A book sat next to her on the table. And next to that was Charlotte's phone.

Sean had an idea.

64

Violet kicked over and over, each blow a triumph as the door gave way more and more. She knew she'd caught the redhead with one of her bullets, so she was probably out of the picture. The short-haired brunette was a screaming mess, so she'd be easy. Sean had been hit once, and she was pretty sure he'd taken a second shot to his side, so he'd be no match for her.

It was almost over. Truth was gone, Anya was dead. She would be free. She would take the Book, proclaim herself messiah—after all, the "chosen one" was dead downstairs anyway—and lead the world into a new revolution. She'd proven she was capable to be judge, jury, and executioner. It was her time.

One last kick and the door didn't swing back shut. She shoved it open. The redhead lay in a pool of blood to one side.

Violet saw the back of the short-haired brunette's head as she ducked into Truth's sitting room.

I've got you now. She held the gun in front of her and stepped into the hall.

And then her faith came crashing down on her.

65

Sean stepped from behind the door and swung the Book suspended over him with all the force he had left. It smashed into Violet's head. Her neck contracted into her shoulders and she fell backwards, cracking her head on the wall behind her. She crumpled to the ground, limp and unconscious. Sean kicked the gun down the hall as Mags poked her head out of the room.

The Book slid through Sean's fingers and fell to the floor. He didn't have any more energy to hold onto it. It landed open, its front flap hitting Violet in the arm.

Mags approached, holding Sean's gun, which Violet had apparently picked up while chasing them. She pointed it at their would-be murderer.

"Don't worry," she told Sean, her hands surprisingly

steady after such an ordeal. "I will keep an eye on her until the police show up."

Sean smiled a thanks. He looked down with a start as bloody fingers grasped his hand.

It was only Juliette.

"It's over," Juliette gurgled. Dark red liquid coated the side of her face. "Bring on the cavalry." Her eyes rolled backwards.

Sean's knees buckled, unable to hold him up any longer.

"Anytime, cavalry. Anytime."

66

Bright white lights.
Scent of bleach.
Incoherent voices.
Pain. Unbelievable pain.
Relief.
Blackness.

67

March 21ˢᵗ
1:30 p.m.

Sean opened his eyes. Fluorescent lights shined above him.

He blinked several times and became aware of two things: he no longer lay on the floor of the corridor under the Soldiers and Sailors statue and he hurt. A lot.

He turned his head to look around, but a curtain enclosed the hospital bed, blocking his view. His right arm lay immobilized next to him, wrapped in sterile bandages, lined with a full-length arm brace.

Mouth dry, his attempt to call out failed. He ran his parched tongue over his lips, coughed, and tried again.

"Nur—" The word trailed into a cough. The movement shook his whole body and his side, where he'd been shot, protested angrily.

Moments later, a nurse pulled open the curtain.

"Good afternoon, Mister Trann," she said, pulling up his chart. "How's the pain?" She deftly held a cup of water with a straw to his lips. He took a couple sips, sighing with relief as the moisture spread through his mouth and throat.

"Painful," he said. Suddenly, thoughts of what had happened rolled over him. "How is everyone? Charlotte? Detective Tay? Mags? Where's Violet?"

Sean hadn't realized he'd been trying to sit until the nurse pushed him back down. She turned a dial connected to a wire on his I.V. "Just rest, Mister Trann. Just rest."

Sean fought the drugs as long as he could, but the pain faded and the drug-induced void of oblivion pulled him under without his consent.

68

March 22nd

3 p.m.

"He's waking up."

"Don't hover, Mags. He'll see you in a minute."

Mags.

Sean awoke to the sight of the short-haired brunette chewing on her bottom lip. Millan sat next to her, a look of relief washing over his face. The two of them slowly came into focus.

"Hey, Sean," Mags said, sitting on the edge of her chair.

"Mags." He paused. "Mags?"

"I'm okay," she answered the unasked question. She took his good hand in hers. "I'm fine."

His forehead wrinkled.

Mags nodded in understanding. "Juliette just got out of ICU yesterday. That stray bullet hit her in the stomach. She's recovering slowly—I guess there might be some hearing loss because of her ear—but the doctors think she'll be all right. The ear wasn't salvageable though, unfortunately. Charlie—Counselor Eth—didn't make it." She paused. "Doctor Salla is still in intensive care. They say they're hopeful, but there was a lot of damage to her lung."

"Violet?"

"Under arrest and awaiting trial."

"Victim?"

"We found him with plenty of time to spare," Millan chimed in.

Mags pushed her glasses up the bridge of her nose. "After the paramedics arrived and took you all out, I went through the compound's computer system. Every person Truth had chosen was listed. So this last victim wasn't hard to find."

The nurse had come back, telling them Sean needed to rest. As she turned up his I.V., Mags leaned in close. Sean could see the tears that streaked her face.

"It's over, Sean," she whispered. "It's over."

Sean felt her squeeze his hand before the waves of painkillers pulled him back under.

69

March 25th
11 a.m.

It was Sean's turn to sit at the edge of a hospital bed. He'd been in the room for three days, wrapped in a hospital blanket, his braced arm propped awkwardly on the armrest. He'd refused to go home and since no one dared kick him out, he was allowed to stay.

Mostly he stared out the window. He couldn't watch the television, which seemed only to air news about the 'Spider' serial killings and upcoming trial. Reading worked in small stints, but he'd already exhausted the hospital's magazine supply. So he just stared, drifting in and out.

A moan pulled him back to the present. He blinked away

his sleepiness and sat up.

Charlotte stirred. Her skin was pale, her hair oily, her lips dry.

She was still beautiful.

"Hey," he said when her eyes opened.

"Hello, Sean." She took in her surroundings. "How long have I been here?"

"Five days."

She raised an eyebrow. "How long have *you* been here?"

"I was released two days ago, but decided to hang out until you woke up." He smiled. "It's good to see you awake."

"What happened? The last thing I remember was a knife in my chest."

"Long story really short? Truth called me and told me how to find you. Truth is dead. Angellica—I mean Anya—is dead. Violet, the one who threw the knife at you, is under arrest and awaiting trial. The book is a murder weapon, since it's in evidence, though we've gotten over a dozen calls from different museum curators and universities wanting to see it. And the underground bunker is being thoroughly searched. Not sure what's going to happen to those involved. Some have been kept against their will, sort of. It's pretty much a mess."

Charlotte blinked heavily, as if absorbing all the information with some difficulty. "Angellica is dead?"

Sean nodded, wondering how to explain. "She and Anya. . . they were kind of the same person. It's—it's complicated." He hadn't really sorted out how he felt about that yet. The best term was probably denial. Or numbness. Either way, he didn't want to think about it.

Charlotte seemed to understand. "How are Mags and Detective Tay? Did you find them?"

"Mags had some superficial wounds. Tay wasn't so lucky. . . but the doctors say she'll be all right after some physical therapy. Don't worry," he said at her concerned look, "she's tough. She'll be fine."

Charlotte nodded slowly, her eyes a bit clearer. She gazed out the window. "I requested them, you know. To be my scientists." She let out a sigh. "But I guess it does not matter. The Triad is broken." She placed her hands on her bandaged chest. "And I did not die."

Sean wasn't sure what Charlotte meant, but he supposed it might be shock. "You're right. You're alive," he told her softly. He took her hand in his. "It's over."

Tears rimmed her eyes, but the look in them stayed hard and strong. For the first time ever, Sean heard her use a contraction.

"No, Sean, it's not over."

70

Three months later
10 a.m.

Sean's shoulder ached as he strode through the light drizzle of rain into the precinct. He made his way to Millan's office. It was the first time he'd been back since his stint in the hospital. He inhaled deeply, taking in the scents of stale coffee and body odor from bustling officers.

He felt at home.

Millan looked up as Sean knocked on his door.

"Hey, kid. Good to see you."

"You, too." He took a seat across the desk from Millan. "Anything exciting going on?"

"Not for you. You know you're on restricted duty until

you recertify with that mangled shooting arm of yours."

"It's not *mangled,*" Sean said, rolling his shoulder. "And don't forget the mandated counselor's approval."

"Yeah, they brought in some new woman to replace Eth. She's not local, but I'm sure it won't be that bad. A few months and you'll be back, fully active." He paused. "No news yet on a trial date either."

Sean shrugged. He'd given his official statement to the authorities, but a trial would bring everything out again, fresh and new. Until then, he didn't want to think about Angellica or Violet or Truth or any of it.

Millan nodded with understanding. "Tay is back next week. Wilt has been beside himself with worry."

"I'm not surprised."

"Your new partner is here, too."

"I heard. Detective Payne, right?"

"Yeah, he got here a couple of days ago. He'll be partnering up with Wilt until you and Tay are fully back in action. Have you met him yet?"

"Not yet."

Silence fell as both men avoided what needed to be discussed. Millan broke the quiet.

"Have you heard from her?"

Sean didn't need Millan to say who he meant. They both knew he meant Charlotte.

"Mags called me yesterday and said she and Doctor Salla are diagramming the locations of all the other Triads."

"I still can't believe she's planning to take them all on and shut them down. And that she got Mags to go with her."

Sean shrugged. "Mags is the best. If anyone can crack their system, she can." He hoped Millan would let the subject drop. He'd been furious at Charlotte when she'd told him she was going to continue as this "messiah" and convince the other Triads to stop killing. If it didn't work, at least she'd have names and coordinates for officers to shut the operations down, but spread over multiple cities and countries, it was no small task.

Charlotte had stayed calm the whole time, which infuriated Sean even more. Didn't she realize he'd just found her and she was leaving? Didn't she realize she'd only be putting herself back in danger?

Sean had ignored Charlotte's calls. He knew he was being petty and childish and pretty much a giant dick, but he didn't care. She'd made it out alive. And she was leaving, just like that.

"Do you know how long they'll be gone?" Millan asked.

"No idea. Couple months. Couple years. Who knows?"

Millan shifted uncomfortably in his seat. "I'm sorry."

"For what?"

"For this." He nodded behind Sean. There she stood, framed in the doorway, her hair in an elaborate braid, her hands tucked into her coat's pockets. She didn't look at all like she'd had a knife thrown into her chest three months earlier.

Millan rose and gestured for Charlotte to take his seat. He left the office, closing the door behind him.

"I apologize for the deception," Charlotte told him.

"Don't worry. I'll kill Millan later."

"I find that I miss you, Detective Trann."

Sean blinked, completely thrown by the comment. "Wow. No small talk, huh?"

"It has never been my forte."

Sean forced himself not to grin. He reminded himself he was angry with her.

Charlotte continued. "Though the project I undertook is important and can save millions of lives, I found I was not satisfied with my work." She flipped her braid over her shoulder. "Your presence over the past few months has had a strange effect on me. I found myself thinking of you often and wondering when I would see you again." She paused. "This is not like me."

Sean swallowed. "What are you saying?"

"I care for you, Sean. And I could not leave until I told you that."

"But you're still leaving."

"Yes. I must. People are counting on me, whether they know it or not."

Sean actually understood that. It's how he felt about his job. That people out there needed him to stop killers so they wouldn't become victims, too.

A huge sigh left his mouth. All his selfish reasons drained away. He knew she had to leave. How could she not? If the situation were reversed, he would do the same thing. He still didn't like it, but he understood it.

"Where does this leave us?" he asked.

"I am unsure. This is a new area for me."

He took her hands in his. "How about hopeful?'

She smiled. "Hopeful is good."

ABOUT THE AUTHOR

Christa Yelich-Koth is an award-winning author (2016 Novel of Excellence for Science Fiction for ILLUSION from Author's Circle Awards) of the Amazon Bestselling novels, ILLUSION and IDENTITY. Her third book in the *Eomix Galaxy Novel* collection is COILED VENGEANCE.

Christa has also moved into the world of detective fiction with her international bestselling novel, SPIDER'S TRUTH, the first in the *Detective Trann series*.

Looking for something Young Adult? Try the YA fantasy *Land of Iyah* trilogy, starting with book 1: THE JADE CASTLE.

Aside from her novels, Christa has also authored a graphic novel, HOLLOW, and 6-issue follow-up comic book series HOLLOW'S PRISM from Green-Eyed Unicorn Comics. (with illustrator Conrad Teves.)

Originally from Milwaukee, WI, Christa was exposed to many different things through her education, including an elementary Spanish immersion program, a vocal/opera program in high school, and her eventual B.S. in Biology. Her love of entomology and marine biology helped while writing her science fiction/ fantasy aliens/creatures.

As for why she writes, Christa had this to say: "I write because I have a story that needs to come out. I write because I can't NOT write. I write because I love creating something that pulls me out of my own world and lets me for a little while get lost inside someone or someplace else. And I write because I HAVE to know how the story ends."

You can find more about Christa and her other books at:
www.ChristaYelichKoth.com

Made in the USA
Monee, IL
20 April 2021